Blood Visions

Blood Visions

L.J. Hamlin

Torquere Press Publishers
P.O. Box 37, Waldo, AR 71770
Blood Visions by L.J. Hamlin Copyright 2016
Editor, Jaymi Lynn
Cover by Kris Norris
Published with permission
www.torquerepress.com
ISBN: 978-1-644449-70-4
PRINT ISBN: 978-1-946058-04-1

First Torquere Press Printing: May 2016
Printed in the USA

Blood Visions

L.J. Hamlin

Table of Contents

DEDICATION

This book is dedicated to my mother, my hero, the one of the only people who has and never will give up on me. I love you mostest.

DEDICATION

In loving memory of my grandparents, you may never have gotten to see me as an adult, but you raised great kids who have supported me and my dreams.

Blood Visions
by L.J. Hamlin

Private detective Ronan Bayne is a former cop who now runs his own agency specializing in all things paranormal. After several women have gone missing, Ronan gets called in by the police chief.

Dustin McPherson is a psychic who's worked with the police in the past. After having a vision of one of the missing women, he meets Ronan. Together, they must solve a case more complicated than either of them expected.

Prologue

Somewhere in Oregon

The floor is hard and cold, very cold. That's the first thing Ann Beth notices when she wakes up, which confuses her at first—why is she on the floor? Why is she cold? It's dark. She should be in bed. Ann Beth reaches out, wondering if she has fallen out of bed. And her arm rattles, or more accurately, the chain connected to her arm rattles.

"What the hell?" Ann Beth lifts her arm to her face. It's so dark that she can't see the metal cuff around her wrist until it is right in front of her face. It's old and rusty, not the sort of thing her sorority sisters would use in a prank. No, if they were going to handcuff her, it would be with pink, fluffy handcuffs, and probably to a stripper or a naked frat boy.

As she feels along the chain, she realizes it's connected to a wall. Panic starts to creep in, because this doesn't feel like a prank. The room she is in is almost pitch-black, but Ann Beth strains her eyes trying to look around anyway. It's most certainly not her bedroom. She can't see a bed, or furniture, or her window that faces campus. In fact, there are no windows, like maybe she's in a basement? It smells damp like a basement.

Ann Beth looks at the thick cuff on her wrist, to see if she can get it off, but it's tight and locked. It pinches a little, making her skin sore. She doesn't think she has been here long, at least she hopes she hasn't.

She can remember getting out of class, but then it starts to get fuzzy. Her last class had been Women's Studies, and they'd been given a reading assignment. Ann Beth always does her assignments right away; she loves the course and the teacher, Ms. Grace. She thinks she remembers going home, back to the sorority to do that reading.

Feeling down her body Ann Beth can just tell that she is

wearing her own nightgown. Her friends all say it makes her look frumpy, but it's light and cool in the summer heat without showing everything off. So she must have changed in her bedroom. Ann Beth uses her free hand to feel her shoulder-length hair. It's in a braid, so she did get ready for bed, but did she go to sleep? She can't remember.

She doesn't try to stand up. Her legs feel weak, and there is no point when she is shackled to the wall.

"Hello?" Ann Beth calls out; she hopes this is a prank, but if it is, it really isn't a funny one. To get her here, to another room—one other than her bedroom—she thinks she must have been drugged for that, because surely she would have woken up otherwise.

Ann Beth knows some sororities and frat houses take pranks too far, but there haven't been any cases of drugging at Reed University. There have been a few cases of alcohol poisoning at the Portland school, but it's a good school, and Ann Beth's friends are good people. They like to party and have fun, but they wouldn't do something like this, not to a friend, not to anybody. Not only are her friends not this cruel, none of them would want to risk getting a police record.

She's trying not to panic, but she's afraid. If this isn't a prank, then she's been kidnapped.

No one answers her first call, so Ann Beth takes a breath, trying to gain some courage.

"Is anybody there? Hello, this isn't funny," Ann Beth yells, and her voice echoes a little off the walls.

If there is anybody around who can hear her, they don't answer. Ann Beth listens carefully, but she can't hear anything. Maybe they are just being really quiet, maybe they are behind a door or something.

"Please, let me go. I won't call the police, I promise, just let me go," Ann Beth pleads, and she can't keep the tremble out of her voice.

"Please!" Ann Beth shouts.

She keeps yelling, tugging at the chain, but it doesn't budge. It just makes her wrist hurt and makes her cry out in frustration. Even though it seems useless, and her legs are still shaky, Ann Beth stands up, and pulls against the chain some more. She's not sure when she starts to cry, but she suddenly notices the change in her voice, as it becomes thick with tears.

And then suddenly there is a noise Ann Beth is sure she didn't make and she goes quiet. She's silent apart from her slightly heavy breathing. She's out of breath from trying to escape and crying, but she tries to even it out, to make less noise. Ann Beth stands very still; she's never listened more carefully in her life. And then she hears something. It sounds like movement.

"Hello?" Ann Beth says, hoping someone is here now, but terrified at the same time. This could be someone here to rescue her, or it could be the person who brought her here and they might want to hurt her. Why else would they have taken her? Her family isn't wealthy, so it's unlikely that this is about money.

Yet again, no one responds, but there is a sound like faint footsteps. There's a dim light coming from somewhere in the room. It doesn't show her much, but it's something.

"Please, please don't hurt me. Just let me go and it'll be like nothing ever happened. Just throw the key close; I won't open the cuff until you leave. Or drug me again. I'll have never seen your face, I won't be able to get you in any trouble," Ann Beth bargains. She's seen enough TV shows to know that if your attacker-slash-kidnapper ever lets you see their face that means they are planning to kill you.

The sound of footsteps gets closer, louder. Ann Beth tries to see through the darkness, willing her eyes to work just that little bit better. The shadows seem to shift in front of her, coming closer, the darkness itself moving.

Her kidnapper is there, in front of her in a black cloak, the material as dark as the room. The cloak has a hood that covers the person's face, hiding it in shadow.

"I... please. I've never hurt anyone, just let me go." Ann Beth feels like she is running out of time, her heart has started racing, beating wildly in her chest.

And then movement again as the hood is lowered. Ann Beth looks up, and begins to scream.

Chapter One

Fresno, California

Being called into a police station at seven a.m. when you haven't worked there for five years would worry some people, but not Ronan Bayne. When he was twenty-six, he became an ex-police detective, turned private detective. But he knows when his old boss, Police Chief Wilkinson, sends him a message to see him that he's needed, not in any trouble.

So Ronan arrives at the Fresno police station bright and early with a to-go cup of coffee from home, because he'd known he wouldn't be on time for his early meeting if he stopped on the way. But Ronan needs to feed his caffeine addiction in the morning or he's useless.

He plans to just rush through and go straight to Chief Wilkinson's office once he's let in, but he is stopped by a detective he used to work with named Scott.

"Hey man." Scott shakes his hand.

It's not that Ronan doesn't like Scott, it's just he's curious about what the chief wants, so he's in a rush, and Scott can be a talker.

"Been undercover or did your wife kick you out again?" Ronan asks; he's not rude enough to blow Scott off right away. He'll have a quick chat, even though curiosity is killing him.

"What do you mean?" Scott asks.

"The way you look?" Ronan raises his eyebrows.

"What do you mean?" Scott says, playing dumb.

"You look like a hobo," Ronan says bluntly.

And Scott does. His clothes are old and ratty, his beard is long and unkempt, and he looks like he hasn't washed in a while either.

"Compared to you I always did, but yeah, I've been undercover." Scott nods.

"What do you mean 'compared to me?'" Ronan asks.

"You're always so perfect." Scott says "perfect" like it's a bad word.

"Nothing wrong with the way I look." Ronan is taller than Scott, at just over six feet, with short blond hair that he keeps neatly cut. He has stormy gray eyes and a muscular body he works on in the gym when he can. He's clean shaven, freshly showered, and wearing smart shoes, black slacks, a dark blue shirt, and a black leather jacket. When he was a police detective, he would have worn a suit and a tie. He dresses more casually now, still putting in effort though; he hates to look like a slob. Maybe he's a little straitlaced, but who cares?

"You just need to let loose sometimes. I know you gay guys like to dress well, but that doesn't mean you can't wear sweats every now and then," Scott says it casually and without bite; Ronan knows that Scott doesn't even mean to be offensive.

Scott is the type who isn't really homophobic, but he's not the most enlightened guy either. He believes in all the stereotypes, and he'll say stuff that shows his ignorance. He doesn't mean to offend, but he does.

"I wear sweats to the gym. I'd better go now, Scott. I don't want to keep Chief Wilkinson waiting, you know how he is." Ronan isn't lying. The chief doesn't like to be kept waiting normally, but Ronan is here as a favor, so Wilkinson won't get mad at him if he's a few minutes late. But he knows it's something Scott will believe.

"Oh yeah, you'd better go. I should be heading out anyway; I'm in the middle of a case. It's good to see you, man." Scott smiles and gives Ronan a wave as Ronan heads for the chief's office.

Ronan knocks on the office door and hears the chief call out.

"Who is it?" the chief yells.

"It's Ronan." Ronan knows he's expected.

"Come in," the chief responds.

Ronan opens the door and heads in, closing the door behind him.

"Ronan, hello, take a seat." Chris Wilkinson is twenty years older than Ronan, and he looks every year of it, with gray hair and a bit more weight than he should be carrying. He's sitting at his desk in a leather chair, and he gestures for Ronan to take the seat on the other side of the desk, which Ronan does, taking a sip of his coffee before putting it down on the desk.

"Hello, Chris. So, what did you want?" Ronan asks.

"Straight to the point as always," Chris laughs.

"Well, when you call me at ten at night I know something is going on, so I'm curious. You know how I am; I hate not knowing things." Ronan shrugs.

"We have a case. I have a feeling it might be your sort of thing," Chris says with emphasis and his meaning of Ronan's "thing" is a complex one.

The government still won't accept the supernatural as real. The police won't even investigate cases as supernatural. They ignore any supernatural elements to a case, which can make it almost impossible to solve. Ronan had never liked this when he was with the police. He'd gotten in trouble for working on those kinds of cases. He'd decided that he would set up his own private detective agency specializing in the supernatural. He'd always had a knack for it, had done his research, and seen lots of things that many people would never believe in.

So Ronan's "type of thing" means a supernatural case, one that Chris can't properly look into himself because the people in charge have tied his hands.

"Might be?" Ronan asks.

"Well, it's not clear what is going on. We've been working with the FBI because the case crosses state lines. Women have been going missing, here in California, but also in Nevada, Arizona, and Oregon," Chris explains.

"I assume there is a reason you suspect all the cases are linked?" Ronan asks.

"Yes, that's the weird part. We have ten women missing so far, no obvious connections, ages between eighteen and thirty, different races, different backgrounds. But at the sites of abduction, that's where it gets weird." Chris runs through the usual connections they look for.

"Kidnapper leaves a calling card," Ronan guesses.

"That they have. At each site we've found blood."

"That isn't really weird. They were injured during the kidnappings, it happens, maybe they were killed and the bodies taken," Ronan suggests.

"Let me finish. The blood at each scene, it doesn't belong to the woman who was taken, it comes from the woman who last went missing. For example, Jamie Harvard is most recent, the tenth, she was taken from her law office. We found the blood of Ann Beth Green in Jamie's office; Ann Beth was the ninth to go missing," Chris says, raising his eyebrow at Ronan.

"That is strange. Is there anything else you can tell me about the blood?" Ronan pulls a notebook and a pen out of his pocket, and he starts making notes.

"It doesn't have any preservatives in it, but it still seems fresh, which ruined the theory that the blood was being drawn and stored and brought to each scene in vials. There's always just a smear of blood, but the wrong person's blood." Chris shakes his head.

"Okay, that's very weird. This could be my kind of case." Ronan is trying to think what kind of supernatural creature could be doing something like that, but nothing comes to mind. Ronan hasn't had a case like it.

"Do you think you have the time to look into it? I'd appreciate it if you could. I've been working all the angles I can, and I'm coming up empty. Ten girls in two months, Ronan, and Christ knows when this thing will stop." Chris looks almost desperate, and Ronan knows how he feels. As a police chief, Chris has his hands tied by the law, and it's frustrating as hell for him. Just like it was for Ronan when he was a cop.

When there are leads you are forbidden from following because the government won't admit the supernatural exists—even though tons of people have seen them—and not being able to follow those leads means that people might be getting hurt or killed, well, it's more than frustrating. It's why Ronan had left the force. The police had too many rules stopping them from getting justice when it came to the supernatural.

"I can make time for ten missing girls." Ronan isn't about to sit here and do nothing. These ten women might already be dead, but if they're not, well, Ronan wants to get moving to find them.

"Thank you. I knew I could count on you. I've already asked if I can put you on this case as a consultant, like we have before, and the governor has approved the request. So you know the drill, do your thing, send in reports, we'll send you information, and save any receipts for your expenses," Chris rattles off; he looks a little relieved.

"Yeah, this isn't my first rodeo. I know what to do," Ronan points out.

"I know. Here's the file of what we have so far, details on the missing girls, where they were taken from, and everything else." Chris hands Ronan a thick police file, but then, it contains the lives of ten girls in black-and-white facts, which strikes Ronan as sad, but he shakes it off.

It's not his job to be sad for these girls. It's his job to find them, and if they are already dead, then it's his duty to find the thing that killed them.

"I'm going to start at the most recent crime scene, so I'll go to Oregon, where Jamie Harvard went missing," Ronan tells Chris, flicking the file open to find the list of names, to make sure he got it right.

"It's a long drive, when do you think you'll get started?" Chris asks.

"I'm going to go home and pack now, then head out. I'll be there by early evening." Ronan stands up.

"I knew you'd want to get started right away." Chris grins.

"You know me well. I'll be in touch, Chris." Ronan takes the file, waves good-bye, and heads out. This time he manages to avoid being stopped by anyone.

Ronan drives home to his apartment, and the first thing he does is take his travel case out of the hall closet. He's going to be hitting three states, all a good distance from each other, but manageable. So he'll be traveling for a while. And multiple women have gone missing from each state, in different areas. It'll take a while for him to visit all the sites where the women went missing and the blood was found. Those sites are not the only places he'll look at either; he'll investigate the victims' lives, and look for places they could be held, or their bodies could have been dumped.

So clothes are a must, enough for over a week. Ronan packs those first, mainly shirts and slacks. A suit jacket and tie goes in the bag just in case he needs to go anywhere with a dress code. Some warmer clothes—sweaters, jeans, thick socks, as well as normal socks. Underwear is also important. Ronan has forgotten about underwear just once, and he'd felt like an idiot.

He has a bag of toiletries ready to go in his bathroom cabinet, and he takes that and puts it in his bag. He puts the police file in the bag too, and his laptop in its case. Ronan looks around his apartment, trying to make sure he hasn't forgotten anything he needs to pack. Ronan doesn't have any pets to feed, or plants to water, no boyfriend to call to let him know he'll be out of town.

He does text the other members of his agency: Alan, Rick, Alice, Lisa, and Harry, to let them know he has taken a case. Alan, Rick, and Alice all work out in the field, solo like Ronan. Lisa works in the office as a receptionist, but she also keeps them all organized and finds them cases. Harry works in the office; he does research for all the private detectives. He's a wiz with a computer, and he always digs up information for them.

Once that is done, he packs his phone charger, sets his alarm system, and locks up his apartment. Taking the bag down to his blue Ford Taurus, Ronan puts the bag in the trunk, and gets in the driver's seat. He takes his satnav out of the glove box and plugs it in, tapping in the address of the victim in Oregon. He doesn't plan to go straight to where she was abducted from, but he wants to get a motel close by, and this seems like a good way of going about it.

It's a long drive, but Ronan is used to long drives. He stops for coffee and a piss break twice, and once for lunch, and another coffee, and to read the police file; the caffeine is enough to wake him up, without making him feel jittery. He'd checked the time when he left his apartment, and it had been about ten a.m.; he crosses the state line into Oregon just after four p.m.

It's still light when he finds a motel. Ronan checks in and takes his things to his room. He unpacks a little, hanging up a few bits of clothing, putting his toiletries in the bathroom. Ronan sets up the desk with his laptop and the file on the case, with some folders and notebooks to make his own notes and files.

Ronan opens the file that Chris had given him that morning. Ann Beth Green had gone missing three days ago from her room, in the middle of the night. Ronan writes down the address of the college and her sorority house on a scrap of paper torn out of a notebook, and then he's on the move again.

The drive was long and tiring, but Ronan can't bring himself to take a nap before he gets started. So he gets back in his car, and drives to the Reed University campus. Ronan parks in the visitors' parking lot, and then gets out of his car. He's aware that he doesn't really blend in—at thirty-two, dressed like he is, he doesn't look like a student. Maybe he could pass for a teacher, though.

Ronan wants to start by checking out the building Ann Beth was taken from. Ronan read in the police file that there were some drag marks in the mud behind the sorority house. So Ronan decides he'll look to see if the marks are still there, and if he can tell anything from them, like what might have taken this girl, did she leave under her own power or not?

Ronan finds the right building without having to ask for directions, which he's thankful for, because asking for directions would make him stick out more than he wants to. Ronan makes his way to the back of the building. Ann Beth's bedroom was at the back of the dorm building on the second floor, and the markings had been in the dirt on the ground. Ronan knows from the files that the area behind the building is taped off, so there might still be evidence.

But when Ronan rounds the side of the building, he sees that there is someone over the tape line. He's not a cop, Ronan can tell from this distance because of the long curly mop of bright purple hair. Ronan stops where he is, trying to see if the figure has flowers, if he could be making a memorial to the missing girl.

But the short man doesn't have flowers, and as Ronan watches, he squats down and looks like he's examining the ground. Ronan moves toward the slight figure slowly, one hand on the gun in the holster at his hip. This man could have come back to cover his tracks, if he's a man at all.

Ronan draws his Glock, and points it at that purple head.

"Stand up slowly," Ronan orders.

The man freezes, but he doesn't stand up.

"Hands above your head and stand up slowly," Ronan repeats.

The man raises his hands above his head—they look human enough, but he could be a shape-shifter. He has long, delicate-looking fingers, broad palms, short fingernails painted black. The polish is chipped. He has traces of dirt on his fingers. He begins to stand up slowly.

Ronan keeps his gun pointed at the stranger, his heart beating at the possibility that he's stumbled onto the bad guy so soon into his investigation. Ronan doesn't want to be forced to shoot—if this man is the kidnapper, then Ronan wants to question him to find out where the missing women are.

"Turn around, and don't make any sudden movements. I have a gun, and I will use it," Ronan warns.

And slowly, like he's been told, the man turns.

Chapter Two

Oregon

He wakes to a searing pain in his head, and his sheets soaked in sweat. Dustin McPherson reaches out to his bedside cabinet, and switches his lamp on. Bright light floods the room, hurting his eyes.

"Fuck," Dustin grumbles, rubbing his eyes with his fists. When the black spots stop dancing in front of his vision he looks at his alarm clock—it's five a.m. Dustin groans at that, and punches his pillow.

For a moment he doesn't know what woke him up so suddenly, what has his skin slick with sweat, his heart racing, his sheets tangled around his legs. But then it starts to come back to him. The girl. She'd been alone somewhere dark, begging for help, and there had been blood.

It was too real to just be one of his nightmares. Dustin had learned to tell the difference between his dreams and a vision while he was asleep by the age of twelve, and he is twenty-one now. Dustin sits up in bed carefully, his head swimming a little, his ears still ringing with the girl's heart-wrenching sobs.

He gets out of bed and goes to the bathroom. He takes some Tylenol out of the cabinet and washes it down with a glass of water. He hopes that will help with his headache, and he won't have to take the tramadol his doctor has given him.

Dustin looks at himself in the mirror above his sink. He looks pale even for him, and sweaty. His dyed purple hair is matted, some of it slicked down, stuck to his head, and other bits are sticking up wildly. The whites of his bright blue eyes are a little bloodshot, but there is no blood below his nose this time, so that's something.

Splashing some water on his face to try to wake himself up a little, Dustin dries off his face with a towel, and then heads back to his bedroom. Dustin sits on the edge of his bed and pulls out the sketchbook he keeps there, and the charcoal.

He starts sketching the girl from memory. He can remember what she looked like, but Dustin can't remember anything about the room she had been in, only that it was dark and cold. She'd been chained up; her wrists were bleeding. Dustin had been able to feel her fear; she'd been terrified.

Once his sketch is done, Dustin boots up his laptop and goes on the Internet. He searches for local missing girls—tons of different news stories come up. It takes some searching before he finds an article with a picture of the girl he saw in his vision. Her name is Ann Beth Green, and she was taken from Reed University, which is only an hour's drive away.

Dustin goes into the main room of his apartment, and to the small, open-plan kitchen. He opens up the cupboard and looks at his selection of teas. He decides on a chamomile and honey blend, as it's meant to be soothing. He brews his herbal tea, and sits on a stool in his kitchen. He's killing time, because he knows he can't call the police this early or they'll be more likely to think it's a prank phone call, even though it has started to get light.

Dustin drinks his tea, then goes for a shower, washing the sweat off himself, and trying to clear his mind, but the sight of Ann Beth, hurt, afraid, and alone keeps coming back to him. He finishes his shower, and brushes his teeth, then he dries himself off, using a blow-dryer on his hair.

Then he opens up the medicine cabinet again, and takes out his Xanax and Klonopin like he does every morning. He hates that he's medicated, that he has to take pills to stop him from panicking over every little thing. But he knows he needs to take it. Dustin has become more at peace with his anxiety disorder with the help of a therapist.

After taking his meds, Dustin goes back to his bedroom to get dressed. He puts on black boxers and black socks. Then he finds his black skinny jeans—they have rips in the knees from where he had fallen over last month, but personally Dustin thinks it adds to the look. He finds a clean T-shirt, also black, but he adds some color to his outfit with a bright red hooded sweater.

Next he puts on and laces up his Doc Martens boots; black, of course—it's one of Dustin's favorite colors. His first therapist had said that it was a reflection of his dark personality and depression. His most recent and preferred therapist had disagreed, and just got that Dustin was into punk and goth fashion because he liked it.

Dustin tries calling the police first, to say he may have information about the disappearance of Ann Beth Green. He wants them to know that she is still alive, so they keep looking for her, not a body, because he's sure the urgency with which the police search is affected by if they think the missing person is already dead or not.

He plays phone tag for hours, trying to talk to someone who is on the case. Some of the people he talks to seem to think he's just trying to get information on the case, like he's a reporter or just nosy, and they tell him nothing. When Dustin finally tells them that he is a psychic and he's had a vision regarding the case, well, the first person he tells laughs at him, and the second hangs up.

It's infuriating. Dustin paces his apartment, trying to think what to do. He decides to go down to the police station in person. He grabs his bike and rides down to the local police station.

Dustin chains up his bike outside, pretty sure it'll be safe—who would break a chain on a bike outside of a police station, after all? He goes inside and asks to see the person in charge of the case of the missing women.

"Can I ask who you are?" the man on reception asks.

"My name's Dustin McPherson." Dustin has a bad feeling, from the way the man is looking at him, that this isn't going to go well for him. His name tag reads Officer Grey, he's not—from Dustin's reading him—in charge of the case.

"And are you a relation to any of the missing women?" Officer Grey asks.

"No, but I have information about one of the women who is missing," Dustin explains.

"You saw something?" Officer Grey asks.

"In a way—I had a vision of one of the victims." Dustin takes a breath and braces himself. He had to try, but he can feel it coming, and it doesn't take a psychic to see the disdain coming off Officer Grey.

"Oh, you're that psychic that's been calling all morning. Listen, kid, I don't know if this is a prank, a hoax, or what you're playing at, but this is a serious case, and we don't have time to interview the local crazy. Get out of here," Officer Grey orders.

"This isn't a joke. I'm serious. And I'm not crazy," Dustin argues.

"Don't make me arrest you. You won't enjoy a day in the cells," Grey warns.

"Arrest me? What for?" Dustin asks.

"Wasting police time. Now get out of here," Grey barks, and with a frustrated sigh, Dustin does leave.

He's unchaining his bike outside, thinking of what to do, when he decides he'll go to the college—maybe if he goes to Reed University, he'll be able to pick more up, get another vision. He can't get Ann Beth's face out of his head.

Dustin has had a lot of visions before and sometimes they were of people in danger and in need of assistance Dustin has always done his best to do something for them, because he feels like whatever power sends him his visions, wants him to help.

To ignore the vision would be to ignore a girl in danger, to leave her to whatever horrible fate her captor has planned. So Dustin gets on his bike and starts peddling toward the university— it's a long ride, but he knows the way; he's lived in Oregon all his life.

It's late afternoon by the time Dustin makes it to the college. He makes his way on to campus and finds the right sorority house. Dustin chains up his bike again, and then starts looking around. He decides to do a circle of the dorm, and that's when he sees the police tape at the back. To some people that would look like something to stay away from, to avoid, but to Dustin it looks like a clue.

It's not until Dustin crosses under the police tape that the hairs on his arms stick up. It's not because he's cold—there is no breeze around, cool or otherwise. Dustin moves toward the weird feeling, using the sinking sensation in his stomach as a guide.

He stops when he sees faint marks in the dirt. Dustin leans down, removing his gloves and putting them in his pocket. He touches the disturbed earth, and images start to flicker in his mind, just pieces, flashes. Ann Beth's face, first laughing, in sunlight, bright, happy, then again in a dimly lit room, her cheeks tearstained. Dustin sees flashes of other girls, some that he saw in reports on the Internet, but others he can't remember seeing in his research.

Dustin hears the rattling of chains, sobbing, a scraping sound. He feels cold to the bone. And he can feel their fear—his heart starts racing. And that is when someone speaks, throwing Dustin out of the vision, but not shaking off the fear and weird shaky feeling.

The man's voice tells him to stand up, hands above his head, and to turn around. Dustin does as he's told and turns to face a handsome man with a gun. Older, taller, blond, gray eyes, he looks like he works out, like he could kick Dustin's ass even without the gun.

"Who are you?" Dustin asks.

"I think I'll be asking the questions," the man says firmly.

"Are you a cop? Or am I getting robbed?" Dustin ignores the "no questions" order. He's not sure what would actually suck more. He doesn't have a lot of money on him to steal and a cop will probably arrest him.

"I'm not going to rob you. Do I look like a criminal?" The man snorts, like he isn't holding a gun on Dustin.

"So you're a cop?" Dustin asks.

"Something like that. Who are you? And what are you doing at this crime scene?" the possibly-a-cop guy asks.

"My name's Dustin McPherson. I was just taking a look," Dustin says nervously, unsure of how much he should tell this guy.

"Are you a reporter? Or a student here?" That gun isn't going away; it isn't shaking. This guy doesn't even look like his arms are getting tired.

"Neither," Dustin admits.

"Then what the hell are you doing here?" the man demands.

"Can I at least put my arms down, officer? And maybe you could stop pointing a gun at my head? I didn't do anything wrong." Dustin tries to sound reasonable. He's a little afraid of being shot, and his heart is still racing from the vision-induced fear.

"Put your arms down, but keep them where I can see them, and I'll be keeping my gun out, thanks."

"Thanks, officer." Dustin puts his arms down, glad to stop the strain from holding them above his head, and he very carefully keeps his hands in the man's sight and away from his pockets. He doesn't have any weapons on him, but this cop doesn't know that.

If he sees Dustin move, he might shoot.

"I'm not an officer. I'm a private detective. My name's Ronan Bayne. And I'm not an idiot. If you're not a student here, there is no reason for you to be on campus. Give me a reason not to call the police," Ronan says firmly.

A private detective. Dustin guesses that makes sense, and at least this guy can't directly arrest him. But how to stop him from calling the cops? With Dustin's luck, he'd get Officer Grey, who would happily press charges against Dustin for him entering a crime scene.

"You won't believe me," Dustin sighs, because he can only think of the real reason for why he's here, and he doesn't think a private detective will believe him.

"Try me. Just go for the truth. I'm real good at knowing when I'm being lied to," Ronan pretty much orders.

"I had a vision of the girl who went missing, Ann Beth. I came here to see if I could pick up more," Dustin explains.

"So you're a psychic?" Ronan asks.

"Yes. Let me guess—you don't believe in psychics," Dustin sighs.

"I do believe in psychics—doesn't mean I believe in you." Ronan shrugs, holstering his gun.

"Well, I don't know how to make you believe in me. I'm not like some Vegas act. I don't do visions on command, but I do usually pick up at least something from people. Let me touch you and I'll tell you what I see. I'm not a scam artist either. I don't get paid by old ladies to talk to their dead husbands or find their cats. I've helped the police before," Dustin says truthfully, glad he doesn't have a gun pointed at him any longer.

"Don't try anything funny." Ronan takes off his glove and steps closer, holding his hand out. His other hand hovers over the gun he has holstered at his waist.

"I won't do anything, like I could take you down without the gun anyway. I'm half your size," Dustin grumbles.

"For all I know you're armed." Ronan looks at him with suspicion in his eyes.

Dustin reaches out and takes Ronan's hand. Holding it like you might in a loose handshake. Dustin empties his mind, and lets the images come to him.

He sees a little girl, blonde, in a blue dress. She looks like a doll, and she's holding a toy cat. Then he sees a gun, he doesn't know what type. He sees a bed made up perfectly, an empty apartment. A cat's collar on the dresser table. The flash of a tattoo gun at work. A badge next to a bottle of scotch.

Dustin takes his hand away, cutting the connection.

"Same blur of flashes I always get when I try to trigger a vision. Nothing too long and detailed. But I know you used to be a cop before you became a private detective. You're really neat; maybe one of your parents was Army. And I saw a little blonde girl, in a blue dress, holding a toy cat," Dustin explains—he hardly ever gets a strong vision from touching a person; his visions come to him when they choose to, not the other way around.

"You saw a blonde girl dressed like that? Have you looked into me at all, researched me? You could have found out I was a cop easily, and that my dad was Army." Ronan clearly doesn't believe him, not from the questions he's asking, and he doesn't seem to like him, but the mention of the little girl seems to have shaken him.

"I had no reason to look into you. Until you said your name was Ronan Bayne, I didn't know who you were, and from looking up this case I didn't see your name come up as part of the investigation," Dustin points out.

"I only just got asked to help with this case, so there hasn't been time for reporters to find out and do a story about me. Okay, you didn't know who I was, or that I was working on this case. I believe that much—doesn't mean I trust you, or even believe you are psychic. So why are you here?" Ronan still seems on edge.

"I told you. I wanted to see if I could see more after my vision last night," Dustin points out.

"But why? Is the family paying you? Are the cops?" Ronan asks.

"No one's paying me. The police here wouldn't even listen to me. They think I'm crazy or wasting their time," Dustin says honestly.

"Then why bother coming to the crime scene? Why would you want to know more?" Ronan frowns.

"Do you ever have nightmares?" Dustin says, changing the way things are going, voicing his own question.

"Yes, what does that have to do with anything?" Ronan sounds confused.

"Well, imagine having a terrible nightmare of someone being hurt, and then when you wake up you realize it wasn't a dream, but real. I woke up last night still hearing Ann Beth's sobs in my ears. I could feel the cold of the room in my bones. What kind of person could ignore that?" Dustin can't imagine ever ignoring that—how could he? He never has, not from his first vision.

"You're not a cop. It's not your job to find these girls, no matter what you say you saw."

"How is it anymore your job than mine? You choose to be a private detective; I was chosen by something to get these visions—I didn't choose to get them." Dustin has gotten used to having his visions, but he doesn't know if, given the choice, he would still choose to get them. He likes helping people if he can, but he hates the awful things he sees.

"So you want to help these girls, even though you're not getting paid and you're putting yourself in danger?" Ronan asks.

"I guess so." Dustin shrugs.

"Just in case you're telling the truth, I'd like you to tell me what you saw in your vision?" Ronan presses getting a notebook and pen out of his jacket.

"I didn't see a lot. I saw the girl, Ann Beth. She was in a white nightdress. It had a few black stains on it, especially the hem, like she was someplace dirty. And it was cold, really cold. She hadn't been given a blanket; she was chained up. She was screaming and crying, but I didn't hear any other sounds." Dustin runs through what he can remember, not that it's easy to have perfect recall when you are asleep and terrified.

"Cold, dirty, it's not a lot but it's something. Think carefully, is there anything else you saw? Even small details?" Ronan asks.

"I thought it was weird that there were no rats or mice there, in a place like that, but there was damp. I remember the damp on the walls. I think it was a basement, no windows, there must have been light coming from another room, because I could see Ann Beth, but I couldn't see a whole lot else of the room, no furniture or anything." Dustin rubs his forehead, trying to think, but that's all he's getting.

"I'll look into those things. But you need to stay out of this case. You can't be involved. Ten girls are missing, something big is going on, it's dangerous, and you're a civilian," Ronan warns.

"Well, not to be rude, but the cops don't seem to be getting anywhere. Ten girls in and they have no idea who's behind it, do they? That's why they've hired a private detective, to get more eyes on the case. I want to help, I can help, and I'm going to help," Dustin says, stepping around Ronan and walking away from him and the crime scene.

"I find you someplace you're not supposed to be again I will call the cops on you, for your own safety," Ronan warns.

"That won't stop me—might make it harder, but you're not the only one who can look into things, detective." Dustin glances back, and then walks away.

Another time, another place, maybe Dustin would have asked Ronan for a drink. He's older, sure—that has never bothered Dustin—but cops, even ex-cops, aren't usually his thing. Ronan is very good-looking though, nothing like Dustin, but he doesn't really have a type.

Usually when he felt a spark like this he would be hoping to see the guy again, but this time seeing Ronan again would be a bad thing. It would mean being arrested, which is the last thing Dustin wants, but he's not giving up on the case.

He's not giving up on the girls who are missing.

Chapter Three

Ronan's cell phone rings as he's getting in his car in the campus parking lot—it's the chief, so Ronan answers.

"Hi, Chris, you got more info?" Ronan asks.

"No, but I've got you an appointment with the detective on the case there, Hicks. She's willing to talk to you about what she's seen, maybe show you some of the scenes. Try not to offend any of the local cops. You know they don't always appreciate outside help, so the fact that Hicks is willing to talk to you is a good sign—don't ruin it," Chris warns.

"I'll play nice, I promise. I did have a weird moment at the crime scene," Ronan admits.

"Weird like supernatural? You have an idea of what took the girls?" Chris asks.

"I have no idea what took the girls, but it might have been supernatural. I ran into this punk-looking kid—purple hair, painted nails, and he says he's a psychic. Says he had a vision of the case, of one of the missing girls. I don't know if I believe him, or what he's up to, but I don't think he's the kidnapper returning to the crime scene," Ronan explains.

"Want me to run a search on him? This kid?" Chris asks.

"Yeah. I'd like to know if he's up to something, if I need to watch my back. He touched me, and said he saw a blonde girl, in a blue dress, holding a toy cat. That's the last image I have of Sarah alive. It was never in the papers, not the blue dress or the cat. How did he know that?" Ronan had been shaken up the moment Dustin had described Ronan's dead sister. She'd been just ten years old.

"I know how Sarah affects you. Give me his name and I'll see what I can do. I'll make sure he's not playing you," Chris says.

"Thanks. His name is Dustin McPherson, no idea on age, living in Oregon somewhere," Ronan sighs.

"Hopefully not too common a name. I'll call you back later, and I'll text you Hicks' details—talk to you soon." Chris hangs up.

Ronan makes his way to the Portland Oregon Police Department, making good time, as far as he can tell. He's never been to Portland before—maybe his driving time would be considered slow to a local. But either way, he's sure he hasn't been long enough to keep Detective Hicks waiting.

He parks his car at the station and heads inside. He goes to the officer on the desk, a guy whose name badge says Officer Grey.

"Hello, I'm here to see Detective Hicks," Ronan tells him, after waiting for the man to look up and finally make eye contact.

"Do you have an appointment?" Grey asks, not looking at the open book of appointments in front of him.

Ronan has met cops like him before, total assholes. No wonder they had him working the front desk at his age.

"Yes, I should. Under Ronan Bayne. My chief just spoke with your detective about it," Ronan explains, trying to stay pleasant sounding, even though he's taken an instant dislike to this guy's attitude.

"From out of town, then?" Grey asks, instead of looking for Ronan's appointment.

"California. Now, I don't want to keep Detective Hicks waiting," Ronan says a little tightly. He doesn't like being played with by some pencil-pusher cop who likes the power of controlling people's actions.

"So, what's it like being a cop in California?" the officer asks, ignoring the fact that Ronan clearly wants to see Detective Hicks.

"I'm not a cop; I'm a private detective. And the city is paying my bill. I think they'd appreciate if I got on with my job, instead of talking with you, as fun as that's been." Ronan can't help the hint of sarcasm that slips into his voice.

"PI, huh? I thought you guys just investigated cheating housewives and businessmen. What do you want with Hicks? Is she banging someone's husband?" He smirks.

Ronan is about to tell the asshole in front of him where he can stick his smirking face—right up his own ass—when a pretty, middle-aged woman in a suit walks over, glaring at Officer Grey.

"Want to repeat that?" The woman—Ronan is betting she's Hicks—looks straight at Grey, challenge in her eyes.

"Just men talking, don't get your panties in a twist." Grey snorts at his own clever little joke.

Ronan bets the female detective would have heard that and a lot worse a thousand times.

"I see sensitivity training really did you wonders. I guess a one-week course wasn't enough to cure you of your mommy issues." Hicks rolls her eyes.

Before he finds his voice again, Hicks has turned to face Ronan, giving him her attention, and cutting off the indignant officer.

"Are you the private detective? Ronan?" she asks.

"Yeah, that's me." Ronan nods.

"Follow me. We have all the case evidence we have put together in one room—ten girls' lives takes up more than one board." Hicks starts walking, and Ronan follows her, not even bothering to look at the asshole. It's cops like that who give the rest of them a bad name.

Hicks takes Ronan to what he thinks must have been the family room. It's not an interrogation room and it doesn't look like a break room. But in a station, there is always somewhere private to take people you need to talk to who aren't guilty of anything, like the families of victims or even victims themselves.

The room is full of whiteboards covered in writing and pinned up sheets of paper, news articles, school reports, arrest records. Every piece of information that has ever been recorded about the ten missing girls is probably on these walls.

"We're working with the FBI, where the case crosses state lines. And now someone suggested bringing in you, after they made the link about the blood. The man I talked to, Chief Wilkinson, he said you had an eye for the weird ones." Hicks sounds a little skeptical.

"I know it sounds like a whole lot of bullshit, but sometimes, not always. The cases without a straightforward answer, the ones that seem like an unbreakable mystery. That's because something's involved that we weren't trained to look for as cops, something we were taught to believe isn't real," Ronan says softly.

He hadn't believed once. And then there was Sarah, beautiful Sarah, dead at just ten. And there is all he's seen since. Things that can't be explained away by science. Things that most people think belong in the fiction section of the library.

"Life will make a believer of you if you if you let it," Ronan adds.

"So you're trying to tell me that something like a werewolf took these girls?" Hicks says, her disbelief clear.

"Not likely. The pattern of the abductions is wrong. Werewolves like to hunt around the full moon; it gives them a power boost. And they don't often carefully break in, leaving no trace of themselves, and take girls. If it was a werewolf, you'd be seeing busted down doors and a whole lot more blood, in my experience," Ronan explains.

"You're totally serious aren't you? You're not pulling my leg, and I don't think you're crazy, so this is real." Hicks shakes her head.

"I know it's hard to take in, it was for me at first too. But yes, the supernatural is real. There are things out there that we can't explain away and one of those things has probably taken these girls," Ronan says.

"And you take on these kinds of cases all the time?" Hicks asks.

"Yeah, I mean I've never seen one quite like this before, but I'll figure it out. I always do." Ronan sounds more confident than he feels. He has so little to go on.

For all the information that has been gathered by the cops in each state, they really have nothing. Nothing that really connects the girls. They are different races, different ages, they work different jobs, they have different family lives.

"So what do you think it is? Do you have an idea?" Hicks seems more open-minded than a lot of cops, hell, a lot of people.

Ronan hates to admit the truth. "No, I'm really not sure at this point."

"So you don't know something that marks its crime scene with the blood of its last victim?" Hicks sounds curious.

"I haven't seen that before. But I have a lot of people researching books on the supernatural. They'll tell me about anything that comes close to these disappearances, and I'll go from there." Ronan is confident that Harry, back at the agency, will be doing excellent research, and he'll find something soon.

"Well, take a good look at everything here and let me know if there is any information you need, anything I can get to help you. I'll leave you to read some stuff for a while, and get you a file box to take away of all the files. In case what we put together has something different from what your chief gave you." Hicks excuses herself and leaves the room.

Ronan takes out a notebook and pen, and starts going over the boards, making notes, trying to make connections, even though there don't seem to be any beyond all the missing people are women, and they are just that, missing.

He's deep in his note-taking when noise from out in the station catches his attention. There is yelling and at least one of the voices belongs to that asshole. Ronan puts his notebook back in his pocket, and cracks the door open.

He spots Hicks first—she looks furious, but Grey is the one yelling and making a scene.

"You can't just undermine my authority like that," Grey snaps.

"Yes, I can. You are trying to arrest someone linked to my case! If someone says they have information on *my* case, you come and get *me*," Hicks says very firmly—it's clear she won't be backing down.

"He's a nutcase, not a lead," Grey growls.

"If he is mentally ill, Grey, I will order a psychological exam, but that's my call. Now get out of my face," Hicks orders.

Grey walks away, but even from where Ronan is standing he can see that the douche is muttering under his breath. Probably vile things about Hicks and whoever started the augment between them.

Hicks comes over to Ronan, looking calm again by the time she reaches him, but that might be a mask. Ronan wouldn't be surprised if she was hiding anger over the encounter.

"I have a sort of lead. Would you like to interview him with me?" Hicks asks.

"What kind of lead?" Ronan wants to know.

"A psychic." Hicks sounds skeptical even as she says the word.

"Let me guess, purple hair? Young, had a vision?" Ronan can't believe he'd run into more than one psychic in the same town, in the same day, relating to the same case.

"How did you know that?" Hicks frowns.

"I met him earlier at a crime scene," Ronan explains.

"And what's your take on him? Is he mentally ill? Or an attention seeker? Scam artist?" Hicks asks.

"I'm not sure. He might be the real deal. Let him sweat in interrogation for a bit while I call my chief back. He was going to look into this guy for me and maybe you can run a check on him too. He said his name was Dustin McPherson." Ronan hadn't thought he'd see the young psychic again; he's not sure how he feels about it.

He doesn't like the idea of a stranger who can look inside his mind to his deepest secrets. He doesn't like the fact that he feels attracted to that stranger, even though he's young, and probably trouble. Ronan doesn't need to be involving himself with guys who trespass on to crime scenes.

"Okay, let's call your chief. This kid might actually come in useful. I can't believe I'm considering that a self-professed psychic could be a good lead." Hicks shakes her head and they go back into the room Ronan had come from.

Ronan takes a seat and pulls his cell phone out. He calls Chris and gets through quickly.

"Hey Chris, do you have the report on that psychic yet? Is he a scam artist?" Ronan asks.

"You're keen to know about him." Chris points out.

"He showed up again. At the police station. We have him in interrogation. I need to know if I should be treating him as a lead, a suspect, a crank, or whatever the hell he is." Ronan tells himself that is the only reason he wants to know. It's not personal. It's not because when the guy touched his hand he saw Sarah. If he is a fake, if he did learn about her some other way, Ronan will be pissed.

"Well, I don't think he's a scam artist or a suspect. He's either the real deal or he believes he is the real deal," Chris says.

"Mental issues?" Ronan asks.

"I found that he dropped out of college because he had some kind of breakdown. And he sees a psychologist and a bunch of doctors, but I haven't found out what for. He can't be too nuts; he's been linked to at least twelve cases I can find that he helped solve," Chris explains.

"So he's either the real deal, or he's gotten really lucky a lot of times. They're sure he wasn't more involved in the cases, like he wasn't to blame and passing it on to someone else?" Ronan needs to be sure.

If he's going to go listen to this guy, and use what he says on the case, he has to believe in him. If he ends up wasting time on false leads, anything could happen—more girls could go missing, or the ones missing could be killed if they haven't been already. Ronan doesn't have room to be getting things wrong here. He knows he's not the only one on the case, but he's the only one with experience in the supernatural.

"Everyone I've talked to says he's a stand-up guy, a good kid. That he really helped, that he sees things that other people don't—trained cops. He could be an asset." Chris sounds like he believes in Dustin.

"So I'll talk to him. See what else he knows. Tell him to keep in touch if he has any more visions regarding the case," Ronan says thoughtfully.

"I was thinking more you maybe take him with you to a few crime scenes, see if he sees anything? I know you like to work alone, but think of him like a gun—he's a tool to use," Chris suggests.

"You want me to take a psychic with me to crime scenes, when I don't even take a partner?" Ronan doesn't even go to crime scenes with people from the agency. Alan and Alice partner up, Lisa and Rick do too—sometimes they work alone, sometimes they take Harry if there is a computer problem they can't crack.

But Ronan goes alone—all the team does for him is research.

"I think it could be a good idea. But talk to him. See if you think he's the real thing and stable. If you think you can stand being around him, get him to help. This is a big case—I'm throwing everything I have at it; we all are. You're my best chance of solving it—if he can help, that's great."

"What if he doesn't want to be dragged around to crime scenes by a private detective?" Ronan asks.

"The city is willing to pay him. Same fee as you. From what I can tell, he lives in a crappy apartment in a worse neighborhood, so I'm sure he can use the money." Chris isn't one to throw around money. He's a sensible guy, a good chief. He must think Dustin is a decent lead. The other cops he's worked with must have said nice things.

"Okay, I'll go talk to him, and I'll consider working with him, but if he slows me down at any point I'll cut him loose," Ronan warns.

"It's your call. Text me your decision. Oh and get this, he's got a record—a few charges for entering private property and crime scenes, but those were dropped. He got probation for one thing though, but that's ended." Chris sounds amused.

"What did he get probation for?" Ronan is curious.

"He was arrested at a marriage equality demonstration for fighting," Chris says.

"I'm guessing he was for marriage equality, and this isn't your way of telling me I might be working with a homophobe?" Ronan doesn't think Chris would sound so amused if that was the case.

"He hit a member of the Westboro Baptist Church. So gay or straight, I'm thinking he was on the right side of the fight that day. I mean, I thought you had gaydar—can't you tell if he's gay?" Chris asks.

"Please, I wish it worked like that. Anyway, I'm going to go interview him," Ronan says, not wanting to talk about the times he'd been unsure of a man's sexuality with Chris, his ex-boss, even if they are friends now.

"Let me know how it goes," Chris orders.

"Yes, sir," Ronan says before hanging up, because old habits die hard.

"So you're gay?" Hicks asks as Ronan puts his cell phone away.

"Yep, that going to be a problem?" Ronan raises an eyebrow. Hicks wouldn't be the first homophobic woman he'd met.

"Not at all. Must have been hard, being a gay cop. It's hard enough being a woman and everyone thinking you're gay, a slut, or a tease." Hicks shakes her head.

"People can suck, one of the many reasons I went out on my own. You ready to interview Dustin?" Ronan asks.

"As ready as I'll ever be to interview a psychic." Hicks nods, getting up from her chair, and together they head for interrogation.

Chapter Four

It's far from the first interrogation room Dustin has been in, but it doesn't mean that he likes them. They are so soulless, without character—Dustin doesn't like that. He's not sure how long he's been sitting at the small desk when the door opens again. Two people walk in—a woman, and the private detective from the crime scene.

"You're not a cop," Dustin points out.

"Neither are you, doesn't stop you from showing up at crime scenes. But I'm working with the police as a consultant," Ronan tells him, taking a seat; the woman takes the other seat.

"I'm Detective Hicks. Ronan told me he'd already met you." Detective Hicks smiles.

"And what did he have to say?" Dustin asks her, but he's looking at Ronan, trying to get the measure of this guy.

"That you might be the real deal, so I'm coming in here open-minded. Doesn't mean I'm a believer though. I've never met a real psychic, but there are cops who vouch for you. So convince me." Detective Hicks raises her eyebrow.

"You've looked into me," Dustin guesses, because that is the only way for them to know he's worked with other police before. It's not like Dustin told Ronan.

"Yes. I had someone look into you," Ronan confirms.

"Awfully skeptical for a guy who runs an agency specializing in the supernatural," Dustin responds.

Ronan looks surprised. "How did you know that?"

"You're not the only one who can look into people. I might not have your resources, but it's called Google. Dude, you guys have an ad on there and a website." Dustin rolls his eyes.

He'd googled the name Ronan gave him as soon as they'd been apart. He'd wanted to know more about who he was dealing with. Ronan hadn't seemed like the cops Dustin usually met trying to look into cases, even though he used to be a cop.

Dustin had touched him, skin to skin, and he had seen things that left him with questions, ones he didn't think Ronan would be quick to answer, and ones he hadn't found out through a Google search. Dustin can't help but be interested, and not just because Ronan has this kind of brooding, sexy, mysterious thing going on.

"So you know I'm a believer. Not something I hid when I met you at the crime scene. But like I said, I believe in psychics— doesn't mean I believe you have real powers." Ronan shrugs.

Dustin has an idea. "Can you get me something small and metal, like a spoon?"

"Why?" Ronan asks.

"So I can show you something," Dustin says.

"I'll get it." Detective Hicks gets up and leaves the room.

"What are you playing at?" Ronan presses once they are alone.

"Reading you wasn't enough proof to you that I can do stuff, so I'm going to show you something different," Dustin explains. He'd seen a few things when he touched Ronan, maybe not enough to convince the guy though. Dustin could go again, try and force a vision, but he has a feeling that Ronan wouldn't like that at all.

Dustin is surprised Ronan let him read him once, but then Ronan thought he was fake, so maybe that was why he let Dustin touch him. Because Ronan has this closed off thing going on, a guarded look in his eyes. Dustin's seen it before, in other cops— Ronan is a closed book, shut down, and he's not interested in opening up.

"You'd better not be playing me," Ronan warns, and before Dustin can say he's not, Detective Hicks comes back.

"Can't hurt to give you a spoon." Detective Hicks sits down, and sets a teaspoon on the table between them.

"And if you are stupid enough to try and use a spoon as a weapon, I'll shoot you," Ronan says.

"Real ray of sunshine isn't he?" Dustin says to Detective Hicks, who looks like she is fighting a smile at his words.

"You behave, and Ronan, maybe try not to threaten him. He's not a suspect at this time. He's here with information." Detective Hicks tuts at them both.

"Just show us whatever it is you think will prove you're the real deal." Ronan has a lot of disbelief in his voice for someone who hunts ghosts and monsters for a living.

Dustin puts his hand down on the table, palm up, away from the spoon. And then he focuses on the small metal object—it wouldn't work if it was something big. The teaspoon begins to shake, and then it moves slowly across the table and into his hand. Not finished, Dustin takes hold of the spoon. Holding it up, he focuses again, and the spoon slowly starts to bend in half. Once the metal is twisted and bent, Dustin puts it down onto the table—the room is silent apart from the three of them breathing.

"Proof enough?" Dustin asks, breaking the stillness. He takes a tissue out of his jacket pocket just in time, ready to catch the small trickle of blood.

"You're bleeding." Detective Hicks sounds worried.

"Which would be why I don't pull out that trick often. Not just because of the headache." Dustin grimaces, cleaning away the small amount of blood.

"You can move objects?" Ronan asks.

"Only metal and only small things. And even then, well, you can see for yourself, it's not easy on my body and not something my neurologist recommends I do." Dustin has a headache now, but he doesn't want to tell them. Dustin doesn't like to admit how weak his powers can make him, how it hurts.

"You see a neurologist?" Detective Hicks asks.

"I have issues with headaches." Dustin doesn't want to go into it. It's not like his powers are going to kill him, not like they once thought. But they will always cause him pain, a lot of pain.

"So a small amount of telekinesis and visions, anything else we should know?" Ronan asks.

"Made a believer of you, have I?" Dustin asks instead.

"Made me a believer in you and I didn't know this shit was real," Detective Hicks says honestly.

"And you?" Dustin presses, focusing on Ronan.

"I was always a believer," Ronan shrugs.

"But do you believe in me now?" Dustin asks.

"I'd be stupid not to. There was no way to fake that, not here and now. Between that and the crime scene, I find myself believing you really have powers." Ronan is still just as grumpy, though. Dustin is used to most cop types being excited when he proves his powers. But then, Ronan has probably seen more than Dustin's small shows of power, if his website was anything to go on.

"So we know you're for real now—what brought you here again after being sent away?" Detective Hicks asks. She seems more interested, more open. A little shocked by what she's seen, but not afraid.

"I left the college, but I stopped for a coffee nearby, but that's not important, it wasn't the place that was important. Sometimes visions come to me later, after I've tried to make a connection," Dustin explains.

He'd been sitting down to a latte when he'd zoned out, the images coming to him.

"What did you see?" Ronan asks.

"Cages," Dustin says simply.

"Cages?" Detective Hicks repeats.

"A room full of cages," Dustin explains.

"For animals? What makes you think that this vision links to this case?" Ronan asks.

"I think they were animal cages, but big ones, and I don't think they were being used for animals. They had chains in them, blankets, water bottles, food. And it was cold and damp, just like the first vision I had of Ann Beth." Dustin is sure the place he saw has something to do with the missing women. He's not often wrong about what his visions link to.

"You think the missing women are being kept?" Detective Hicks asks.

"Yes. The first vision I had, I told Ronan about, I saw Ann Beth in a basement somewhere. She was alive, but alone, chained up. But I think at some point some of the women have been kept together." Dustin has no idea why, who, or what is going on with the women. All he knows is they aren't being killed as soon as they are taken, so there is a chance of saving them.

"I'm going to be straight with you. I was hired to look into this case by the police. The police and FBI are working together. But they want me on the case because of the things I specialize in. They also want you on the case; you'll be paid," Ronan tells him.

"Okay, I'd like to help." Dustin isn't going to argue wages. He's on the case, that's what he wants. He wants to help.

"You'll be working with me." Ronan doesn't sound too pleased about that fact.

"I can do that." Dustin is sure he can put up with Ronan's

closed off nature—as long as the guy isn't a total jackass, it should be fine.

"You should tell him about the weird thing about this case, the reason you were called in," Detective Hicks says to Ronan.

"Ah yes, the blood." Ronan frowns.

"What about the blood?" Dustin asks.

"At each crime scene the blood of the previous woman has been found," Ronan explains.

"Which is weird as hell," Detective Hicks adds.

"Found how? Like painted on the walls? What?" Dustin hadn't seen any blood in his visions so far, not like that, not at the crime scenes—the only blood he saw was on the woman's bleeding wrist.

"No, just traces, usually on the ground, sometimes on the furniture. No one can work out what's going on. I've started researching possibilities, but I haven't seen anything like this before, and I've seen a lot of weird shit," Ronan comments.

"That is strange." Dustin frowns—who takes blood from one crime scene to another?

"I'll be staying on the case, but I'll only be working the crime scenes here, so I might see you again. But are you all right to travel to the other states?" Detective Hicks asks.

"There's nothing to stop me going, but I can't drive, so that might be a problem." Dustin has never had a driver's license. He never took his test, because of his visions. He always knew there was a risk that he could have a vision while driving and crash. He doesn't want to risk killing himself or anyone else.

"I can drive you, seeing as we're working together." Once again Ronan sounds reluctant.

Dustin has a feeling that Ronan isn't going to be the easiest person to work with.

"That's decided then. Ronan has copies of all the files you need. Let's get you out of here and send you two on your way. If these women are alive, we need to work quickly." Detective Hicks stands up, clearly ready to be on the move.

Dustin thinks she'd probably be easier to work with than Ronan. She seems nicer, more open. Even though she didn't know about the supernatural before today. But Dustin knows that he doesn't get to choose who he works with. He's lucky to have been let on the case.

They all stand up and leave the interrogation room together, getting lots of looks from other officers. Detective Hicks shakes both their hands and says good-bye to them. Ronan gathers his files and leads the way out of the station, giving Dustin no choice but to follow.

"So we're going to check out the other locations in Portland first, right? See if I can get a vision, and if you can detect anything?" Dustin asks as they get outside.

"There are two more we can probably get to today, then we'll start traveling. You have anything that'll stop you from leaving town without notice? Job? Family?" Ronan asks.

"I volunteer at a few places, but I don't have a job or set hours. And my family—let's just say they won't notice. I'll text a few friends so they don't end up putting in a missing person's report on me. But no, there's nothing at the moment that will keep me from leaving town." Dustin doesn't want to explain about his parents.

Mr. and Mrs. Perfect, the ideal couple, good careers, well-off, nice house. All the shiny dressing hiding the truth from the outside world, like his father's affairs and his mother's drinking. And, well, Dustin had never fit into their picture-perfect world, not with his "issues" as they called them. So they were happy for him to stay out of their lives.

They send money every month. Dustin donates most of it, only keeping enough for things like his medications when he hasn't been able to earn money himself. It can be hard to get a job when any simple Google search of your name shows an article about a breakdown and several about being a psychic.

"Where do you volunteer? My car's this way, I can drive us to the scenes. Did you get a bus here?" Ronan asks, leading the way—he seems to like being in charge.

"I rode my bicycle, but I'll pick that up later. I work at a domestic abuse shelter and an animal rescue center." Dustin likes his jobs, even though he doesn't get paid. He likes helping people and animals.

"Not a lot of men work in domestic abuse shelters. Aren't the women afraid of you?" Ronan frowns.

"It's a mixed shelter, for men, women, and children. I haven't had anyone be more afraid of me than anyone else there. The kids tend to like my hair, and the moms like it when the kids are

43

happy." Dustin shrugs—he doesn't like to brag, but he's good with people, especially people society would class as damaged.

Dustin might not have been through what they have, but he can understand it, because he's felt it. His visions give him an insight into lots of other kinds of lives. He feels what they feel when he has visions of them.

"Yeah, the hair's interesting. Why purple?" Ronan's face is blank, so it's hard to tell if he thinks Dustin's hair is interesting in a good or bad way.

"Why not purple?" Dustin asks, a little defensively.

"I guess being an ex-cop I was taught to blend in, not stick out in a crowd. Someone sees you, with that hair, well, it's memorable," Ronan explains.

"I'm not a cop or a private detective. I don't go sneaking around or trying to blend in. When I help the cops, it actually helps to stand out, to be different. People hear psychic and they don't expect a wallflower or some military-looking dude. They think of hippies and gypsies, which isn't my style, but this is, and it hasn't stopped me from helping people," Dustin says truthfully.

"Don't get me wrong, I like it, it suits you. I just can't imagine going to crime scenes looking like some kind of goth runway model." Ronan sounds a little flustered toward the end, maybe because he realizes he just called another man attractive. Dustin hopes Ronan isn't the uptight homophobic type of ex-cop. He has that strict military vibe, and that type of guy can often be the kind who try to kick Dustin's ass.

"Thanks, I think. I do fine at crime scenes, though. I mean, people stare and whisper, but I figure they'd do that anyway; people find it kind of interesting to be around a psychic. Even cops—they'll be wondering if I'm the real deal, what kind of powers I have, can I tell them if their wife is cheating, the usual." Dustin shakes his head.

"This is my car." Ronan points—it's a nice-looking Ford, not like super fancy, but well looked after, no scratches or dents. Dustin would bet money that Ronan is a careful driver, probably never breaks the law.

Ronan unlocks his car, and they both get in the front. Ronan passes Dustin some files.

"Can you read while I drive? It might help you get caught up on the case. I'm taking us to Jamie Harvard's house first. She's the most recent to go missing." Ronan fills Dustin in.

"I can read it. I saw some stuff online. They thought it was the boyfriend to start off with?" Dustin asks, opening the first file as Ronan pulls away from the curb.

"They never should have—it was BS racial profiling. Missing white girl, African-American boyfriend, so of course they were looking at him when she went missing. Tony, the boyfriend, he had a solid alibi for when Jamie went missing. He reported her missing right away, there was nothing suspicious in his behavior, and no one had reported them fighting or having any problems." Ronan shakes his head, clearly a little pissed off at the cops for that one.

"That's messed up. Just because they were different races they what, think he must be a killer?" Dustin asks.

"There is still a lot of racism in the police force—even though the higher-ups say it's not tolerated, it happens, I've seen it happen. I had it easy in that respect—white, blond, I couldn't fit in California more. But people even stereotype that. I've had people think I'm some dumb beach bum. I know that's not as bad as what people of color get, but it still used to piss me off." Ronan clearly isn't a racist, which wins him some bonus points with Dustin, but that still doesn't mean Dustin is going to enjoy working with him.

Ronan, it's like he has a brick wall around him—the only time it had really been down was after Dustin had read him, then he'd been shaken up by the things Dustin had seen. It makes Dustin wonder who the girl had been, what all the images had meant.

"So no dumb blond jokes? Fair enough. Just don't call me a faggot or a fairy and we have a deal," Dustin throws out, not making eye contact, waiting for Ronan's reaction.

"Sounds like a fair deal, no name-calling," Ronan agrees. He doesn't even ask any questions about Dustin being gay, so it seems outing himself to an ex-cop wasn't a stupid idea after all.

"No name-calling," Dustin echoes.

Dustin reads Jamie Harvard's case file while they drive, occasionally asking Ronan questions, but otherwise keeping quiet. Ronan doesn't have the radio on, even though the car has one— Dustin wonders if it's broken or if Ronan just doesn't like music.

Jamie's house is in a nice area. At thirty-two, she's a successful lawyer, working for a reasonably large firm, a firm that the file says

45

has offered a reward for information that leads to her safe return. Ronan parks in the driveway.

"How are we going to get in?" Dustin asks.

"The boyfriend's staying in the house in case someone calls with a ransom; he can let us in," Ronan tells him.

"You don't think that'll happen do you? That someone will call? This isn't about money—if it was, someone would have made demands about the girls already." Dustin doesn't believe these are kidnappings for ransom. It's been two months since the first girl went missing. They would have called by now or sent a note. Which doesn't mean it isn't about money; someone could be selling the girls. But that wouldn't explain the blood at each scene.

"No, I don't think someone will call. Are you ready for this? Have you dealt with loved ones of missing people before?" Ronan asks.

"I'm ready. I was once on the case of a missing five-year-old boy. The parents were losing their minds; I think if I can handle being around them, I can do this," Dustin points out.

"All right. I'm going to ask some questions, look around. You do whatever it is you do. The boyfriend's name is Tony, it's good to try and connect, but don't share too much." Ronan opens the driver's door and gets out of the car; Dustin follows suit.

They walk up to the door and Ronan rings the doorbell. Dustin feels Tony's sadness before he even reaches the door; the air is thick with it—Tony must feel like he's drowning in it. The door opens and there's Tony. Dustin tries to look at him with a cop's eye, to see why they thought he was to blame. Tony is tall, strong-looking, black, but Dustin must not be wired like those cops, because that isn't enough to make this man seem dangerous to Dustin.

Tony has kind brown eyes, a little bloodshot from crying and probably a lack of sleep. He looks weary, and lost, and not at all like a man who has done anything to harm his girlfriend, let alone nine other women across the country.

"Hello, Tony. I'm a private detective with the police, I've come to ask you a few questions." Ronan shows his private investigator's badge, before putting it away.

"And who are you? You don't look like a cop, or a private detective," Tony says to Dustin.

"I'm a consultant. I sometimes help police with cases. I'm here to help find Jamie, that's all that matters right?" Dustin doesn't want to have to explain that he's a psychic to Tony; it'll take up valuable time. If Dustin stopped to prove what he is to every person he meets, he'd never get anything done.

"All right, come in." Tony steps back and lets them in, leading the way to the family room.

"Some of my questions might seem strange, and I'm going to try and not ask you too many things you've already been asked—your answers are on file. I know it must be frustrating to be asked the same questions over and over again, when you only have the same answers to give," Ronan says as he sits down.

"Do you mind if I look around while you talk?" Dustin asks.

"No, not if it helps get Jamie back," Tony says.

So Dustin leaves Ronan to question Tony, and heads upstairs, looking for Jamie's bedroom, because that was where the blood was found, and where they think she went missing from. There is crime scene tape on the door, which Dustin ignores. He always ignores police tape, but at least this time he knows ignoring it won't get him arrested, seeing as he's officially working for the police this time.

Jamie's bedroom is stylish, well-kept, with lots of light colors—it's a bright beautiful room, which makes the way Dustin feels when he enters it strange. He feels like he's in somewhere dark and cold, even though warm sunlight is shining through the window.

Something bad definitely happened here—someone, or something dark was in this room. Dustin walks farther into the room, the dark feeling clinging to him as he makes his way to the bed. The sheets are pulled back, and there is a book propped open on the nightstand Dustin has seen pictures of Jamie; he can imagine her reading in bed, just a few chapters before she had to go to sleep, because she had work early in the morning.

Only Jamie hadn't made it to work; they had called her and gotten no answer, so they called Tony, who had come over to the house. And he had found it like this, but with the window open and all the lights still on from the night before.

Dustin places his hand on Jamie's pillow, where she would have rested her head each night to sleep. He begins to sense more of that dark feeling as soon as he touches the cool material, and he hesitates to open his mind.

But that is what he is here for—no matter what he might see, he has to look. Even if he sees something that will haunt his nightmares. Because for Jamie it isn't a nightmare, it's her life— she might be living it right this second.

He sits down on the bed carefully, not wanting to disturb it, but having a feeling he'll need to be sitting down for this. Dustin opens his mind, and lets the images in.

There is darkness and screaming. Someone begging to go home, pleading and bargaining. But Jamie doesn't speak, she's too afraid, has been since she saw that face, that inhuman face. Another voice joins the screamer, saying, "No," over and over. Jamie hears one of the cages open in the dark, and the, "Nos," turn to screams.

Dustin opens his eyes, and he's back in Jamie's bedroom. He still feels cold, so cold, like he was in that basement for real with those girls. But at least Dustin has something to tell Ronan. He gets up off the bed, feeling slightly dizzy. He takes a few minutes to regain his composure, running a hand through his hair, messing it up the way he likes it.

Once he feels more like himself, Dustin leaves Jamie's bedroom and goes back downstairs, where Ronan is thanking Tony for his time, and promising to do all that he can to get Jamie back.

"Are you ready to leave?" Ronan asks.

"Yes. Thank you for letting me look around, Tony." Dustin tries to smile, but it feels frozen and awkward.

"I have your number. I'll be back in contact if I think of any other questions, and the local police will keep you informed of the case," Ronan promises.

Tony walks them to the door, saying good-bye, and he looks so sad, so heartbroken—how could anyone have ever thought he would have hurt Jamie?

They go back to the car before Ronan speaks—he doesn't turn to Dustin until they are inside the car.

"Did you see anything?" Ronan asks.

"Yes, Jamie is still alive. And she's being kept with other girls. I heard at least two others," Dustin explains.

"Anything else?" Ronan presses.

"Jamie thought of the face she had seen as 'inhuman.'" Dustin bites his lip. He might be psychic, but he doesn't have much experience with the supernatural.

"So it's as we suspected—something, not a person, is taking girls, keeping them for some reason. Did she know what it was? Or where she was being kept?" Ronan asks, starting the car and pulling out of Jamie's driveway.

"I didn't see what she saw, but I know it frightened her, so much that she was afraid to make a sound. But she didn't know what it was, or where she was. All I could tell, again, was that it was dark and cold, like a basement. I know that's not very useful, but I didn't see more." Dustin is a little frustrated, and he's worried that he's not doing enough, that he isn't helping.

"It's good that we know that the women are alive and being kept together. We weren't sure about that. And we can rule out any humans in their lives. I was already sure that Tony had nothing to do with it, but your vision saves us time. We don't need to look into people in the women's lives unless we suspect they are not human," Ronan says thoughtfully.

"Some cops I've worked with, they don't really know what to expect from a psychic, they think I'll see everything, the whole story, when it's more like snapshots. I'm just… I want to be straight up with you—hopefully I'll be able to help, but I can only see what I'm shown, if that makes sense," Dustin rambles.

"I get what you're trying to say, I think. Some people you've worked with have had too high expectations of what you can do with your powers. I've met psychics before. I know it's not always simple. I don't expect you to have all the answers. I just hope you'll have some." Ronan seems quite reasonable.

"I want to help, but I've been lucky so far to see what I have— the likelihood of me seeing an address is slim to none, but I could see something that will lead us to where the women are being held." Dustin hopes at least that he can see something that will show him the way to the missing women.

"Just do your best. There are a lot of people on this case—the FBI, the cops—they might find something. And I have a researcher looking into what could be taking the women. I can tell him now that they are being kept alive, that'll help Harry with his research. There are only so many creatures that keep their victims alive,"

49

Ronan tells Dustin as he drives.

"Are we going to where the third woman went missing?" Dustin asks.

"Yes, and then I'm going to crash for the night. I've done a lot of driving today. I'll do some research, get some sleep, and then pick you up in the morning and we'll head to Arizona, where four women went missing, then to Nevada, where two went missing, and then back to California, where just one woman is missing. At least, that's what we'll do if we don't find anything that sends use elsewhere." Ronan lists off the places the women have gone missing from.

"So next is Lisa Green?" Dustin asks.

"Yes, twenty-five, waitress, went missing on her cigarette break at the diner she works at," Ronan says, taking a turn down a busy street.

"It was nighttime, right, but still, it must have been very quick. Her break was fifteen minutes long, I read in the file. She was seen at midnight, she should have been back sooner, but no one went looking for her until half an hour had passed, and she wasn't outside, and they found blood in the alley." Dustin checks the time in one of the file folders as he talks.

"So at the most the window to take her was half an hour. The alley is quiet, but it's next to a busy diner. We need to look and see what's around it, how something got her away so quickly." Ronan hums, clearly thinking out loud.

They drive the rest of the way to the diner talking over what they have read in the files, then they park across the street from the diner.

"I want to see what's at the other end of the alleyway first. Because Lisa Green should have been seen if she was taken from the front, unless she was lured away, but the blood suggests some violence—even though it's not hers, it's very confusing," Ronan says before getting out of the car.

Dustin follows him. And they cross the street. The mouth of the alley opens into the street; it goes down along the length of the diner, which is next door to a nail salon, separated by the alley. But Dustin sees as soon as he gets into the alley that at the other end there is a parking lot—it's on the other side of a wire fence, with barbed wire, but Dustin still thinks it's more likely Lisa was taken that way, and not out onto the street.

"The blood was up here, near the diner's back door," Ronan tells him, walking farther into the alley.

"When her boss went looking for her, did he say if he found any lit cigarettes? The file said she was a smoker. I was just wondering, if she was still smoking when she was taken, then she was taken sooner and by surprise, not just as she was getting ready to go back inside," Dustin reasons walking to where Ronan said the blood was.

"I don't know, good question. I'll ask her boss afterward. I think they must have taken her over the fence. It's not that high, a lot of creatures would be able to get over it with Lisa, especially if she was unconscious. Do you agree?" Ronan presses a hand against the fence, like he's working out how hard it would be to climb.

"That was what I thought too, but I have no idea what kind of supernatural things are real. What strong things are there?" Dustin asks.

"Ghouls, shape-shifters, werewolves, vampires, skin-walkers; people who are possessed often get strength from the ghost possessing them; you can get a kind of zombie, they are pretty strong, but they aren't smart enough to kidnap and keep someone, they just kill and feed," Ronan explains.

"All those things are real?" Dustin is surprised.

"You're a psychic—have you never met anything like that?" Ronan asks.

"Not like a monster. I mean, I was always a believer, because of what I am, my abilities, but I never saw anything. When I've helped the cops before, the bad guys always been human." Dustin spots what he thinks might be the remains of blood, and he kneels down to touch it.

Pain shoots through his body, but it's not his body, it's Lisa's. There is a rush of images and when Dustin forces his eyes open again, he's fallen onto his side on the ground, and Ronan is crouching beside him looking worried.

"Well that sucked." Dustin moves slowly into a sitting position, his head spinning.

"What happened to you? Are you okay?" Ronan asks.

"Vision—they can be like that sometimes. I'm all right.

51

Probably a little dirty from the ground," Dustin complains, trying to get up.

Dustin is a little unsteady on his feet though, so Ronan reaches out, steadying him, helping Dustin stand.

"Thank you," Dustin says softly, a little too aware of how close Ronan is. Ronan is a big, solid presence, very manly, and Dustin finds himself drawn to the heat coming from Ronan. But Dustin isn't an idiot. He knows he's just being a fool. He's shaken up from his vision, and Ronan is an attractive man, but that's no reason for Dustin to go and do something stupid, like make a pass at a straight ex-cop the first day they are working together.

Dustin makes sure he's steady, and then he steps back from Ronan, who doesn't look like he noticed Dustin having a moment. If he has, he's not having a straight guy freak out over it.

"So what did you see?" Ronan asks.

"Lisa was hurt here. And scared. She didn't see whatever it was coming. So it must have been quiet. And I think she was taken to a car? Do any of those monsters you talked about know how to drive as well? Because I would swear it took her to the parking lot and put her in the trunk of a car." Dustin frowns.

"In theory some of them could drive. Shifters, for example, have human forms. It would be strong in human form still, but I don't know of any shifters that carry around the blood of their last victim," Ronan sighs.

"Let's go talk to the people who worked with Lisa, and maybe get something to eat. I'm starving. And dizzy—some food would do me good after that," Dustin explains.

"I should eat too. It's been a long day," Ronan agrees; they go into the diner.

They get a table and both order burgers and fries, and while they wait they talk to the staff. Everyone is worried about Lisa, but no one really knows anything. They didn't see anything that night. They do mention a few creepy customers who paid Lisa too much attention, but none of them sound dangerous.

"I'll give the names to Harry to see if they have any supernatural connections, but I don't think any of them sound right. I don't think this kidnapper would sit in the diner and have a meal or give their name," Ronan sighs.

"I'm not used to monster hunting. Anything I should pack?"

Dustin asks.

"Just treat it like a road trip. Bring a few days of clothes, toiletries, anything you need. I'll have some weapons, but unless you have a carry permit, you can't have a gun," Ronan says, patting his side where the gun he pointed at Dustin earlier that day is concealed.

They eat their meal and talk about the case, the different women, trying to hunt out hidden connections. Then, once they are done, Dustin gives Ronan his address, and Ronan drives him home.

"I'll see you at eight tomorrow. We have a day of driving. Be packed and ready to go. Try and get lots of sleep," Ronan instructs.

"Will do, see you tomorrow." Dustin gets out of the car and goes up to his little apartment.

He packs a bag for their trip, and then settles down in front of his laptop, researching the list of types of monsters Ronan had mentioned. Sleep can wait.

Chapter Five

It's early when Ronan pulls up to the curb outside Dustin's place, but seconds later Dustin appears with a travel bag in one hand. He's wearing a huge black coat that swallows him up, hiding his body from chin to knee. The jeans he is wearing beneath the coat are a bright red, and tight, showing off long legs, well-defined. He's wearing a beanie as well, pulled down over his head, but bits of purple hair peek out from beneath it.

Ronan opens up the car to let Dustin in, and he opens the back to put his bag on the backseat before coming around and getting in the front passenger seat.

"Morning," Ronan says, taking another look. He knows from the e-mail Chris sent over of a few of Dustin's cases that he's only twenty-one, eleven years younger than Ronan, which makes Ronan feel a little bad for checking Dustin out. But Ronan can't lie— Dustin is good-looking, striking, not really Ronan's usual type, but he can't help looking.

"Morning," Dustin says, tugging his scarf down a little so his mouth isn't covered. He has nice lips, and Ronan is a little worried that he's going to allow himself to be distracted by Dustin.

Ronan is here for the case, he's here to help the missing women, he isn't here to get laid. So no matter how intrigued he is by Dustin, it can't go anywhere. Most of what he knows about Dustin comes from files on his work as a psychic. He doesn't really know much about the man, other than he's the real deal, a genuine psychic who seems to like helping people.

Ronan pulls away from the curb, keeping his focus on the road, but at the same time trying to get a read on Dustin. Not because Ronan is attracted to him, though he is, but because he has to work with him.

"You look tired, are you ready for this case? We'll be traveling most of the day," Ronan points out.

"I'm fine. I just had a late night looking into the case. I

was hoping I'd read something that would trigger a vision, it's happened before," Dustin explains.

"And did you see anything?" Ronan asks.

"No, not really. I kept getting this weird feeling when I thought of the women, like, drained. I think I was feeling what they are feeling, and they were drained of energy," Dustin says thoughtfully.

"If they are being kept somewhere cold, with not much food, it would make sense them not having a lot of energy. It's been cold out; if they're in a basement they must be freezing." Ronan turns up the heating in the car just at the thought of being in a basement in January.

"I don't think it's just that. They were really weak, but alive, I'm sure they are still alive." Dustin sounds hopeful.

"I read through some of your cases. I know you've dealt with losing people you've been looking for before. Can you handle that? If we don't get all these women back?" Ronan asks, slowing down as he hits a little traffic.

"I won't like it. I'm sure you won't be happy if any of them die either. But I can handle it. I might not be a cop, or an ex-cop, but I can deal. Like you said, I've done it before. This might be my first supernatural case, but I'm not a total newbie. Why do you think I won't cope?" Dustin asks.

"You've connected to three of these women already; you've felt what they are feeling. I was just thinking that must connect you to the case more, make it more personal," Ronan says honestly, not mentioning that he knows Dustin had a breakdown in college, but not what it was over.

Ronan can't help being curious about that. Ronan was a cop, he saw people go through a lot of shit, and some cops ended up lost in a bottle trying to cope. It's not like Ronan is judging Dustin for having issues, but he's curious, and he would like to know if there is any chance it'll affect the case.

But other than Dustin's association with the police, it was hard to get any other information on him. Harry had gone as far to say in his e-mail that it was like someone was hiding something. Harry hadn't been able to find any real background on Dustin—family, friends. All he could find were arrests and working with the police, and they all started in his college years.

"Did you always get visions?" Ronan asks, wondering if they started for Dustin in college.

"When I was about five I think. I was always a creepy kid, knew things kids shouldn't know or notice. But I didn't really get that I was different until I was older. What is this anyway, twenty questions?" Dustin raises an eyebrow. He has a faint scar under the left one; it looks like he used to have a piercing there.

Ronan wonders if Dustin has more piercings. He has several in each ear, but no other visible ones, like nose, lip, or tongue. Ronan has never had a thing for piercings really, but he thinks he'd like them on Dustin, and those are the kind of thoughts he shouldn't be having. Ronan is a professional. He always puts work first and that's not going to change here.

"We have a long trip, and we could be working together for a while, I figure we should at least know some basics about each other. We don't need to be best friends to work together, but I think it'll be better if we're not total strangers." Ronan isn't looking to make friends, but he knows he'll go crazy if he doesn't learn to get along with Dustin, who seems like a very different type of guy to Ronan.

"So I get to ask questions too?" Dustin asks.

"If you even need to. I'm sure you can guess plenty from your vision when we met." Ronan has been a little on edge about that, about how much Dustin might know, how much he saw.

"Well I know you were a cop, we covered that, and that your dad was Army. I know you hunt the supernatural, but I don't know why. I don't know much about you. I didn't see much. I don't think you want me to try and read you again, so maybe you should tell me a little about you instead."

Dustin might look young and wacky, but he's smart, perceptive. Ronan doesn't want to be read again.

"I have things I'd prefer to keep private. I'm sure everyone does. How about from here on out if we want to know something about each other, we ask, we don't look into each other in any other way," Ronan suggests, mainly because he doesn't want Dustin looking into Sarah, what had happened to her, and how it had affected Ronan.

"Sounds fair enough. Even though you already had the cops look into me, from now on, if you want to know something ask me,

not your cop friends or that researcher, Harry, you told me about."
Dustin doesn't sound too worried about the fact that Ronan had
researched him—maybe he doesn't have much to hide.

"I won't have anyone look into you again. I'll ask questions
from now on. Like I said, we don't need to be close friends, but we
need to trust each other enough to work together." Ronan is curious
about Dustin's breakdown, but he doesn't think their second day
together is the best time to ask something so personal.

Besides, if he starts asking really personal questions, then
Dustin will have every right to ask the same kind of stuff back, and
Ronan isn't ready to be an open book. He wants to be trusted, sure,
but he doesn't want to bare his soul.

"I only looked at your website, which was pretty cool by the
way. So I guess ask me anything you think is important," Dustin
offers.

"Can you shoot?" Ronan had been wondering about setting
Dustin up with one of his guns.

"Not well. I've been to the range a few times, but I'm not
skilled." Dustin sounds apologetic.

"Can you defend yourself though? If it comes to a fight?"
Ronan asks.

"Yes, believe it or not I'm a black belt in judo, and I've dabbled
in a few other martial arts," Dustin says.

The road's pretty clear, so Ronan lets himself take a good look
at little Dustin bundled up in that big coat, wearing boots that give
him a few more inches of height.

"No offense, but you look kind of small to be great at hand-to-
hand combat," Ronan says skeptically.

"I'm all muscle." Dustin shrugs.

"Really?" Ronan hasn't seen Dustin without a ton of layers,
so maybe he does have a toned body under all those clothes—he
looks slim with them on, but he might have muscle.

"Yep, I'm great with my hands." Dustin winks.

"Can you use any weapons?" Ronan asks.

"I'm good with knives, handheld weapons. But of course I
never carry a knife, detective, because that would be illegal."
Dustin's eyes have a sparkle in them as he speaks.

"I think, given that we are hunting a mystery monster who has
ten women captive, I'll let that go. Not that I encourage people to

break the law. I was a cop once." Ronan is a believer in the law, and upholding it, most of the time. But he also sees that sometimes the law hasn't caught up with the world they are living in—it's certainly not designed to deal with the supernatural.

"So why did you stop being a cop? It seems like you love that kind of thing. And at the police station yesterday you fit in, it was like you belonged there." Dustin sounds curious.

"I wanted to help people, so I became a cop, but as a cop I couldn't go after the supernatural. The government knows that there are things that exist in this world that most people think are just stories, but they refuse to acknowledge it, they think it'll cause a panic. So cops' hands are tied. I didn't like that. I wanted to be free to investigate anything," Ronan explains.

"I can get that. It would be frustrating to know that your criminal was actually a monster, and not be able to look into it properly." Dustin frowns. "So teach me about some monsters," Dustin says.

"You want a monster lesson?" Ronan asks.

"Yes. If I'm looking for one then I think I should know more about them," Dustin says.

Ronan knows a lot about monsters, so telling Dustin about them takes up a lot of the journey. They only stop for gas and lunch, because talking about monsters in public isn't a good idea. But once they are back in the car Ronan continues his lesson.

It's afternoon by the time they cross into Arizona, so Ronan drives straight to a motel, his second in two days.

"It would make sense if we share a room so we can keep working on the case. But I totally understand if you want your own room." Ronan wants to be able to keep an eye on Dustin, but he doesn't want to share a room, because of his attraction to Dustin, because he is determined to ignore that.

Dustin isn't even his type—young, slightly odd, outgoing and out there. To compare them Ronan would say he is the kind of person to color inside the lines, and Dustin wouldn't even see the lines—he clearly doesn't believe in rules and regulations.

"I'm okay with that, as long as you don't snore," Dustin jokes.

"I don't snore. Do you?" Ronan asks as they get out of the car and head for the motel office.

"No. I occasionally have visions while I sleep. It'll just look like I'm mumbling in my sleep. When they wake me up I always make notes on what I saw so I don't forget in the morning," Dustin explains.

"That's fine, feel free to wake me if you see something really important," Ronan offers.

They go into the office and a young woman checks them into a double room. She's not nosy, doesn't ask why they are in town, but she's pleasant. She gives them their keys and tells them to come see her if they need anything.

They get their bags from the car and head to their room, for at least the night.

Ronan is unpacking his things, setting up the desk in the room with his laptop and the files from the case, when he notices something out of the corner of his eye. Dustin is sitting on the edge of one of the beds, the one closest to the bathroom, because Ronan had claimed the one closest to the door.

On the nightstand, Dustin has placed several small pill bottles and a bottle of water. Even as Ronan watches, Dustin takes out some pills from the containers and takes them with the water, before he continues unpacking his bag.

Ronan thinks about saying something, but he thinks that might be one of those questions that comes under the umbrella of too personal. And Ronan wants to keep things professional.

"We should probably eat and get an early night. We don't want to be lurking around crime scenes in the dark. I want to let the local police know we are here and check in with Harry as well," Ronan suggests.

They go out to a local restaurant and eat together. Ronan talks a little about being a cop, how they are taught to investigate, and the clues the Phoenix cops might have missed. And he tells a few cop stories, none too personal, but from his years as a cop—Dustin seems to find them interesting.

Dustin adds his own cop stories, about the police he has worked with, and the places his visions have taken him. He doesn't brag, but Ronan already knows from what Harry e-mailed him that in a lot of the cases, the situation was only solved because of Dustin and his visions.

Toward the end of their meal a group of teenage girls come in and are seated at a table close by. Ronan notices them giggling and looking over a lot, but Dustin doesn't seem to notice it. When they pay their bill, one of the girls gets up and comes over. She's good-looking, red hair, curves, too young for Ronan even if he liked women.

"Hi." She smiles, and it's clearly directed at Dustin.

"Hello," Dustin says politely, but Ronan can see the lack of interest in his gaze.

"Can I give you my number?" the girl asks, twiddling with her hair.

"Sorry, I'm with someone." Dustin reaches across the table and puts his hand on top of Ronan's, and the girl seems to notice him for the first time.

"Oh, I'm sorry, I didn't know." The girl blushes and turns away, hurrying back to her table.

"Let's get out of here," Dustin suggests, and he stands, letting go of Ronan's hand, which feels slightly cold now that it's not in contact with Dustin's.

They don't talk again until they are out of the restaurant, in the parking lot, heading for the car. Dustin puts a hand on Ronan's elbow to still him then.

"Sorry for using you like that, I hope you don't mind. It seemed like the easiest way of turning her down. I didn't want to upset a—what? Fifteen-year-old girl? And I thought maybe you'd be okay with it if it avoided a scene." Dustin looks a little worried, like he's afraid of how Ronan will react.

"That's fine. Does that happen a lot? Should I expect to see women throwing themselves at you?" Ronan asks as they get back in his car.

"I guess for a gay guy I get a fair amount of attention from women. It's weird, like, I'm a total shy loser, always have been. I was the quiet kid in class, but girls always pay attention to me. I don't know why." Dustin shrugs.

"You were shy?" Ronan asks as he starts driving them back to the motel.

"Yeah, really. I know I seem pretty out there, but I live in my own little world most of the time. I'm not the life of the party. I'm sure you've probably dated more than me. I can still be shy now."

Ronan is kind of surprised. Dustin seems so comfortable in his own skin. It's a little shocking that he's maybe not great with people. Maybe Ronan was judging a little too much on appearance, because of Dustin's colorful style, because he's gorgeous. He could see how embarrassed Dustin was by the young girl's attention, but he still tried to be kind about letting her down.

"You touched my hand," Ronan realizes.

"Yeah? And? I wasn't making a pass at you." Dustin is clearly used to dealing with homophobic cops.

Ronan could just tell Dustin that he is also gay, but he doesn't want to share that. If he does, it might be easier for Dustin to guess that Ronan finds him attractive. And he just doesn't want to talk about his personal life.

"I know that. I was just… you didn't have another vision, did you?" Ronan doesn't want Dustin seeing more of his secrets.

"Oh, no, no I didn't. I wasn't trying to see anything. I don't get them every time I touch a person. That would be really annoying. So you don't have to worry about me reading you all the time, like if you pass me a coffee and stuff. But it could happen—it just doesn't happen often unless I'm open to it," Dustin explains.

"Cool, no offense, but I like the inside of my head to stay private. I know we agreed to be honest with each other, but I'm sure you'd like some boundaries still. I don't like the idea of someone I've been working with for two days knowing every detail of my life," Ronan says honestly.

"I totally get that. I don't think there is anyone in my life I share every detail of what's inside my head with. Including my friends, so I get not wanting to do that with someone you hardly know," Dustin agrees.

"Good. I don't want to be an asshole, but I don't want to be read," Ronan says as they pull up outside the motel.

"Sounds fine to me. I won't read you on purpose. And If I accidentally get any visions about you, I'll tell you," Dustin says, getting out of the car.

They go back to the room they have rented; Ronan settles in front of his laptop, to check on his e-mails, while Dustin goes and takes a shower. Ronan tries not to think about Dustin naked and wet in the other room. He hasn't had a stupid, instant crush like this since he was a teenager.

Ronan is glad that Dustin comes out already dressed, in black sweatpants and a big black hooded sweatshirt. He's completely covered, but he still looks good. Ronan is careful not to stare as Dustin goes over to his bed, getting on it, but propped up with the pillows, with a book in his hands, his feet covered in fuzzy purple socks. Ronan has an idle thought about what Dustin might look like without those clothes on, but he shakes his head and goes back to reading e-mails—this is going to be a long night.

Ronan needs this case to go as quickly as it can, and not just for the missing women's sakes.

After Ronan has looked through his e-mails, full of Harry's theories, and lists of sightings of different creatures in each state, he goes to his bed, turning the TV on quietly.

Dustin gives up reading his book after awhile, and goes to sleep with the TV still on. Ronan offers to turn it off when Dustin starts to doze, but Dustin says it's okay to leave it on. Ronan watches a few crappy shows and ends up falling asleep watching the TV, and waking up to infomercials. He turns the TV off then and gets under the blankets. If he dreams, he doesn't remember.

***

Ronan is the first one awake in the morning, so he goes and has a shower. By the time he's done, Dustin is sitting up in bed, looking rumpled from sleep. A grown man should not be able to look adorable, but Dustin does—looking at him now reminds Ronan of a sleepy kitten, a thought he is most certainly keeping to himself.

Once again Ronan notices Dustin shaking out pills from the white bottles and taking them with water. Again he pretends not to see, but he's getting more curious. Daily medication is different than having to take something occasionally, and Ronan wonders if Dustin has some kind of health problem. The only way to find out is to ask, because Ronan promised not to snoop into Dustin's life. But Ronan isn't ready to ask such a personal question.

They eat a quiet breakfast out of the vending machines outside, and then they get dressed, agreeing to visit the most recent of the crime scenes first. They have four of them to visit here. The first being a path along the Gila River where Charlotte Carter, aged twenty, had been seen going for her usual jog before she went missing.

They drive out as close to the scene as possible, and then walk the path. It's been weeks since Charlotte went missing, and the police tape has been taken down, but Ronan can work out the spot that the blood was found from the photos in Charlotte's file.

"There was one set of footprints here that roughly matched Charlotte's, right size. And there were what looked like drag marks in the dirt near the blood." Ronan points out where he thinks the marks would have been, before dozens of people walked through here, taking away any evidence Ronan would be able to see.

"Did what took her leave prints?" Dustin asks.

"There were faint impressions of another footprint, but I don't know if that's from what took her. Some creatures have quite human bodies, so human-looking feet and footprints are a possibility," Ronan explains.

"So this is a popular path, right, lots of people visit the river. Again, it seems like it must have been quick to have gotten Charlotte out of here without being seen or heard," Dustin says thoughtfully.

"No one heard any screams or shouting. There is the possibility that this creature looks normal enough that it lured Charlotte away, but it's unlikely from how her friends and family described her. She was street-smart, she wouldn't have gone off with a stranger she met while out running, not even if it was another woman." Ronan doesn't think this creature is luring the women away, he thinks it must be strong enough to take them by force.

"So the blood was here?" Dustin points to the ground.

"I think so," Ronan nods.

Dustin leans down, taking his gloves off, and tucking them in his jacket pocket, before touching the ground.

"It's muddled from all the people who have been here. But I think I'm picking up on Charlotte. She saw a man, he looked normal, and then something changed, something made her afraid. She tried to run, but he grabbed her, put something over her mouth and nose, and then she was gone, out like a light," Dustin says, straightening up.

"Did you see what took her?" Ronan asks. Knowing what they are facing might help them find the women, because certain creatures are more likely to be found in different areas. If they find out what the monster is, they might have more of an idea where its nest is.

"No, it was too blurred, but I know it was the face that gave it away as not human, does that help?" Dustin asks.

"It might. There are only so many creatures that look human, and then only change their faces. I'll text Harry that info and get him to narrow down his research. You're doing a good job, it couldn't have been easy to pick up on Charlotte when so many people have been here—not just cops, and FBI, but it's a public path, used every day." Ronan is a little impressed.

"It helps that the case is in my head. I've seen the girls; I've seen where he's keeping them. If any energy connected to the case is left behind, I can probably find it," Dustin says simply.

"Well, let's get you to the next crime scene. It's a coffeehouse in Mesa. She was co-owner—Jade Able, forty, our oldest missing person. We'll be able to talk to her business partner; she's kept the place running," Ronan suggests.

"I could use a coffee." Dustin smiles brightly.

They walk back to the car and drive to Mesa. It takes them a little while to find the coffee shop, but eventually they do, parking up the street from it.

They go into the shop, a kind of bohemian place called "The Green Bean" and go to the counter. They both order lattes and then ask to speak to the owner. They are shown to a table in a corner, and not long after their coffees arrive, a woman in her forties comes over and sits down.

"Hello, I'm Mary Right. You wanted to speak to me?" Mary asks.

"Hi, Mary, we're both working with the police on your friend Jade's case. We'd like to ask you about her disappearance." Ronan shows his private detective badge, to prove he is who he says he is, not a reporter or anything.

"I'm happy to answer any questions. I just want Jade back," Mary says, with a voice thick with unshed tears.

"You and Jade are very close?" Ronan asks.

"Friends since high school. We've been running the Bean for ten years together, we both live above the shop," Mary explains.

Ronan was sure that he read that the apartment above the coffeehouse only has one bedroom, and he has a theory.

"Please excuse me asking such a personal question, but are you and Jade a couple?" Ronan asks.

"Yes—the other police people didn't ask, so I didn't tell. We're very private people, Jade and I. I didn't want people in our business like that. I was afraid if they knew we were a couple they wouldn't take Jade going missing seriously, that they'd think we must have just had a fight, that Jade had run off. But we weren't fighting, and Jade would never just run off. If she wanted to leave me Jade would tell me, she's no coward." Mary pulls out a tissue and dabs at her eyes—she's only crying a little, but it's clear this is hard for her.

Ronan can only imagine what it must be like to have a lover go missing without any explanation. He'd be going crazy looking for them. And it would be frustrating that the police's first suspect would be the missing person's partner.

"Did Jade have anyone in her life you thought might be a danger to her?" Dustin asks—Ronan had mentioned to him in the car ride here that if the creature could appear human, it may have made its way into some of the victims' lives.

"You're not a detective are you?" Mary asks, looking Dustin over—his goth platform boots, his skinny jeans—green today— and his huge black coat. He's not wearing his hat so his purple hair is all on show. He looks so very different from Ronan; Ronan knows he still dresses like a cop.

"No, I'm not a detective. But I am consulting with the police and the FBI. I'm a psychic," Dustin says.

"A psychic? That's fascinating. Jade would love to meet you, she loves things like that, unusual people. Is there any way you can do a reading? Tell me if she's still alive?" Mary says hopefully.

"Yes. This place is full of her energy—I'm already picking up flashes of her life, but do you have something she touched a lot?" Dustin asks.

Ronan finds it interesting to watch him work. He's good with people, but not like the charming con men a lot of so-called psychics are.

"She has a favorite coffee cup. I haven't washed it since she went missing. It was still in the sink when she didn't come back from locking up the shop that night. Would that work?" Mary says, standing up.

"That should work." Dustin nods.

"I'll go get it; I'll only be a second." Mary smiles, and hurries away.

"What will you do if your vision tells you Jade is dead?" Ronan asks.

"I'll break it to Mary gently. I think she'd rather know the truth, than spend the rest of her life with false hope," Dustin says softly.

"Have you had to tell someone that a loved one was dead before?" Ronan has, as a cop, and as a private detective.

"Yes." Dustin doesn't add anything else, and before Ronan can question him on it, Mary is back with a flowery mug.

Mary sits down and puts the mug in front of Dustin.

"This might not work at all, don't get your hopes up," Dustin warns.

"I won't. I'm just grateful that you're going to try." Mary smiles weakly.

Ronan watches as Dustin places his hands on the mug and closes his eyes. His face goes very relaxed, very still. And he doesn't say anything for a few long moments.

"Jade is alive, she's with the other women. She's telling someone not to cry, that it'll be okay, that they'll get through this," Dustin says, opening his eyes, but still holding the mug, like maybe he's trying to keep the connection.

"She's alive? You're sure?" Mary sounds so relieved.

"Yes, I'm sure. She has a very strong energy; it's easy to read. She's afraid, but she's trying to keep the other women calm. She's cold, and uncomfortable, but she didn't seem to be in pain," Dustin explains, taking his hands off the mug.

"Thank you, thank you so much. Please tell me you'll be able to find her. I'd be in your debt forever. Do you know why she was taken?" Mary says in a rush.

"We don't know why the women are being taken, but we are doing our best to get them back, and so are the police and FBI." Ronan isn't going to make any promises, because he doesn't want to break them. And so far neither he nor Dustin have found anything that is helping them to find the missing women.

"We'll do everything we can to get Jade home to you," Dustin says, taking Mary's hand.

"Do you ever see the future?" Mary asks.

"Sometimes," Dustin nods.

"Can you see my future? Am I alone, or am I with Jade?" Mary asks.

"I can't see that, I'm sorry. It's harder to see the future. I'm good at seeing people's pasts, things that have happened, and things in other places. But the future hardly ever comes to me, and I can't force it," Dustin explains.

"Well, thank you anyway," Mary says softly.

Ronan asks her a few questions about the day Jade went missing while they drink their coffees, making notes to see if he comes up with any connections to the other women, or if anything gives away the creature for what it is. Once he has finished questioning Mary, they say good-bye, and head back to the car.

The next crime scene is in Tonto National Forest, which is a fair drive from the coffeehouse.

"This woman, Cassandra Clark, she was out for a run as well, but she is eight years older than Charlotte, and Hispanic, whereas Charlotte is white. Is that a connection or not, what do you think?" Dustin asks as they get closer to the forest.

"Maybe it's a connection. Both women were strong and healthy, but probably tired from running. From the paths they took, both Charlotte and Cassandra had been running for quite a while before they were taken. Maybe the creature followed them, waited until they were weaker," Ronan says thoughtfully.

Thinking about it, from their records, not one of the ten missing women had any health problems. They were all different ages, but even the oldest woman, Jade, was in great health.

"All the women were healthy," Ronan mutters as they pull into the forest's parking lot.

"You think that's a connection?" Dustin asks.

"It could be. It at least rules out some of the creatures Harry has sent me info on. Certain creatures only prey on the weak and sick. This isn't the case with our women," Ronan says, getting out of the car.

"The path Cassandra took is a bit of a walk from here, can you manage it in those boots?" Ronan asks, looking at Dustin's choice of footwear. The boots reach just under his knees, and they have a platform of several inches.

"I can manage it. Walking in a forest can't be any harder than dancing on a slippery bar top," Dustin says casually, heading toward the paths leading into the forest.

"You've danced on a bar?" Ronan asks, trying to picture it. For some reason his brain decided to picture Dustin dancing in his underwear, all oiled up, even though Ronan doesn't know what Dustin looks like with his clothes off, as Dustin has always dressed in the bathroom.

"I've had a wild night or two." Dustin shrugs.

"I thought you said you were shy?" Ronan points out, taking the lead.

"I am, but after a certain amount of tequila I forget I'm shy. I think everybody does." Dustin smiles.

"I'm not really a tequila man, give me a good whiskey or a beer any day. But I don't drink often, too busy with work, and I don't drink on the job." Ronan doesn't know why he's sharing, other than he likes talking with Dustin. He finds himself being more open and honest with Dustin than he usually is with people. And it's not because Dustin is good-looking, or at least not just because; it's more because of how vibrant and open he is.

"I don't drink often either. I find it blocks and muddles up my visions. Makes it harder to get a clear read on people. Besides, my mom's a drinker. I don't want to end up like her, drinking away every problem." Dustin shakes his head.

"She's an alcoholic?" Ronan asks, dodging an overgrown branch.

"High functioning, most people don't even notice. But living with her, I did," Dustin sighs.

"I'm sorry, that's shitty," Ronan says, for lack of anything better to come up with.

"Thanks, but you don't need to be sorry. And it's something I'm used to. I only talk to her every few months anyway." Dustin shrugs, like he doesn't care, but Ronan suspects he does.

"I guessed you weren't close to your family. You never mention them. Are you close to any of them?" Ronan asks, breaking his own rule not to get personally involved with Dustin.

"No, I'm not close to any of them. None of them even know I'm in Arizona, and I won't tell them about it. How about you? I hear you talking about your agency and the people who work there all the time, but no family. Do you have one?" Dustin asks, and Ronan had been afraid that asking Dustin about his life would lead to this, having two choices—open up or lie.

Ronan doesn't want to lie to Dustin after Dustin has been so honest, so he decides to open up just a little.

"My family sort of fell apart after my sister passed away. My dad shot himself, my mom remarried and moved away, had new kids. She likes to pretend her first family never happened." Ronan hates his mother a little for that, how easy it was for her to move on, to forget him, his dad, and Sarah.

And he's still mad at his dad for leaving him like that. He'd thought about going the same way at the time. But he knew that wasn't what Sarah wanted for him. She'd been like an angel even in life—she wouldn't want them rushing to join her in the afterlife.

"I'm really sorry, that's awful, were you young when it happened?" Ronan asks, and he looks sympathetic, not pitying, like he understands.

"I was sixteen when we lost Sarah. My dad made it until I was seventeen. And I'm thirty-two now, so it was a long time ago," Ronan says, trying to brush away the subject, and the heavy feeling inside of him.

"I'm still sorry. Pain like that, it doesn't just leave you. It leaves an imprint on your soul, on your heart. Was Sarah the girl I saw when I read you?" Dustin asks.

"Yes, it was her. But I don't really want to talk about her. It's not you, I don't talk about her with anybody," Ronan says honestly.

"That's okay; we don't have to talk about anything you don't want to. We agreed not to snoop, and to ask questions if we wanted to find stuff out about each other, but both of us still have the right to not answer, to keep things private," Dustin says softly.

"Thanks. I've had a lot of people complain that I'm too much of a closed book. It gets on people's nerves." Ronan doesn't mention that it has been the cause of friction in several relationships.

"You're the stoic type, it works for you. You don't need to bare your soul to everyone you meet. I totally get that." Dustin nods, and he doesn't seem bugged by Ronan's behavior.

"I think this is the part of the trail they found the blood on," Ronan says, recognizing a tree and a bolder from one of the many pictures he had looked at.

"I haven't seen another person out here. But then, it's cold.

Only the diehard runners and joggers come out to the woods to run in this weather," Dustin says.

"He had privacy to take her, but he would have had to travel to take her to a car, carrying her. So he's definitely strong. And I'm certain he drugged her to make sure no one heard her screaming or calling for help," Ronan says, wandering around the path, looking for missed clues, signs of something supernatural.

"Do you have any idea why he's keeping the women? I mean, it would have been easy to kill her out here, no witnesses, good place to dump a body," Dustin says, running his hand over the trunk of a tree.

"I can think of a few things. It needs them to breed—some creatures use human women as hosts. Or he's fattening them up for a better meal, storing food before he hibernates," Ronan suggests.

Ronan is examining the trees when he finds a claw mark; it looks a few weeks old to him.

"Come look at this, Dustin," Ronan calls; he's hoping Dustin will be able to see something.

"Did a bear do that?" Dustin asks.

"Touch it and find out," Ronan suggests.

Dustin takes his gloves off again, and places his right hand over the claw mark, eyes shut. He doesn't look peaceful for long, and he jumps back like his hand has been shocked.

"Definitely not a bear," Dustin says, sounding out of breath.

"What did you see?" Ronan asks.

"I didn't see his face, because he was wearing a hood, it looked like a man, moved really, really fast though, and it clawed the tree making a grab for Cassandra. It got a hold of her, and then, with this creepy fucking clawed hand, it pressed a cloth over her face until she passed out. Then he slung her over his shoulder like she weighed less than a child," Dustin says in a rush.

"I can use this. I'm going to get Harry to send me some files. There are only a few things I think this can be, unless it's something new, which I doubt—good job, Dustin." Ronan is excited—the more they know, the closer they get to finding the women.

"I wouldn't have seen anything if you didn't find that scratch." Dustin shrugs.

"We make a good team then." Ronan can hardly believe he's

saying the words. He's known Dustin three days—there are people Ronan has known for years that he can't partner with.

"Yeah, we do," Dustin agrees, and there is a look in his blue eyes that Ronan can't read.

"Let's get out of here."

"Yeah, it's kind of creepy out here," Dustin admits.

They start the walk back to the car.

Chapter Six

Dustin sits quietly in the car while Ronan calls the mysterious Harry back in California. Dustin can't help but wonder about Ronan's life back home, what it's like, what he's like on his own turf. Ronan intrigues him; Dustin can't help it. And he normally doesn't have a thing for older guys.

But if he admits it to himself, he's been having a few thoughts about Ronan, like what that strong body would look like naked, how it would feel to be pinned underneath Ronan, or maybe up against a wall.

"Dustin?" Ronan calls.

Dustin startles; he hadn't even realized that Ronan had finished his phone call to Harry.

"I'm sorry if I scared you," Ronan apologizes.

"No, it's fine. I was in my own little world," Dustin says, cursing his cheeks for blushing.

"I was thinking it's getting late and it's been a while since we ate. We should probably call it a night. Go get something to eat. And hopefully Harry will have sent me the narrowed-down list of possible creatures once we've finished dinner," Ronan suggests.

"Sounds like a plan to me." Dustin nods.

Ronan starts the car, heading back in the direction of the motel.

"Any food you're really craving?" Ronan asks.

"Do you like Mexican food? I'd love a burrito," Dustin admits.

"I love Mexican food—has to be spicy though. Do you have Wi-Fi on your cell phone? Can you search for a local place?" Ronan asks.

"Yeah, sure." Dustin gets out his cell phone and searches for Mexican restaurants. Once he finds one not too far away he gives Ronan the directions.

"I like it spicy too," Dustin comments as they make their way toward the restaurant.

"My ex-boyfriend used to hate it, always bitched about my

cooking," Ronan says casually, and then he freezes, like he's just realized what he's let slip out.

"Boyfriend? You're gay? Bisexual?" Dustin asks.

"Gay." Ronan looks a little embarrassed.

"Why didn't you tell me when I told you?" Dustin says, a little offended. He'd been so worried that Ronan would be homophobic. He'd been scared to be honest about his sexuality, but he'd done it anyway, because that's who he is—he doesn't hide from things that scare him.

"I still think like a cop sometimes. I got really used to hiding that part of my life." Ronan shrugs.

"I can imagine that it wouldn't have been easy, being a gay cop." Dustin can understand that. They go into the restaurant and are shown to a table.

"Most people didn't know, until I was spotted at a gay bar. I thought I was far enough away from home that no one I knew would see me, but I got outed. My chief was really good about it, some of the other cops not so much—they were assholes," Ronan says, taking a menu.

"I've met a lot of homophobic cops, *a lot*. And I'm not like you," Dustin says, taking his own menu.

"What do you mean? Not like me?" Ronan asks.

"If you want to pass as straight, you can. The way you dress, the way you act, you're not going to set off some bigot's radar. I do. People see the dyed hair and stuff, and they assume, and I won't lie about it, even when it would be safer to. If someone asks if I'm queer, I'll always say yes." Dustin breaks off when the waitress comes over to ask about drinks.

Dustin doesn't think a person "looks" gay or that they look "straight" but he knows there are stereotypes. Ronan is butch, manly—short hair, practical suit, good-looking, but in a very masculine way. Ronan might not be a cop anymore, but he fits the stereotype of a straight, sensible cop.

"I'll have a Coke please," Ronan says.

"And you, sweetheart?" The waitress is older than them both, with graying hair and a kind face.

"Can I get a lemonade please?" Dustin asks.

"Of course. I'll be over with those in a second, and I'll give you a little time to decide what you want to eat. If you need me, my name's Anne." Anne taps her name badge before heading off to get their drinks.

"I think what you're saying, Dustin, is people don't make assumptions about me being gay, but they do make assumptions about you because you're pretty, and you dress well, but with a lot of color and it makes more of an impact," Ronan says.

"You think I'm pretty?" Dustin's never had a cop, ex or otherwise, call him pretty in a nice way. He's had "pretty boy" sneered at him like an insult, but Dustin doesn't think Ronan is being cruel.

"Yes. You have to know how you look, right? I mean, I see people looking at you wherever we go, you have to notice that," Ronan says softly.

"People look at me because I'm weird, because I'm a psychic in huge shoes, with purple hair," Dustin points out.

"The way I see people looking at you, it's not like they think you're weird. I might not be a psychic, but I can read people— being able to is part of my job. People look at you with desire, maybe you should notice that more," Ronan says, blushing slightly.

He looks cute when he blushes.

"I guess the same way you're used to acting like the cop you were, I'm still stuck thinking I'm the loser I was in high school," Dustin admits.

"You didn't have a lot of friends?" Ronan asks.

"I had some friends—the other weird kids, the goths and stuff. But I was far from popular. I went to an exclusive private school. Those places are hell if you don't fit in. And I was a gay psychic, half convinced I was going crazy back then—school wasn't easy." Dustin had hated high school, and it's not like his home life had made up for it.

Mom was always out with some committee or another, chairing some social group, at some kind of fundraiser, always with a glass of wine or champagne in her hand, and the beauty of being rich meant every time she emptied the glass, there was someone to fill it. She hadn't cared about a single cause she worked for; everything was about appearances and being in the right social circle.

Why look after your child when a series of nannies and staff can do it, leaving you free to have a dazzling social life. And it wasn't like Dustin was the kind of kid she could even show off to her friends—sure, he got pretty good grades, but he was strange. As a teen, it had been harder to control his powers, harder to be around people. Dustin had drawn into himself, happy to be labeled a loser, and not paraded around at his mother's parties.

And then there was his father, the lawyer, always "working late" with his assistant. Such a cliché, screwing his much younger staff, and ignoring his family, apart from when he needed them for social functions.

"I didn't know your parents had money, that didn't come up in my snooping before we agreed not to snoop," Ronan says.

"You wouldn't find anything about my parents from looking up my name." Dustin shrugs.

Anne appears with their drinks, and they both order burritos— Dustin grilled chicken, Ronan pork.

"Why wouldn't your parents come up when I searched you? Your police record did." Ronan points out once Anne has left.

"I legally changed my name during college. McPherson isn't my real surname, I picked it out of a list of surnames I found online," Dustin admits.

"What's your family name then?" Ronan asks.

"Greenfield," Dustin says, taking a sip of his lemonade.

"Isn't there a law firm in Oregon called Greenfield?" Ronan frowns.

"Yes, that'd be my dad's law firm." Dustin knows a lot of people have heard of his dad, especially people in law enforcement. Ronan had been a cop, and he didn't live that far from Dustin's hometown, and Dustin's dad had offices in several states, including California.

"So you don't just come from money; you're like super rich, a socialite?" Ronan sounds surprised, but then Dustin doesn't blame him—Dustin knows he doesn't give off the rich vibe.

"You dropped me off at my apartment; did it look to you like I'm rich?" Dustin asks.

"No, no offense but it kind of looked like a shitty neighborhood, and a basic place." Ronan frowns, clearly confused.

"I don't have a lot to do with my parents, or their money." Dustin doesn't explain that he gets an allowance of guilt money that he takes just to make life easier, and to guarantee that he can always have his meds, and see the doctors he needs to.

"Can I ask why not?" Ronan looks curious.

"My parents never handled me being psychic very well. They didn't like me being different, and then I came out as gay. They wanted me to change, to pretend I didn't have visions, to marry a woman. They wanted me to be their idea of a perfect child. I wouldn't do it. I ended up finally moving away, and changing my name so people would stop linking me with my family," Dustin explains.

"Did it bother them that you changed your surname?" Ronan asks.

"No, I think they preferred it; it meant when I got in the papers for helping the police on cases no one linked me to them. It's better for everyone this way; I don't embarrass them, and I don't have to live with the pressure they used to put on me," Dustin sighs.

"I'm sorry your family life is like that," Ronan says softly.

"It's okay, I don't need them." Dustin doesn't really miss his parents, because he was never close to them. It had always been like living in a house with strangers who were constantly disappointed with his every action.

"Seems we both don't have much to do with our families," Ronan says as Anne brings out their food.

"No we don't, for different reasons," Dustin says, digging into his food.

Ronan changes the subject to a lighter one after that and they talk while they eat. Ronan is a smart guy, quite funny, and charming. Dustin isn't sure what to think of Ronan being gay; he hadn't guessed. But Dustin tells himself that it doesn't matter that Ronan is gay. They are still two totally different people just working together. Just because Dustin finds Ronan attractive doesn't change a thing.

After they've eaten and paid for their meal, they leave and drive back to the motel. Dustin asks for some more monster lessons and stories, and Ronan tells Dustin about them while they watch some old action movie on the TV.

It's fascinating to hear about all the things that Ronan has seen, and dealt with, things that Dustin never even imagined. Ronan asks him about some of the cases that Dustin worked on too, and they talk about those as well.

It's soon late enough to go to sleep, and they both get ready for bed. Dustin gets changed in the bathroom, and brushes his teeth. He takes his evening medications. He gets into bed, feeling oddly unsettled. He lies there for a while, and hears Ronan fall asleep before him, but eventually his wired brain begins to settle, and he finally falls asleep.

***

Dustin wakes to the smell of fresh bread, Ronan coming through the door with sandwiches and coffee.

"I didn't feel like eating out of the vending machine again," Ronan says, sharing out the food.

They start eating, Dustin still in bed and Ronan at the desk.

"Harry has a theory about what could be taking the women, based on what we've told him, and the blood at the crime scenes," Ronan says, taking a sip of coffee.

"That's great, what does he think it is?" Dustin knows that finding what they are hunting is a big step, because Ronan knows where different types of monsters are likely to be found.

"A kind of demon called a *Sanguis*; it's Latin for blood, bloodshed, and carnage. It's similar to what you've seen in vampire movies, but it doesn't just feed off blood, it needs spinal fluid too. They often feed in cycles, feeding on lots of victims, and then resting for long periods of time," Ronan explains.

"And would this *Sanguis* demon leave blood at crime scenes?" Dustin asks.

"Yes, they have this weird trait where they cry blood from their last meal each time they hunt. They also look human until they are about to attack or feed," Ronan says, taking a bite from his sandwich.

"That would make sense. I'm no demon expert, but it would fit with what I've seen. Where do they like to stay?" Dustin asks.

"Dark, damp places, basements, near a fresh source of water. You've been seeing a basement," Ronan points out.

"This'll help us, right?" Dustin asks.

"I hope so. We'll finish eating and then go to the last crime scene here and then head to Nevada. Harry is looking for sightings of a *Sanguis*, any police reports of people claiming to see demons, that sort of thing. We need to keep trying to see more of the crime scenes," Ronan says.

"I'll get dressed. Do you know how to kill one of these things?" Dustin asks, getting out of bed and taking a last sip of his coffee, using it to down his morning medication. He takes his antidepressants twice a day, and his painkillers whenever he gets a bad headache. Once again, Dustin notices Ronan watching him swallow the pills, but yet again Ronan doesn't say anything about it, he just looks away, even though Dustin can see the questions in his eyes.

"Yes, pretty simple, you stab it through the heart. Which isn't as easy as it sounds. They are strong and dangerous. They have razor-sharp claws and teeth. But I've faced things as hazardous," Ronan tells Dustin, while he starts packing up his things.

"Have you ever seen one before?" Dustin questions as he grabs clothes to take to the bathroom with him.

"No, I've only read about them, and no one in the agency has faced one that I know of; they're pretty rare. I'll get Harry to ask Alice, Lisa, Rick, and Alan what they know about them. Get dressed, and pack your things—we'll start heading to Nevada straight from the next crime scene," Ronan suggests.

"I'll be quick." Dustin goes into the bathroom, brushes his teeth and has a quick wash. He packs up his things in the bathroom, and then gets changed as fast as he can. He feels like they are finally making progress.

Dustin wiggles into a pair of black jeans that have both knees torn out, but he loves them because they make his ass look great. It's cold so he puts on layers—a black Ramones T-shirt, and his red hoodie. Once he's dressed, he goes back into the bedroom and packs away his things, before finding some shoes to put on.

"How do you walk in those shoes?" Ronan asks as Dustin buckles up his boots.

"They're easy to walk in once you get used to them. I've been wearing them for years." Dustin shrugs.

"Why do you wear them? I mean they're cool-looking. I couldn't pull them off, they suit your style though, but is it a height thing?" Ronan asks.

"Yeah. I've always been on the short side, so I like that about them. They make me a little taller. How tall are you?" Dustin asks, standing up straight, and starting to check the room to make sure he has packed everything.

"I'm six foot one," Ronan says, zipping up his bag.

"I'm only five foot six, so you have a good few inches on me," Dustin points out.

"That's not that short. Are you ready to go? One last crime scene in town to go to. Thirty-year-old Grace Smith who went missing between the grocery store and her house," Ronan says, picking up his bag and his laptop.

"I'm ready, and thanks for not calling me short." Dustin grabs his bags, and they leave the room, loading up the car.

"It's kind of cute," Ronan says softly as they are on the way to book out of the room and pay their bill.

"What's cute?" Dustin asks.

"How petite you are." Ronan blushes slightly again, like maybe he's embarrassed to admit he was complimenting Dustin.

"Well, thanks." Dustin isn't going to let the fact that within two days Ronan has called him good-looking and cute go to his head—it probably doesn't mean anything, Ronan is just being nice.

They pay their bill and then get in the car and drive to the grocery store in their file. They park Ronan's car at the store, and get out.

"We should walk the path she would have walked home," Ronan suggests.

"Good idea," Dustin agrees.

They start at the entrance of the grocery store, Ronan looking around as they walk. Dustin just opens his mind and his senses, hoping to pick something up.

"I think she knew she was being followed," Dustin says after a while, breaking the silence.

"Did she see what was following her? I'd like to confirm that we are looking for a *Sanguis* as soon as possible," Ronan says.

"I can feel her in my head—she was afraid, she thought maybe someone was going to try and rob her. She was holding onto her bag tightly, walking fast. And then I just lose the connection," Dustin sighs.

"Do you think that's all you'll see here?" Ronan asks.

Dustin nods. "Yeah."

"Let's go back to the car then, we'll head for Nevada. It's

another long drive; there are only two missing women from there. We might not get to see their crime scenes today, but we can get booked into a motel," Ronan says.

"I feel bad you having to do all the driving," Dustin sighs as they head back to the car.

"It's not that bad. I like to drive. And I'm used to traveling with my job. I often do a lot of driving when I'm on cases. Why don't you drive?" Ronan asks.

"In case I have a vision when I'm driving—I'd crash the car. I totally check out when I have a vision," Dustin explains.

"That makes sense—I never thought about that, how driving and things like that would be affected by psychic abilities." Ronan seems surprised he hadn't thought of it before.

"I would never wish away my powers, because of the people they allow me to help, but they do have a lot of downsides at times." Dustin had moments in his past when he had wished he was normal, but he's become more at peace with who he is over time. He accepts his powers, and he uses them to do good.

They get back in the car, and Ronan starts the engine, cranking the heat back up, because it is a cold day, and they start toward Nevada. Ronan drives all morning, and then they stop at a gas station for a bathroom break and to get some food to snack on.

Dustin thinks Ronan seems a little more approachable today. Ronan is still far from an open book, but he seems more relaxed around Dustin than he was the first day they met, which was only four days ago. Dustin still remembers the feeling of having Ronan's gun pointed at him. It's not the first time someone has drawn a gun on Dustin, and every time it has been a cop, and he's been somewhere he technically shouldn't have been.

They've been talking all morning, not about anything important, just trading stories. It's nice—Dustin can't help but have a small crush on Ronan. Dustin never thought he would have a crush on the cop type, even an ex-cop. Dustin has always been a rule breaker, and Ronan is all about following rules, from his cop background, and further back to his military upbringing.

After their break, they get back on the road. Dustin checks in with a few friends by text. It doesn't sound like he's been missing out on anything. He's already let the places he volunteers at know that he'll be out of town for a while, but he checks in with them too to see if they need anything, because he might not be in town, but he can send a friend to help out if they need it.

Apart from the animal shelter having a new litter of kittens everything seems to be pretty quiet.

"I don't suppose you know anyone who'd like six kittens?" Dustin asks.

"Harry would probably take one or two, he loves cats. But most of the other people I know travel for work like I do. I don't have a big social circle. My closest friends all work for the agency I set up. Actually, my old captain, Chris, he has kids, they'd take on at least two. Why?" Ronan asks.

"One of the places I volunteer just got a litter of kittens. And most people aren't looking for them in January. A lot of people are getting rid of kittens they bought their kids for Christmas and they decided were a bad idea in January. If you could ask your friends, I'm sure someone from the shelter could deliver them to California. They're great people; they'll do anything to get an animal a good home." Dustin loves working with animals; they are so uncomplicated. Animals don't lie, or cheat—if you treat them well, with kindness and love, they will give you twice as much love back.

And Dustin admires animals and their ability to still look for the good in people. He's seen animals that have been abandoned and abused that still love people, still seem to have hope that they'll find that perfect family. Dustin sometimes feels like he could learn from those animals. He's been kicked by life a few times, seen awful things, but that doesn't mean he should give up.

"I'll talk to Harry and Chris when we get to Nevada, and I'll see if they know anyone who is looking for a new family pet. I'll let you know. I wish I could have a pet. Maybe if I lived with someone, a roommate or partner, someone who'd be home all the time, I could have that, I'd like a dog. I haven't had a dog since I was a kid," Ronan says.

"I don't have any pets right now either. The apartment I live in doesn't allow pets. It's small, anyway, and animals need room. I wouldn't want to have a pet somewhere that wasn't good enough for them. But if you ever are in the position to get a dog, I can help you out—rescue dogs need love too." Dustin is always trying to hook up the people he meets and likes with the perfect pet for them. If he doesn't like a person, he wouldn't suggest they get a pet—Dustin only sends animals home with good people.

"Did you have pets growing up?" Ronan asks as they enter the Nevada traffic. It's dark out and the city is lit up. Being January the days are shorter and darker than they usually are in summer.

"No. My parents weren't pet people. Hell, a kid was too much responsibility for them. They weren't good at looking after living things. I really can't imagine my mother walking a dog or emptying a litter box." Dustin shakes his head.

"So you never had any kind of pet the whole time you lived at home?" Ronan sounds shocked.

"Nope, I didn't. And then I moved into a college dorm, so pets weren't allowed there either. I've never had a pet of my own," Dustin admits.

"That's kind of sad. I'm sorry, everyone should have a pet growing up. And you must like animals if you volunteer at an animal re-homing shelter." Ronan turns off the main street and onto a road with a couple of motels, pulling into one with a vacancy sign.

"I love animals. I'll have a houseful one day. But I want to do it on my terms. I'm saving up from the cases I've worked on, and odd jobs. I plan to get a better place. I want to help people, and animals; to use my abilities for the best. I don't want to live a life anything like my parents', empty, and all for show." Dustin doesn't care how good his parents' lives look to outsiders, he's seen it from the inside, and that's not the kind of life he wants.

"That sounds like a good plan," Ronan says as he parks.

"I figure I still have time to work some stuff out," Dustin says as they get out of the car to go to the office.

"You have lots of time, you're only twenty-one," Ronan points out.

They go into the office and rent a double room for two nights. It shouldn't take longer than that to look at two crime scenes. They put their bags in the room and then go at pick up Indian takeout, which they eat at the small table in their room.

Dustin is used to eating most meals alone, even though he has friends at home. He always has breakfast in his apartment alone, and he has dinner there too. Sometimes he'll have lunch with a friend or at one of the shelters. But Dustin can't remember the last time he ate so many meals with the same person and enjoyed it so much too.

"Tomorrow we have two places to go. Kate Reid went missing from her home and Jackie Hunt went missing from her job as a security guard at a warehouse," Ronan says as they eat.

"How are we getting into the house?" Dustin asks.

"This one, I need to call the local police so they can let us in. Chris has contacted all the local police chiefs to let them know I've been hired, and that the FBI agrees with that decision," Ronan explains.

"So they know we're on the case?" Dustin has had mixed reactions to him being put on cases in the past—not all police want to work with a psychic, even after he proves he's not a fake just out to earn a few bucks.

"They know we are on the case, and have been told to give us any help we need, but to mainly let us get on with things. I'll let Chris know that we have an idea of what might be taking the women and why." Ronan takes a sip of his soda.

They talk about their plans for the next day a little more, and eat the rest of their food. After they've eaten, they clean up and take turns showering, and then Dustin settles in with his book while Ronan goes on his laptop again, e-mailing his contacts.

Dustin goes to bed when his head starts to dip while he's reading, and this time he falls asleep before Ronan.

***

Morning seems to come too soon—it's still not very bright, but they had set an alarm for seven. Dustin goes through his morning routine on autopilot—pills, teeth, dress, have a piss, get breakfast. Ronan calls the local police chief and they are told someone will meet them at Grace Smith's house.

Ronan drives them to the missing woman's house, and by the time they get there, Dustin is feeling more awake.

They meet a young officer named Clark who keeps looking at Dustin with wide eyes. Obviously Officer Clark has been told about Dustin being a real deal psychic. But apart from some staring he doesn't give them any trouble, and he stays standing guard outside when Dustin and Ronan go in the house.

"Could a *Sanguis* break into a house?" Dustin asks.

"Yes, in their human form they can do anything a human can, and with the strength, the claws, it's probably easy for one to get into a house. And the original police report said that a window was left open. Which seems weird in January, so maybe the *Sanguis* actually opened it," Ronan says.

"Which window?" Dustin can't remember from the report. He's read all ten, but that's a lot of different facts to remember—ten women, ten lives, and ten crime scenes.

"That one." Ronan points to a now closed window in the family room at the back of the house.

Dustin walks over to the window, and climbs up onto a chair so he can reach the lock. The moment he touches it it's like he's been shocked. His heart starts beating a mile a minute, and he sees it for the first time; the horrible twisted face of the *Sanguis* demon. It has long, sharp teeth, and mottled gray skin, and bloodred eyes. Dustin hears it growl, and he hears a woman's scream, and then he opens his eyes, and he's back, standing on the chair, leaning against the window, but with Ronan holding firmly onto his waist with both his large, strong hands.

Dustin has to focus on the horrible images he saw not to get the world's worst-timed boner, because the feeling of Ronan's hands tight on his waist is really doing it for him.

"You almost fell," Ronan says when Dustin meets his eye, and Ronan slowly lets go of Dustin's waist, like he either doesn't want to let go, or he's still worried that Dustin will fall. Once Ronan has let go, he holds out a hand to help Dustin get down from the chair.

"So does a *Sanguis* have red eyes when it's hunting? Like the whole eye—iris, what should be the white, all of it?" Dustin asks, wanting to keep his mind on the job. This silly little crush is really getting out of hand. It's their fifth day together, and Dustin is just feeling more and more drawn to Ronan.

"Yes it does, did you see it, then?" Ronan asks.

"Yeah, I saw it. It's a scary-looking creature. Are you sure we can kill that?" Dustin asks—he thinks he should probably start carrying the knives he's been keeping in his bag.

"I'm sure. I've fought worse," Ronan assures him.

"Really?" Dustin asks.

"Really. Come on, let's hit the other crime scene and let Officer

Clark go back to his job," Ronan says.

They leave the house, meeting Officer Clark out in front, where he is still waiting.

"Did you, ah, have a vision?" Officer Clark asks hesitantly.

"Yes, I did. Thank you for letting us in." Dustin smiles.

"No problem." Officer Clark still doesn't look like he knows what to make of Dustin. But the officer locks the house back up, and heads for his squad car while Dustin and Ronan go back to Ronan's Ford.

"He was on edge around you," Ronan comments as he pulls away from the curb.

"A lot of people are. Not everyone is as used to the supernatural as you are. You've met humans with powers before. It was probably Officer Clark's first time meeting someone like me. At least he didn't freak out, or ask me to check if his wife was cheating." Dustin rolls his eyes.

"You've had guys ask you that on cases?" Ronan asks.

"Men, women, everyone seems to want to know if someone is cheating—boyfriend, girlfriend, wife, husband. It's the question I get asked the most." Dustin hates getting that question from people. It's not something he wants to answer, because if the person's partner is cheating, they are never thankful to Dustin for being the bearer of bad news.

"That must be difficult." Ronan frowns.

"Yeah, it's never fun. I always knew that my dad was cheating. I knew every time he lied about being at work and he was really with another woman. I always questioned whether to confront him, if I should tell my mom, but then I realized she already knew, so I just stayed out of it," Dustin admits.

"Nobody ever thanks you for getting involved in their relationship. I've had people try and hire me to look into their spouses, to see if they are cheating. But I don't do that. I occasionally do cases that aren't supernatural, but I never investigate cheaters, too much hassle." Ronan shakes his head.

They drive to the warehouse and park. The whole place seems pretty empty. They leave the car and walk around the warehouse— no one is manning the front desk, so they walk to the back where they find another door.

"Maybe we should knock, see if anyone comes," Ronan

suggests.

"Let's see if it's locked," Dustin says, taking hold of the handle. He turns it, and the door opens.

"Huh, open, let's look to see if we can find anyone, or find where Jamie Hunt went missing." Dustin walks into the warehouse, leaving Ronan to follow him.

The lights are on in the warehouse, so Dustin assumes there must be someone there, so he starts moving between the stacks of boxes. He's walking when he suddenly hears something, movement.

"Hello?" Dustin calls out.

"I don't think anybody is here," Ronan says, just as a very large and very vicious dog appears, growling.

"Oh shit," Dustin says.

"Good doggy, sit," Ronan commands.

The dog growls and lunges toward them.

"Run," Ronan says.

Dustin doesn't have to be told twice. He starts running, but he's not quick enough, and he feels a searing pain in his leg as the dog bites down, knocking him off his feet.

Ronan draws his gun and fires into the air; the dog yelps and lets go long enough for Ronan to lean down and help Dustin to his feet. Then Ronan helps Dustin limp outside, and he shuts the door firmly behind them. The dog thumps into the door, clearly having shaken off its fear at the sound of the shot.

"Are you okay?" Ronan asks.

"My leg really fucking hurts, but I don't think it did a lot of damage. There's not too much blood," Dustin groans.

"All right. Let me help you back to the car. Then I'll report this, because I don't want the cops tracking me down later. I have a first aid kit, or would you like to go to the hospital? Do you need a tetanus shot?" Ronan asks.

"I had one recently for work. I don't want to waste time and money going to a hospital. If you think you can patch it up, that would be great," Dustin decides.

Ronan helps him back to the car, and then makes a call to the local police once Dustin is sitting down. Ronan gets everything straightened out, while Dustin sits there cursing to himself.

"How are you feeling?" Ronan asks, starting the car and

driving away.

"It hurts like a bitch. I have painkillers back at the room. I get bad headaches. I can take those, that'll help." Dustin's thigh is throbbing where it has been bitten.

"Are those the pills you take every day?" Ronan asks, finally voicing the curiosity Dustin had seen on his face the past couple of days.

"No, those are for something else," Dustin says honestly, not sure if he wants to share this part of his life with Ronan. "You've been wanting to ask since you first saw them, haven't you?"

"I'm curious. Are you sick? You don't have to tell me if you don't want to," Ronan adds softly.

"I'm not sick or dying or anything like that. They're antidepressants," Dustin admits, and it feels good to be open about it. Now he doesn't have to worry about Ronan finding out by accident.

"You suffer from depression?" Ronan asks.

"And anxiety, yes." Dustin nods.

"I did hear you had a breakdown in college," Ronan admits.

"Yeah, everything just got to be too much; the pressure to be normal, my visions, my family, classes, relationships, everything. I got help, though. I got into therapy, got on medication, and things improved. I have bad days, and bad moments, but I'm a lot better. It doesn't mean I'm crazy."

"I never thought having a breakdown made you crazy. I'm glad you got help. I'm sorry you went through all that. I'm sorry you didn't have a family that helped," Ronan says as he pulls into the parking lot of the motel.

"Thank you. It was a really crappy time, but it got me to a better place. You aren't worried about working with someone with mental health problems?" Dustin knows that some people do have issues with it; they write him off as crazy.

"I have no problem with it at all." Ronan gets out of the car, comes around to Dustin's side, and opens the door, helping Dustin limp to their room.

"Okay, pants off and in the bathroom. I have everything I need to clean and patch up your wound in there," Ronan orders.

Dustin leans against Ronan while he takes his boots off, but then takes an unsteady step away to take off his pants. Dustin shivers at the cold in the room, and partly because he feels exposed.

"It doesn't look too bad. The dog didn't tear your flesh; you just have puncture wounds, but it's going to be sore as hell to walk on," Ronan says, looking at the back of Dustin's leg before they make their way to the bathroom.

In the bathroom, Ronan gets out a first aid kit.

"If you just stand facing the sink, maybe hold on if you're a bit unsteady on your feet. It'll hurt to clean the bite," Ronan warns.

Dustin makes his way carefully to the sink. He can put weight on his leg, but it hurts. He holds onto the sink, hoping he won't make himself look like a wuss, because Ronan is such a manly man, an ex-cop. An injury like this is probably nothing to him. Not that he'd admit to wanting to impress Ronan—but Dustin kind of wants to—at the very least he doesn't want Ronan to think less of him.

"Are you ready?" Ronan asks.

"Yeah, just do it. I know dog bites need disinfecting and everything." Dustin holds on, looking ahead—all he can see is himself in the mirror, so he closes his eyes.

"I'm sorry, but this will really hurt."

Ronan sprays something on his leg, and Dustin feels like his leg is on fire. He grits his teeth, holding in any sounds that might want to escape. It really does hurt.

"Okay, not much longer, I'm almost done," Ronan says, doing something behind Dustin, and before Dustin knows it Ronan is smoothing a piece of gauze over the wound and taping it down.

"You might have a few little scars, but it won't be too bad," Ronan promises.

"Not like it's some place I'll have on show all the time anyway," Dustin says, straightening up and turning carefully so he is facing Ronan.

"Yeah, the only time anyone's going to see that will be if you're naked and they are behind you," Ronan says, then he frowns, and then he starts to blush.

"Just realized when someone would see my wound-slash-future scar?" Dustin asks, because the only time he can think of when someone is going to see the naked top of the back of his thigh is during sex.

"Yep. I was actually going to be stupid enough to say something like, 'I can't think of when you'd be in that position again,' and then I realized. I'm an idiot," Ronan admits, his cheeks still glowing, and it makes Dustin laugh a little.

"You must have an innocent mind not to be able to think when a gay man would be seen naked from behind. Now, since my leg's still sore, can you help me over to the bed? Let me grab my bag. I want to put my sleep sweats on; they'll be loose on the wound," Dustin says.

Ronan takes his arm and some of his weight, walking him back to the bedroom, stopping by Dustin's bag. Dustin grabs his sweats and continues onto the bed, limping away from Ronan and sitting down on the bed to put his sweats on.

"Maybe I have an innocent mind, or maybe I was just trying not to assume you liked to bottom. Because if you were topping no one would see that bite mark." Ronan smirks, before heading over to boot up his laptop.

"I top, sometimes." Dustin shrugs. He's not a prude about his sex life. He can talk about it without getting embarrassed, even if the guy he is talking about it to is very handsome and Dustin has a slight crush on him.

"We are not having this conversation," Ronan laughs.

"Well, you don't need to tell me anyway, I can tell," Dustin says, getting comfortable on the bed. His leg is throbbing like a bitch and he'll probably take a painkiller in a second.

"What do you mean you can tell?" Ronan asks, sitting on the edge of his bed, facing Dustin, while his laptop loads behind him.

"You are way too bossy, self-contained, and self-controlled to be a bottom, even a bossy bottom. You are totally the pushy domineering top type." Dustin smiles. He may have put a little thought into it—a few inappropriate thoughts—and he can't picture Ronan submitting.

Dustin can picture Ronan holding him down though, and his face flushes slightly at the thought. He'd felt how strong Ronan was, dragging him away from that dog—had suspected already from the way he fills his suit, but now he is sure that Ronan is strong enough to pin him to a mattress, or any other flat surface.

"Okay, just because you're kind of right is no reason to be smug. I'm not that hard to read." Ronan rolls his eyes.

"So I'm right? I won't be smug, I promise." Dustin grins.

"I wouldn't call myself bossy, but I guess I like being in charge in all aspects of my life, including sex. I'm not like a Dom or anything; BDSM isn't my thing. But I like to stay in charge." Ronan shrugs.

"You are bossy. And I didn't need to be a psychic to read you either." Dustin moves on the bed to reach for his pills and water, but ends up pulling on his leg and wincing.

"Are you okay?" Ronan asks, standing up and hovering over Dustin.

"I can't reach over without pulling on my leg," Dustin admits.

"Here, let me." Ronan walks around the bed and gets Dustin's pills for him.

"It'll hurt more while it's fresh, as soon as it starts to scab it'll hurt less. Can I check to see if you have a temperature?" Ronan asks.

"You brought a thermometer on a case?" Dustin asks.

"No, but I can usually tell without one," Ronan offers.

"Okay. Probably best to make sure I'm not getting sick from the dog bite." Dustin nods.

Ronan leans in toward Dustin and pushes Dustin's hair gently off his forehead with one hand, and then he presses his other hand to Dustin's forehead.

"You don't feel too hot, even with the heat on," Ronan says, dropping his hand.

"You don't make a bad nurse," Dustin says, glancing at Ronan's mouth; he has nice, strong-looking lips.

"Thanks. I thought your hair might be dry from the dye; it's really soft," Ronan says, reaching out like he wants to touch Dustin's mess of purple hair again, but he doesn't, lowering his hand back to his lap instead.

"Conditioner." Dustin shrugs; the moment feels oddly charged considering they've only been talking about dog bites and hair, but maybe Dustin is just feeling that way from being so close to Ronan on a bed. He can feel the warmth of Ronan's body close to his.

"Can I?" Ronan asks, again lifting his hand toward Dustin's longish hair.

"Go ahead." Dustin nods. He likes the idea of having Ronan's hand in his hair, even if it's not sexual for Ronan, just curiosity.

L.J. Hamlin

Ronan reaches out and cards his fingers through the left side of Dustin's hair, his fingers running carefully through the strands. Ronan is watching his face, and Dustin licks his lips, feeling tension thrumming through his body. He feels like he should act, but part of him thinks if he does anything, this moment will be broken.

In the end, Dustin doesn't have to decide what to do, because Ronan decides for him, leaning in and pressing a soft kiss to Dustin's mouth. Dustin parts his lips slightly and the kiss deepens right away.

It's been a while since Dustin kissed anyone, but it's not something you forget how to do, and he kisses back, giving as well as taking. Ronan keeps a hand in Dustin's hair, keeping control of the kiss, and Dustin doesn't mind at all. For a straitlaced guy, Ronan sure can kiss.

Ronan nips Dustin's lower lip, and Dustin gasps, hands reaching out and grabbing Ronan's shirt, balling in the front of it, and drawing Ronan closer. Dustin wants to feel more of Ronan, wants to feel his body over his, weighing him down, holding him tight.

Dustin thinks things might be heading in that direction when Ronan's cell phone rings—some old rock-and-roll song. Ronan freezes like someone has thrown a bucket of cold water on him. He lifts his head away from Dustin's, letting go of his hair. Dustin has no choice but to give up his hold on Ronan's shirt.

Ronan gets up off the bed and goes over to where his cell phone is resting on the nightstand; he checks the caller ID and then answers. Dustin lies still, not knowing what to do with his body. It's still thrumming with the excitement of Ronan's kiss, heat is coursing through his veins and pooling in his groin, he's half hard.

But at the same time, he's filled with dread. Ronan had dove away from him like a kicked cat. Like he'd suddenly realized what he was doing, and he regretted it. Ronan might be gay, but Dustin doubts he's the ex-cop's type. Ronan probably goes for men like him—sensible, strong, no baggage.

Dustin has a lot of baggage. Like an airport's lost and found's worth.

Maybe Ronan wasn't even that attracted to him. They'd spent almost a week in each other's company, twenty-four seven, and

91

under a lot of pressure with the case. That kind of situation can throw a person off. Hell, maybe Ronan was just lonely and looking for some easy affection.

Dustin is so caught up in his thoughts about Ronan that he doesn't realize Ronan has ended his phone call until Ronan walks over to the end of Dustin's bed. Dustin can't help but notice that he keeps plenty of space between them and feels a little sad. It's not like he's head over heels for Ronan, but he likes the guy. He's attracted to him, and Dustin hasn't really felt that way about a guy in a while.

And his psychic powers haven't scared off Ronan, unlike other guys—well, at least Dustin thought they hadn't.

"Another woman has gone missing," Ronan tells him in a flat voice.

"Oh my God. Where?" Dustin asks, trying to push away the confusion he's feeling; they are on a case after all.

"Back in California. Good thing we're heading back there in the morning. Seems like the *Sanguis* demon might still be there," Ronan sighs. His lips are still slightly swollen from when they had been making out, and it's distracting as hell.

Dustin can't help but wonder where things would have headed if not for that cockblocking phone call. Dustin can tell they won't head there now. It's written all over Ronan's face, his body language, the regret he's feeling. Now he's closing up on Dustin again, just like the first day they met.

"Do you want to go now? It's not that late," Dustin suggests.

"No, I want you to rest your leg for at least a few hours. Maybe get some sleep, eat. So you're good for the drive. I don't want to end up having to stop to take you to a hospital if you start bleeding. Keep your leg still and let it scab up some," Ronan says.

"Okay, we go early in the morning though. I want to see the crime scene while it's fresh; I might pick up on more." Dustin hopes he can see something—eleven girls missing now, being kept in cages so a demon can feed off them, off their blood and spinal fluid. No wonder the women always felt so awful when Dustin saw into their minds, felt what they were feeling.

"I have no problem with an early start. I'm going to go grab us some pizza, okay?" Ronan asks.

"Is that how you're going to play this? Act like it never

happened?" Dustin asks, because he has to know.

"We're on a case," Ronan says, moving toward the door.

"What's that supposed to mean?" Dustin knows they are on a case; it's how they met. How could he forget that or forget the now eleven missing women?

"What happened was unprofessional. I don't want to dwell on it." Ronan sounds so closed off again. Almost like a robot or a wooden actor with lines he's rehearsed, but doesn't know how to put feeling into.

"Unprofessional? You're a private detective, not a cop anymore. You don't have to act a certain way on cases. And it's not like there are any rules about police consultants kissing on a case," Dustin points out.

"We're working together. Working with someone and sleeping with them is a bad idea. I've seen it blow up in good cops' faces. I'm here to work, not get laid. And that's the end of it, I don't want to talk about this anymore," Ronan says, grabbing his wallet and stuffing it in his pocket.

"Fine, it was just a stupid kiss. We don't have to talk about it if you don't want to," Dustin forces the words out. The kiss didn't feel stupid or like "just" a kiss. And Dustin does want to talk about it, he wants to know what Ronan is really feeling, if he feels anything at all.

But they are on a case. Dustin is here for a reason, to help missing women. And he won't let his emotions get in the way of that. He can control his feelings; he's had crushes before that he never acted on. So what if the fact he can still taste Ronan on his lips is driving him mad? A large slice of pizza will soon sort that out.

"Pizza sounds great. Get me something like a meat lovers', no vegetables, especially no onion please," Dustin orders, changing the subject just like Ronan had wanted to.

"Just meat. I'll remember that. I won't be long." Ronan sounds relieved that Dustin is going along with changing the subject.

"Awesome. See you when you get back." Dustin picks up his cell phone and looks at the screen like it's the most interesting thing in the world, until he hears the door open and shut as Ronan leaves.

Maybe it was a good thing they only kissed. If things are this awkward after that, Dustin doesn't want to imagine how tense it would be if things had gone further between him and Ronan.

Seeing as he has his cell phone in his hand, Dustin decides to text one of his friends for advice. He scrolls through until he finds Polly Kite's number. Dustin had met Polly in college, before his breakdown—she was one of the few people who stuck around after it, came to check on him.

Hey Polly, you know how I told you I was on a case with a private detective? Well, we just kissed, but now he wants to forget all about it. I'm confused. Help?

Dustin sends the message and then waits, quickly checking Facebook.

You dog you, smooching with a private detective. Who started the kiss? If it was you, maybe he's intimidated? Wasn't ready for you to make a move?

Polly's suggestion would make sense, if Ronan hadn't been the one to start the kiss, but he had. Ronan had come and sat close, Ronan had touched him, Ronan had asked if he could touch his hair. Everything leading to the kiss had been because of Ronan.

He kissed me. Phone rang, he stopped. Was like a different person after. Mr. Ice was back. And the call was about the case, not sure why that would have him freezing back up.

Dustin sighs as he sends the message. This shouldn't be bothering him so much. It was one kiss, really. Totally PG rated, no nudity of any kind, no heavy petting. It shouldn't be seared into Dustin's memory, but it is. He wants Ronan to kiss him like that again, but to not stop this time. Dustin wants to see where those passionate kisses could lead.

Sorry, honey, I don't know what's up with your private detective. Guys are confusing. Let me know if things change, or if you just need to complain about him. I'm here for you, babycakes.

Dustin smiles slightly at Polly's text. She's always so kind to him.

Oh I have a feeling I'll be complaining plenty. Spending a car journey with him tomorrow, Nevada to California. I have a feeling it's going to be one awkward-as-hell trip. Maybe I can fake sleeping?

Nevada to California is roughly a ten-hour drive. There's no way Dustin can pretend to be asleep for all of that, so he's going to have to talk to Ronan about something. Just not kisses or feelings. He'll talk about the case, that'll be safe. He can ask about the two women who are missing from California, and what the area is like, seeing as Ronan lives there.

There are safe topics they can still talk about, even if there will be a huge elephant in the room, or car, with them.

Dustin texts with Polly until Ronan gets back with two large pizzas and some sodas.

"Do you always eat this healthy?" Dustin jokes, digging into a large, very cheesy, meaty, slice of pizza.

"I'm actually pretty good when I'm at home. I cook a lot." Ronan shrugs.

Sensing a safe subject, Dustin asks cooking questions for the rest of the time they are eating. Ronan seems happy to answer them and things don't feel that awkward. Maybe they'll be able to focus on the case after all.

Still, Dustin goes to bed early, mainly to avoid talking to Ronan. He has to lie still so he doesn't hurt his still-tender leg. Otherwise, he would be tossing and turning. It takes forever for him to settle down. Maybe because he's lying in the bed Ronan kissed him in, with Ronan just a few steps away. It's hard not to think of the other man.

Eventually Dustin does fall asleep and doesn't wake up until Ronan's alarm blasts, waking them both. Ronan seems awake instantly, like the good solider his father probably trained him to be. Whereas Dustin is groggy and out of it. As they get ready to leave, he thinks he might not have to fake sleep for some of the long journey to California.

They get coffee to go at a place near the motel after they have checked out, and then the trip starts. Dustin manages to stay awake for the first hour, which is mainly filled with long, awkward silences, but then he decides to rest. It's a long trip and this case needs for him to be at his best. Dustin dozes for a few hours until they stop for lunch.

Ronan parks the car at a diner and they go in and are seated by a perky Chinese waitress. They order drinks and food. Ronan is on the phone with his old chief, Chris, until the food comes, leaving Dustin to fiddle with his phone, texting all the people he knows in and out of work. When the food does come, Ronan reaches for the salt at the same time as Dustin, their hands graze, and Ronan turns bright red, stammering out an apology, as if he had done something truly terrible.

"This is stupid, grow up," Dustin says.

"What?" Ronan is clearly playing dumb; he's not that dense.

"We kissed, you regret it, whatever. You don't want it to happen again, fine, it won't. But you need to stop acting like we're in middle school and we just broke up. We have five more hours in a car together, and God knows how many days on this case. We need to get along. Your need to keep things professional is causing them to be anything but." Dustin is a little angry. They are both grown men; they can be adults about this.

It's not as if Dustin asked Ronan to kiss him. Sure, he'd wanted it to happen, but he didn't start it, Ronan had. Now Ronan is acting like a total idiot, and Dustin doesn't want to have to put up with it. He had started to think of Ronan as a friend; they had opened up to each other the past few days. He wants to go back to that and he's sad that the kiss took it away.

"Maybe I'm being a little childish," Ronan admits.

"It was just a kiss. It's not the end of the world. You're still a big, bad detective and awesome at your job. You're still going to solve this thing. Nothing's changed. That is, nothing has changed unless you let it." Dustin wants his friend back, maybe more than he wants a lover, even though he'd really like that too.

It's been a while since Dustin was attracted to someone and longer still since that person seemed like they could cope with his psychic abilities. Ronan has seen things much stranger than a psychic. The guy knows about vampires and demons—Dustin's weirdness hardly compares to that.

But just because Ronan is cool with Dustin's powers and just because Dustin wants to get in Ronan's pants, does not mean they are meant to be.

"I just… you are a very attractive man, Dustin. And I don't want you to think I regret the kiss because it was with you. It's more about the timing; the timing is terrible. I can't get involved with someone while I'm working with them. But you're right that I'm acting like a fool. We need to go back to the way things were, and get back to work," Ronan says, stabbing at a fry on his plate.

Dustin doesn't know what to think. With everything Ronan just said, he hopes they'll be able to at least get back to the way things were before they kissed.

"The job comes first—I totally agree about that." Dustin isn't lying; the case does come first. Those poor eleven missing women, being kept locked up by the horrible *Sanguis* demon, with its glowing red eyes and vampire-like fangs.

Getting those women back is the most important thing in Dustin's life right now. He wants to say he shouldn't even have room in his head left over to think about men, but he does. He can't help it; he's only human.

"Good. I was thinking. When we get to California, my place has a spare bedroom. I thought you might like to stay there instead of a motel. I'm not making a move on you or anything. I just think it'll make sense for work. I'll be at my place and maybe the agency's office. I'll work from those places, so you being there makes sense to me." Ronan looks worried, like he thinks Dustin will say no or get the wrong idea about the invite.

"If I have a vision it's better that I'm close by to tell you. And you can be my ride, seeing as I'm going to be in California without my bike. You'd have to come get me from the motel. I think it's a good idea. I'll try to be a good houseguest." Dustin has never shared a house with someone he didn't know well. He's only ever lived with his parents, but he's been a guest at friends' houses.

There's never been any drama, but then Dustin had never wanted to sleep with any of those people. And he very much wants to sleep with Ronan. But Dustin likes to pride himself on the fact that he doesn't think with his dick, so he's hoping he can handle this.

"I'm sure you make a good houseguest. I hope you like my place." Ronan smiles.

"It's probably better than my place." Dustin snorts.

They get lunch and things are easier again, nothing feels strained or forced. So it seems clearing the air was the right thing to do. This morning and last night were just a blip—they made a mistake giving into their physical needs, and it messed things up. They are back on the right path now.

Even as Dustin tells himself that, he finds himself looking at Ronan, looking at his lips and remembering what they had felt like on his. But Ronan has made it clear that he is not interested in a relationship with Dustin, sexual or otherwise.

Dustin hopes what Ronan's saying is true, that it isn't personal. That Ronan wouldn't sleep with anyone while on a case, not just Dustin. But Dustin does have doubts. A lot of people view him as a freak or as troubled. And maybe they can get used to him as a friend, but people don't always want to get close to someone like him.

He tries not to let the depressing thoughts take hold and tries focusing on the case instead. Once they are back in the car and on their way to California, Dustin asks more questions about demons and what Ronan has seen of them, how to deal with their demon, how to hunt it.

It's a long drive, but the tension in the car is all but gone, so that makes it easier. The hours pass by quickly and before Dustin knows it, he's in California for the first time. Ronan drives to his place in West Park, in Fresno. It's a nice area, not too upscale, but not run-down either. Ronan has a house, not an apartment, and he parks outside of it.

Not for the first time since they met, they get their bags out of the car in the dark, but this time there is no motel to check in to. Ronan leads them straight into his house, deactivating his security system. Once they are both inside Ronan locks up again.

"It's late. I'll show you to your room and if you want a shower, I'll show you where the bathroom is," Ronan offers, turning on lights.

"Yeah, I'd like that. After being in the car for so long I could use a nice shower, and then a good night's sleep in a bed—napping in the car isn't the same." Dustin smiles.

Ronan leads the way, pointing to the bathroom when they pass it, and then showing Dustin to the spare bedroom. It's a nice room; it has a few bits of exercise equipment in it, but nothing that gets in the way. It has a double bed, which is enough for Dustin. A double is all he has at home. His apartment isn't big enough for a king, and it's not like he really needs one. He's not a big guy, and he sleeps alone.

Dustin puts his bag into the room, taking out a towel and pajamas to change into once he's showered.

"Try not to get the dog bite too wet," Ronan warns.

"I'll be careful, but it's already feeling a lot better. Thank you for patching me up and for pulling me away from the dog before it did more damage. If you hadn't scared the dog off, my leg would be looking a lot worse." Dustin is grateful for what Ronan did for him. But he doesn't really know how to show it without it looking like maybe he's making a move on Ronan, so he keeps his words simple.

"We'll go to the crime scene in the morning. Then I'll take you into the agency's office to meet everyone. We can have a little brainstorm and see if what you've seen in your vision gives them any ideas. I have a few places I want to look for the *Sanguis* demon from what I know they like, but it's too much ground to cover. We need to narrow it down," Ronan says.

"What are the people you work with like? Do they all believe in the supernatural? Am I going to have to prove I'm psychic? Or will they look at me like I'm a circus freak?" Dustin asks, clutching his towel.

"They all believe, and they won't treat you like a weirdo. You won't have to prove yourself. They know I wouldn't be working a case with a fake." Ronan sounds sure of that.

"So, are you like their boss?" Dustin asks.

"I guess so. I started the agency; I brought everyone together. I don't really give orders though. We all work together and share the workload." Ronan shrugs.

"Well, I look forward to meeting them. Hopefully they can help us work out where to look for the *Sanguis* demon before it takes any more women." Dustin hates the thought of the missing women, so afraid and in pain, captured by a real-life monster, and held prisoner.

"I hope they can help too. Now I'm going to go to my room, it's just down the hall. If you need anything let me know. But hopefully you won't, because after ten hours of driving, I would really like to sleep until morning." Ronan grins.

"I won't need anything. Night." Dustin can't help but smile back at Ronan; he has a charming smile.

"Night," Ronan says, and he heads for his bedroom.

Dustin goes the other way, to the bathroom. Dustin locks the door, putting his clothes, towel, and toiletries where he needs them; he then strips. Dustin climbs into the shower and turns on the spray. He can faintly smell the bodywash that Ronan uses and can't help breathing in the scent.

Ronan smelled like that and a mix of his own smell when they had been on Dustin's motel bed together. Dustin bumps his head against the tiled shower wall. He really shouldn't be doing this; fantasizing about Ronan in the shower, in the man's own house, while Ronan is going to sleep down the hall.

Logic tells him not to do anything, reason also tells him the same. But Dustin's dick isn't feeling reasonable or logical. Feeling guilty, almost like a naughty child, Dustin slides his hand down his stomach, palming his cock—that is already about half hard—and it swells a little in his hand.

He shouldn't do this, but under the warm spray of the shower, he's feeling good. Even though he's sticking his leg back and at an angle so it won't get too wet, Dustin has learned over the years that you don't need to be perfectly comfortable to get off. He feels good enough to start stroking himself.

Dustin tells himself that he won't think about Ronan, so he tries thinking about the last porn film he saw. But the lead's square jaw and dark hair are soon morphing into Ronan's face and blond hair.

It feels too good to stop. He hasn't been alone like this all week and a small voice tells Dustin to make the most of this privacy, and the nice hot shower with no limit on the hot water. So Dustin strokes himself slowly, taking his time.

He thinks back to that all too brief kiss with Ronan, how Ronan's lips had felt against his, and how they might feel against other parts of his body—his chest, his nipples, his cock. Ronan had been warm and he'd smelled good. He'd felt strong and alive in a way that few people are.

Dustin tries to imagine what it would have been like if Ronan hadn't stopped the kiss when the phone rang. Dustin keeps stroking his cock with one hand, sliding the other up his chest to play with his pierced nipples. He tugs on the small barbells and sharp pleasure-pain zings into his chest, traveling straight to his balls. He pictures Ronan tugging on the little bits of metal, using his fingers and his mouth to drive Dustin wild.

Dustin begins to pant; his breathing becoming uneven as the pleasure he is feeling begins to spike, to build. The warm water flows down his body, relaxing his muscles even as some, like his stomach muscles, tense up as he gets closer to orgasm. And the warmth makes him feel less alone, like he's actually being touched by Ronan the way he wants to be.

His balls start to tighten, and Dustin tugs on his left nipple piercing and then his right again, trying to send himself over the edge. It brings him frustratingly close, but he doesn't tumble over the way he had hoped. Dustin lowers his hand from his chest and feels between the cheeks of his ass, finding his hole.

He doesn't push his fingers inside; he just presses against his hole with the pads of his fingers, rubbing the sensitive skin while he jerks his cock. It doesn't take long like that for him to lose control, his hips twitching out of time with his strokes. Dustin rubs his thumb over the head of his cock, and that is it, game over; he comes so hard he can see nothing but black for a few seconds.

Blinking brings back the white tiles into focus, but his body is still shaking, little aftershocks of pleasure traveling through his muscles. Feeling like his body is made of lead, Dustin makes sure to wash away all the evidence of what he has just done. Then he finishes cleaning quickly and turns off the shower.

Dustin gets out and grabs his towel; he rubs his hair dry first, and then pats down his body, careful of his still injured leg. Once he is reasonably dry, Dustin gets dressed, putting on long black cotton pants, and a long sleeved black cotton T-shirt. The socks he pulls on are the only thing he's wearing that aren't a shade of black. They're bright red instead and super fuzzy—Dustin loves comfy socks and hates sleeping with cold feet.

Dustin tidies up after himself in the bathroom, and then he heads back to his bedroom for the night. He turns the lamp on beside the bed and puts away his dirty clothes. If he doesn't wash his clothes soon, he'll run out. Once his clothes are neatly put away in his bag, Dustin gets into bed with a book.

He's not quite ready to sleep, even though it has been a long day, and despite the fact that orgasms make him sleepy. His brain is too awake. He knows if he tries to go to sleep now that he'll think too much about all the wrong things and end up staying up all night. And staying up all night when you are searching for eleven missing women is never a good idea. So Dustin starts reading, because in theory it'll be the story in the book that's in his head— the life of someone imaginary—not his life.

Like he has done most nights of his adult life, Dustin reads until it starts getting hard to keep his eyes open. Until he starts re-reading the same lines over and over again and still not taking them in. When he gets to that point, he puts a bookmark in his book and puts it on the nightstand.

Then Dustin gets under the bedcovers and rearranges the pillows behind him, so they are flat, and in a more comfortable position to sleep in. He's already taken his nighttime meds earlier in the car, so he doesn't have to worry about that now.

He turns the light off and lies down. Dustin has slept in lots of different beds in his lifetime, in lots of different places—he gets used to them pretty quickly. Just this week he's been in several different motel rooms, but somehow being in Ronan's spare bedroom feels different from staying in a room he has rented for the night, and not just because he's not sharing the room this time.

A home can tell you a lot about a person. Ronan normally doesn't like to open up about himself, but by letting Dustin come to his home, it's like maybe he doesn't feel like he needs to hide from Dustin as much. Or maybe in the morning Dustin will find the house to be as soulless as he first thought Ronan was when he saw him at the college crime scene.

Dustin can't tell much from the spare room and the bathroom, so he guesses he'll have to wait and see—until then, he does his best to sleep.

Chapter Seven

Ronan is cooking pancakes in his kitchen when Dustin comes in looking disheveled and sleep rumpled. It's not the first time Ronan has seen Dustin look like that—he pretty much looks like that every morning—but it feels different to see Dustin look that way in Ronan's home. It's not often that someone else is in Ronan's space, but a sleepy man in his kitchen in the morning would mean that Ronan got laid last night. But that's not the case here.

They slept in separate beds; they are colleagues, maybe friends, but nothing more. And he really needs to stop thinking about sleeping with Dustin. He's not some high school boy controlled by his dick. He can have an attractive man in his house without jumping him.

"Morning." Ronan still can't help looking Dustin over. He looks good, warm and soft, sleepy, his hair a mess He's half asleep, clearly, but Ronan thinks, if he kissed him, Dustin would still respond like he had before, when he'd leaned into Ronan with that surprisingly muscular body. Ronan had felt its hardness when they had been on the motel bed.

"Morning," Dustin says back, and Ronan tries to pull himself out of the fantasy. Dustin is a psychic for crying out loud. He might be seeing every dirty thought Ronan is having about him and wouldn't that just be humiliating.

But looking at Dustin as he drops into one of Ronan's kitchen chairs, Ronan doesn't think Dustin is reading anything, let alone borderline pornographic thoughts, staring at Ronan. His pretty blue eyes are half closed and his face is relaxed, tired.

"Want some breakfast?" Ronan asks, trying to focus on the here and now, not what it might be like to pin Dustin to his kitchen table.

Ronan is sure he had his hormones in better check the day before, but then the day before he hadn't known what Dustin's lips tasted like. That small taste has Ronan craving more, and it's all his own stupid fault for giving into temptation.

"I'd love some breakfast. What are you making?" Dustin asks, running a hand through his purple hair, smoothing it out with his fingers, and then messing it up again.

"Pancakes and bacon. You do it on purpose? Mess up your hair?" Ronan asks, curious.

"Yeah, I don't like it neat. I bet it drives you crazy, doesn't it?" Dustin laughs.

"What makes you think that?" Ronan asks.

"Well, look at your hair. It is perfect; you're so neat and your place is neat. Don't get me wrong, it all works for you. But the ultra-neat types seem to not like my style or my hair." Dustin shrugs.

"I already told you I liked your hair. But I wasn't sure the messy thing was on purpose. You like being messy?" Ronan asks.

Ronan was always taught to keep things neat and clean. His father was ex-Army. He had certain standards and hair was one of them. He would have never allowed Ronan to have long hair, and Ronan still follows most of his father's rules.

But it's not the first time he's questioned them, especially given how his father killed himself with a gun from his collection. All those rules, all that proper behavior, it hadn't helped his father deal with the loss of his daughter. Daily routines, working out, keeping everything clean had gone out the window, and just a year after she was gone, on the anniversary of Sarah's death, he had taken his own life.

"I like my hair, neat doesn't suit me. Are you okay? I'm not trying to snoop, but your energy is so strong right now, I can feel it. I can feel that you are sad," Dustin says.

"I, ah, I was thinking about my dad. I got the neatness from him. He was always such a together guy. I tried to be like him, to keep him happy. Even after Sarah died and mom left. But acting like a soldier, it didn't fix him. Sometimes I don't know why I do it, I'm just used to rules," Ronan explains, serving up two plates of breakfast and coming over to the table with them.

"I'm sorry you went through all that. I guess rules are kind of comforting for you, if you're used to them. I never liked rules, never followed them much. But if that's what you like, it's cool.

I just think you should follow them for the right reasons. Don't follow them to keep a ghost happy, you should put yourself first." Dustin looks like he hesitates to say it, and he drops his gaze to his plate after.

"Did you read me again? Or did you just guess that I sometimes do things to please my dad?" Ronan sighs, stabbing at his pancake.

"It's not stupid. And I didn't read you. I promised I wouldn't, remember? But I can't help but pick up on your emotions sometimes. That and guessing made me think that maybe you were trying to make your dad happy or proud. I tried to make my parents proud, while trying to still be me before my breakdown; it didn't really work out so well, hence the breakdown." Dustin bites his lip, and Ronan wants to stop him before he makes his lip sore, but things are already getting personal. If he were to touch Dustin's lips, the situation might become sexual.

Friends can get personal. Ronan can be friends with someone he's working a case with, but sex, that's different, far more likely to complicate things, and distract from the case.

"I guess we're both a little fucked up when it comes to our families. I'm sorry for... is leaking emotions the right way to describe it?" Ronan asks.

"I've never heard it put that way, but I guess you could call it that. But you don't need to be sorry about it. I feel bad for picking up on stuff I shouldn't. It feels like I'm invading your personal space or something, like I'm being nosy. I don't mean to. Sometimes, if an emotion is strong, it creates an imprint, like a vision. I don't just see things that aren't there, I feel them," Dustin explains, picking up bacon.

"What's it like? Having a vision?" Ronan asks as they eat. He's both curious and trying to lighten the mood.

"I'm not sure I can describe it. One second I'm seeing my surroundings, the next I can be in another place or time. It's like I become another person for seconds, or minutes—I see their past, sometimes their present, rarely their future. But it feels like how I hear an out-of-body experience is. I'm not me for a while," Dustin says.

"I can't imagine seeing someone else's life, feeling their feelings. It must be so strange." Ronan is glad Dustin is willing to tell him about it.

"It's weird. And it gives me a headache; it feels like there is too much in my head all at once. Like it's not just me in there. And then I go back to normal, pop a headache pill, clean up if I've had a nosebleed. I'm used to it; I've always been this way." Dustin rubs his forehead like he's feeling the phantom pain of the headaches he's talking about.

"Did feeling my sadness over my father's death hurt you?" Ronan asks.

"Not really. It was just like walking into a room and getting a chill. You notice it, but it doesn't hurt." Dustin shrugs.

"That's good, I don't want to cause you pain because I can't keep a lid on my emotions," Ronan sighs.

"No one can truly keep a lid on their emotions, trust me, even the most self-contained person feels things that I can pick up on. Don't beat yourself up for being human," Dustin says.

They eat breakfast, together, moving on from heavier subjects, and then separate to get ready to go to the crime scenes.

"We'll go to the most recent scene first, then the second most recent, then we'll head to the agency and see what everyone has," Ronan tells Dustin as he locks up his house and sets the alarm system.

"Newest victim—Alice Tree, twenty, right? I'm still a little fuzzy from sleep," Dustin says, as they head for Ronan's car.

"Yep, that's our eleventh woman. She went missing from her backyard. She was covering some garden furniture that had come uncovered." Ronan unlocks his car and they both get in. It's starting to feel a little too familiar, getting into his car with Dustin.

It's been almost a full week of being in each other's company nearly nonstop, no wonder it feels familiar. Ronan doesn't remember the last time he spent so much time with one person, or the last time he shared so much with someone new.

"Do you think he lured her out into the yard? The *Sanguis* demon, is that something they would do? Like, loosen the covering so that Alice would have to come out into the yard? Are they sneaky like that? The demon thing is still new to me," Dustin says, as Ronan pulls away from the curb, heading to the newest crime scene, number eleven—it's far too many missing women.

"It's possible. *Sanguis* demons are smart; it's smart enough to do that, lure a person out of safety. That's a good thought. I'll call Chris and see if they found any evidence on the sheets covering the furniture. *Sanguis* demons still leave prints and trace unless they clean up after themselves. It's not bothering to clean up the blood it sheds, so I doubt it's cleaning up its prints." Ronan likes how Dustin works on the case with him. He's good at figuring things out. He doesn't just get visions; he interprets things he sees and feels.

"It's really weird the way it bleeds like that. Like the thing isn't scary enough, it cries blood? I thought human criminals were bad enough, I don't know how you deal with monsters." Dustin shakes his head.

"It's kind of funny that you find monsters so weird when you're weird to most people. Not to be insulting. Just it's not every day you meet a psychic." Ronan has met psychics before, but not quite like Dustin, not as powerful, or with his exact abilities, like being able to bend small bits of metal or read the emotions in a room.

"What was the first supernatural thing you saw? Was it on a case?" Dustin asks.

Ronan feels his blood freeze at the question. And images of Sarah fill his mind.

"I'd rather not talk about that." Ronan is glad his voice doesn't shake, but he thinks the strain shows in it.

"Yeah, of course, don't worry," Dustin says.

"It's nothing personal." Ronan doesn't want Dustin to be offended by Ronan not answering his question, but he can't bring himself to talk about it, not now.

Only a few people know what happened and Ronan never had to tell them himself. He can't imagine driving along and just blurting it out. He has a lump in his throat just thinking about it. It makes Ronan feel sixteen again, not at all like a grown man who has faced down creatures and criminals.

"I know. I can see it on your face. The reason you don't want to talk about it has nothing to do with me," Dustin tells him, then reaches out hesitantly and puts his hand on top of Ronan's. His pale hand, long fingers, and black painted nails look so different than Ronan's hand, which is stronger, broader, and slightly tanned even in the winter.

"I'm sorry I asked, I didn't know it was something that would upset you," Dustin adds, and Ronan can tell that Dustin's hand on his is an attempt to offer comfort, it's not a come-on, but Ronan can't help but still feel something at the touch, a warmth he's been trying to ignore since he kissed Dustin.

"You couldn't have known, no need to be sorry," Ronan sighs. This is why he likes things neat and tidy—emotions have a tendency to get messy, and apart from Dustin's hair, Ronan doesn't see the appeal in messy things.

They drive the rest of the way talking about the case. Dustin never takes his hand back, and Ronan doesn't ask him to. When he parks outside Alice Tree's house, where she lives with her parents, Ronan hesitates. When he gets out of the car he will no longer have a reason to be touching Dustin. He's pushed things already, the lines between comforting a friend and more is starting to blur.

The simple connection is nice; Ronan wants the comfort being offered. He's starting to enjoy being around Dustin more than he should and that worries him. In the end, Ronan doesn't have to be the one to end the contact. Dustin takes his hand, with its warmth, away and opens the car door, getting out and leaving Ronan behind for a second. Ronan is quick to follow though; he doesn't want to look like he was having a moment in the car.

Ronan would be mortified if Dustin realized he was getting angst-ridden over a bit of hand-holding. Ronan is a grown man. He likes to think of himself as strong-willed and sensible. It's ridiculous that he's getting his head all turned around by a little affection and a pretty face.

He feels a little bad for thinking of Dustin like that. He's more than just a pretty face—even though he is very good-looking, there is more to him than his looks. He's a person with depth. But it's easier for Ronan if he tells himself the reason Dustin is filling his head is because his dick has taken control, not because of anything deeper. It's been a week, goddamn it, how can he be so attracted to a person in a week?

"Do the parents know we're coming?" Dustin asks when Ronan shuts his car door.

"Yes. I sent Chris a text last night. He let them know we'd be coming over today. He says they are a real mess," Ronan warns.

"I think talking to parents with missing kids is the worst," Dustin sighs.

"It's heartbreaking, not being able to help more. I hated it as a cop, having to deliver bad news to parents." Ronan had loathed that part of his job. It never got any easier, telling a parent or a family member that their worst nightmares had come true.

"Hopefully we can help," Dustin says, optimism in his voice.

"Hopefully," Ronan agrees.

They walk up to the front door together and Ronan knocks. After a few minutes, a man answers. He has to be the father of the victim, Roy Tree. He's late forties, quite a big man; he's older than Ronan and taller than him, a big, strong-looking man. But his face and eyes are tired; his eyes really give away the pain he's in.

"Hello. Chief Wilkinson told you we'd be coming. I'm Ronan and this is Dustin," Ronan introduces them.

"Yes, he did, come in." Roy Tree leads them into his family room and offers them seats.

Roy inspects them both intently. He looks at Ronan first. And Ronan knows Roy sees sensible hair, conservative clothes, jeans, and a coat, someone who looks like they'd work for the police. Then Roy looks at Dustin, who's in his big black coat again and his huge boots—Dustin had told him were called creepers. He has on the red skinny jeans again, and Ronan knows nothing about makeup, but he's sure Dustin is wearing black eyeliner today. Dustin looks good, like he'd fit on a magazine cover doing winter fashion. But Roy really doesn't look impressed.

"The chief told me one of you used to be a cop, and I'm betting that's you," Roy says to Ronan.

"Yes, sir." Ronan nods.

"He didn't tell me how you were involved in my daughter's case, boy." Roy looks at Dustin, and there is anger in the lines of his face.

"I'm a consultant with the police," Dustin says. He doesn't seem affected by the hostility coming from Roy. And there is no way he isn't picking up on Roy's mood.

"What kind of consultant?" Roy pushes.

"I'm a psychic," Dustin admits.

"I don't believe in that kind of bullshit," Roy says bluntly.

"And that's your right, but the police believe in me and I'd like to help find your daughter," Dustin says.

"Well, I'm not wasting my time on some fraud. Get out of my

house. My wife is upstairs having a breakdown, my daughter is missing, and what—you're going to talk to my dead grandma?" Roy yells.

"Mr. Tree, please. We're both here to help you." Ronan tries to reason with him, but he just looks angrier.

"I'll talk to you. But the freak show can wait outside," Roy barks.

Ronan bristles at Roy calling Dustin a freak, but before he can say anything Dustin puts a hand on his arm; he leans in close to speak.

"It's okay. I'll go look outside. Questioning is your thing anyway," Dustin says in a low voice.

"Are you sure?" Ronan asks.

"Yeah. If I stay, there will just be a fight. I'll meet you by the car," Dustin says, standing up.

Ronan grabs his hand.

"Here, take the keys. Wait in the car when you're ready—it's cold." Ronan doesn't like the idea of Dustin standing out in the cold.

Dustin takes the car keys from Ronan, and leaves without another word. Ronan hears him let himself out the house. Once Dustin is gone Ronan turns back to face Roy.

"How can you work with someone like him?" Roy asks.

"What do you mean?" Ronan isn't sure what bothers Roy about Dustin, because he'd clearly taken an instant dislike; it's not just that he doesn't believe in psychics.

"He belongs in a circus someplace, not investigating crimes. I could tell he wasn't a cop from the way he looked, but a psychic? You've got to be kidding me. How is he any help to a real detective?" Roy asks.

"He's actually been very useful. But I understand that not everyone believes in the supernatural." Ronan doesn't tell Roy that they are certain that what took his daughter is supernatural, a demon.

"How is he useful? And you believe in psychics? Is that why you're not a cop anymore?" Roy asks, and the guy is clearly an ass, missing daughter or not.

"I chose to become a private detective so I could pick and choose the cases I took and the people I work with. I was asked to work with Dustin, and I've been around him while he's seen things to do with the case. Things no one else could know. But I'm not here to argue. Can I ask you some questions about your daughter?" Ronan asks, forcing himself to be professional. Once again, Dustin has him wanting to act unprofessional, but this time it's nothing to do with wanting to sleep with Dustin and everything to do with wanting to defend his new friend.

"All right, as long as it has nothing to do with this psychic rubbish or weird feelings shit. I want my girl found and the bastard that took her locked up," Roy growls.

"We all want the missing girls found. Now, tell me everything about Alice's day yesterday, every detail, no matter how small," Ronan says, because this is about Alice, not Roy. The guy might be an ass who took a dislike to Dustin just because he looks different, but he still might be able to help, and he still deserves to be able to see his daughter alive again. And Alice deserves to be found, regardless of who her father is.

Roy grumbles a little, but then he starts going through everything he knows about Alice's day, and when he had seen her and not seen her during the day. Ronan takes notes of everything, even details they already have on file, in case they spark something different this time.

From what Roy says it was very unusual for the covers to come off the garden furniture, no one had been at the back of the house when Alice called to say she was going to fix the covers. Roy and his wife hadn't heard any screams or sounds of a struggle.

From everything Roy says, Ronan believes Alice was lured into the backyard, and knocked out with something like chloroform, then carried away. The backyard backs onto another street, where a car could have been waiting. Dustin had seen a car in one of his visions.

If Alice had been in the trunk of a car, it would explain why she hadn't been seen leaving the area. Ronan questions Roy until he's sure Roy didn't see anything he has dismissed, being a total nonbeliever.

Once he's done, he gets up, trying to think of something to say.

"Find my little girl," Roy says; for the first time, an emotion other than anger crosses his face.

Ronan doesn't know if he could ever handle being a parent;

losing Sarah had killed his father and almost killed him. He doesn't want to know what it would be like to lose a child.

"I'll do my best, sir, for Alice and the other missing women. I know you don't want to hear this, but Dustin is a big part of the reason the cops and the FBI are still looking for the missing women so urgently. He's the one who believes they are alive. Pretty much everyone else is ready to write them off as dead," Ronan says.

"Do you believe him, then? That my daughter and the other girls who have been taken are alive?" Roy asks.

"I believe in Dustin. I believe there is hope that we'll bring all these women home. Keep believing that she'll come home," Ronan says.

"If some sick bastard has touched my baby…" Roy's voice breaks off as it fills with emotion, and Ronan knows what his fears for his daughter are. Because of the most common reasons women are taken and not killed by criminals.

"We don't believe that the man who took Alice is that kind of predator," Ronan says, twisting the truth a little. The *Sanguis* demon isn't really a man, even though it is male—it's not human, but it is a predator. Its need isn't sexual though, that is truthful enough.

"Thank you," Roy says, walking with Ronan to the door. Roy might be kind of an asshole, but he's still a father with a missing child and Ronan does feel bad for him.

"The police will be in touch." Ronan wishes he had the words to give more comfort, but he doesn't know what to say.

The truth, if Roy even believed, it would horrify him. How do you tell a father that his daughter has been taken by a demon that feeds off blood and spinal fluid? And then tell him not to worry? Ronan thinks in this case it's better if he doesn't try to tell the truth.

When Ronan leaves, he finds Dustin waiting in the passenger seat. Ronan walks around the car and gets in.

"How did it go?" Dustin asks.

"He wasn't as horrible once you left. I'm sorry about that. Some people are just bigoted. I don't know if he suspected you were gay because you wear makeup, or if it was your age, or just because you don't look like what he was expecting from a police consultant, but it was shitty the way he acted toward you," Ronan apologizes.

"He wasn't that bad; I've had worse, a lot worse, than Roy. And that's not the first time I've been told to get out of someone's house. It happens when you're a gay goth psychic. A lot of people hate at least one of those things, so I've had my share of crap, don't worry about it." Dustin shrugs.

"Did you see anything?" Ronan asks, wanting to move on.

"Yeah. I saw the car the *Sanguis* demon is using. It's a green Honda. I didn't see the license plate, but that could be useful, right? It was older too, not sure on model. I know there are probably a lot of dark green Hondas that have been in all the states with missing women, but the cops and the FBI can look to see if a car like that has been caught on tape leaving any of the crime scenes," Dustin says in a rush.

"That could be a really good lead. Let me call the chief so he can pass that info on to everyone." Ronan gets out his cell phone and calls Chris, giving him the update.

"Ready to go to Sally Glass' crime scene? It's our last crime scene. Then we can go to my agency. It's in the tower district, so not too far a drive from the park where Sally was last seen. They found blood from one of the other women on some leaves," Ronan says.

"Yeah, I'm ready." Dustin nods.

They drive to the park and walk around until they find the crime scene tape. Apart from the tape you wouldn't know that anything had happened in the park, it's just a patch of grass. It looks almost peaceful, like any other small park. But for Sally Glass this place was the start of a nightmare.

"Do you want to walk the crime scene alone? Would being alone make it easier?" Ronan asks, thinking about how Dustin had a clear vision alone at the Tree home.

"No, it's not easier alone. And as you've seen I fall over a lot with strong visions," Dustin says, absently rubbing his knee.

"Did you fall at Alice Tree's house?" Ronan asks.

"Yeah, hurt the dog bite more than anything," Dustin complains.

"Do you think you need to see a doctor?" Ronan worries as they enter the ring of crime scene tape.

"No, it hasn't bled through my jeans or anything, and it doesn't hurt that badly now. I just pulled it when I fell. The bruises I got will probably hurt worse, but then I always have some kind of bruise somewhere," Dustin says, wandering ahead of Ronan.

"Are they from falling during visions?" Ronan asks.

"Half the time, the rest of the time I'm just clumsy," Dustin laughs, but then he stops—reaching out, he grabs Ronan's arm to steady himself. His grip is quite firm on Ronan's arm, might be tight enough to leave some of those bruises they had been talking about. But on Ronan instead of Dustin.

"Are you all right?" Ronan asks. He can see strain on Dustin's face.

"Hmm? Yeah, yeah. I saw it again," Dustin says, letting go of Ronan's arm with a guilty look.

"The *Sanguis* demon?" Ronan has never seen one in person.

"Yes. It's a creepy looking fucker. And you're going to try and kill it yourself?" Dustin asks.

"Shoot it to incapacitate it, then stab it in the heart to kill it. I have a plan. I've killed other things before, like a werewolf, once." Ronan isn't bragging; he just wants to assure Dustin that he's up to the job of killing this monster.

"Silver bullets?" Dustin questions.

"No, you don't need silver to kill a werewolf. I just shot it with a hunting rifle, head shot. I wasn't alone. There were a bunch of police in the forest too," Ronan explains.

"Well, I hope you can do it without getting hurt. Have you been hurt before?" Dustin asks. As they leave the taped-off area, he looks equal parts curious and concerned.

"Not too badly, a few broken bones and stitches over the years." Ronan shrugs. He's never been hurt badly enough to consider stopping going after the supernatural.

"You need to be careful," Dustin says as they walk back to the car.

"Are you just worried about me or did you have a vision?" Ronan asks just as they reach his car.

"I'm a little worried. I haven't had a vision of you getting hurt, but I've seen that monster—it's a little bit terrifying. So yeah, it has me worried for you," Dustin says softly, opening the passenger door of the car.

"I won't get hurt, but I appreciate your concern." Ronan gets in the car, and Dustin does the same. Ronan is touched by Dustin's concern. It's been awhile since anyone outside of the agency or Chris really worried about him doing his job.

"This thing is a badass," Dustin points out as Ronan starts to drive.

"Well, good thing I'm a badass too," Ronan jokes.

"It's not funny. I know you've done stuff like this before, but it doesn't mean there isn't a risk involved. And you strike me as someone who puts the job before his own safety," Dustin says, looking concerned.

"Don't worry about it. I was a cop for years—sometimes that's what you have to do; you put the case first, the victim first. You should be used to this—you've worked with cops before, an ex-cop can't be that different." Ronan heads to the agency on autopilot. He could find his way there from anywhere in the city.

"None of the cops I worked with were like you. Maybe because you knew psychics were real before we met, something, I dunno, but you've been different from the start," Dustin finishes, looks at Ronan, and blushes slightly.

It looks gorgeous on him, the faint redness to his cheeks. Ronan wants to reach out and touch the soft skin of Dustin's cheek, see if it is warm like it looks from the blush, but his self-control is better than that.

"Well, I guess I'm glad I'm different, thanks," Ronan says roughly, not sure what else to say.

"So, ah, tell me about the people at your agency?" Dustin asks, thankfully changing the subject. Ronan really doesn't know what to think about Dustin finding him different from any other cop he's worked with.

"Well, I told you a little bit about Harry. He's not a detective the way the rest of us are. He doesn't deal with people or go into the field. But he's our backup, our eyes and ears. He'll find out anything we ask about anything so we can focus on the case, the hunt." Ronan loves his team. They are great people. He's a little nervous about them meeting Dustin—for some reason he wants them to like Dustin. Ronan isn't going to read into those thoughts.

"How old is Harry? Was he a cop or anything? Were any of them cops?" Dustin asks.

"Harry is thirty, but he acts more like a twenty-year-old. He's not straitlaced like the rest of us. He looks kind of like a Billy Idol wannabe? With the white blond hair and leather, but he's around your height and about as hard-core as a kitten—I haven't forgotten about kitten homes—and the only other ex-cop is Alice," Ronan explains.

"Harry sounds interesting, how'd he hook up with your agency?" Dustin asks.

"He'd worked as a technical consultant for the Army, which was where he met Lisa and Rick. They were both in the Army. They were somewhere classified when they all saw a pack of coyotes turn into men, which is also meant to be classified. But they had questions when they came back. They found me doing my thing. I helped fill in the blanks," Ronan explains.

"So Alice is an ex-cop, and Lisa and Rick are ex-Army. So I'm betting no wildness there? Like no dyed hair, no style, just sensible like you? Buttoned up with fifty foot walls?" Dustin asks.

"I guess you could describe us like that. Lisa actually dyes her hair, but only brown—she's forty. I think she might be going gray but I've never asked. Lisa and Rick both have tattoos, ones they can hide, from their time in the service. Lisa and Alice have their ears pierced once each, but as far as I'm aware that's all they have done," Ronan says, glancing at the row of silver rings and studs in Dustin's ear.

"And the last one's Alan, right, what's he like? What got him into this?" Dustin asks.

"Alan was part of a private security team. We met him after a yeti killed one of his clients. He's a lot like the rest of us. Sensible I guess you'd say, reserved, focused on the job," Ronan says. He's never really talked about his team with anyone before. No one has ever asked like this.

"A yeti? You're making this shit up, right?" Dustin looks shocked.

"No, I'm not making it up. Yetis are real and very violent. Their kills, if they leave anything behind, are usually blamed on bears. Alan has a scar from a yeti hunt on his leg, ask him about it if you want, but I swear it's true." Ronan grins, because it's kind of fun sharing these stories and seeing Dustin's disbelief.

"Wow, a yeti, that's kind of cool... wait? Do they live in forests? Does that mean when we were in the woods we could have been yeti food?" Dustin asks, sounding a little alarmed.

"Don't worry about it. Yetis hibernate during the winter; we were safe enough." Ronan shrugs.

"You're crazy." Dustin snorts.

"You've agreed to help hunt a *Sanguis* demon, how sane are you?" Ronan fires back as a joke, but then he freezes, thinking of the pills Dustin takes every day, and the breakdown in college. "I didn't mean it like that..." Ronan starts but Dustin holds a hand up to stop him.

"I'm not sensitive about words like that. I just called you crazy! Crazy, insane, nuts they're just words, ones that, as a psychic with mental health issues, I've been called a lot. I have a tough skin for when people mean them with spite. But you were just joking, it's cool, you can do that," Dustin says and Ronan feels a wave of relief.

"I didn't want to hurt you," Ronan admits. He almost wishes he hadn't. He sounds so vulnerable—telling Dustin he doesn't want to hurt his feelings is coming close to admitting he cares about how Dustin feels. Ronan does care about Dustin, but he doesn't want Dustin to know that. He sure as hell doesn't plan to tell him.

"You didn't. I would tell you if that kind of thing bothered me, I swear. I don't want you to tread on eggshells around me because of my mental health. You haven't been doing that so far, and I like it. Even once you knew about the depression and anxiety, you still treated me the same, that's all I want. No special treatment, just treat me like a man," Dustin says.

"Sure, I can do that. No kid gloves. I'll still be an asshole when the urge strikes." Ronan grins.

"You can be kind of an asshole," Dustin agrees as Ronan parks his car in his usual space outside the building where they rent a large office.

"And you're kind of a bitch, so I guess we're even." Ronan smirks. He gets out of the car listening to Dustin splutter. Keeping the grin that wants to break free to himself.

"Never knew you had a sense of humor," Dustin grumbles.

"Come on, follow me, everyone will be waiting." Ronan smiles and leads the way. He doesn't mention that it's rare for him to joke around with someone, especially someone he's only known a week, because once again that feels like he would be giving too much away about himself. Dustin is different to Ronan, he can't lie to himself about that, but that doesn't mean he has to share the truth with anyone else.

Ronan types in the code to open the door and heads inside, with Dustin following. They're on the second floor. So they go upstairs, and then Ronan lets them into the office, where he finds his whole team waiting. Harry is on his laptop on the couch, Lisa is cleaning her gun at her desk, and Alice is at her desk typing something on her keyboard. Rick and Alan are standing in the little kitchen area, drinking coffee.

They all look up when he walks into the room. They knew he was coming from the moment he keyed in his code, but to anyone else it would look like they just sensed him.

"Boss is back!" Alice grins, looking much younger than her forty years—mainly because of her smile, partly because of the fact she's wearing her hair in pigtails and a Hello Kitty T-shirt.

"I've been gone a week," Ronan points out.

"Yeah, but you know this place isn't the same without you. They slack," Rick laughs.

Rick is African-American and the tallest of the bunch at over six feet. He tends to intimidate people, but he's nice as pie with a good sense of humor that has gotten them through some tough times.

"I haven't been slacking!" Harry yelps.

"Who's the cutie?" Lisa asks, putting her gun away. She looks good. When Ronan left, she'd still been sporting a black eye and bitching that there wasn't good makeup for women of color to cover up blemishes, let alone huge bruises.

Ronan freezes for a second. If he responds, everyone will know he thinks that Dustin is cute, and suddenly Ronan feels like he's back in high school all over again.

"If you read your report you'd know he's the psychic, Dustin McPherson," Rick says, sipping coffee. No caffeine in it, though. Rick never drinks caffeine, but he loves coffee. He says it makes him too jittery.

"I read the report. It didn't say he was cute. I thought maybe Ronan had picked someone up on the way here," Lisa says, winking at Ronan. She's such a tease. She's always lifting their spirits, somehow less worn down by Army life than Rick.

"I think he's a little young for the boss man." Alan shrugs, which makes Ronan wince inside, because he did kiss Dustin despite the eleven-year age gap.

"Is it always this hectic?" Dustin asks him.

"Pretty much," Ronan says, then he takes a step farther into the room.

"As some of you have already guessed, this is Dustin, the psychic. We'll be working with him on this case, please make him feel welcome," Ronan orders.

"Hello, Dustin, welcome to our little operation." Alan smiles, just a hint of his Italian accent coming out as always.

The rest of the team echo Alan's hello.

"Hi everyone. Ronan's been telling me about you and what you do here. I hope I can help out on this case." Dustin looks almost shy, faced with a room full of people. His hands are shoved into his pockets, and he's hunched in on himself a little.

Ronan remembers that Dustin said his anxiety often comes out when meeting new people. So being faced with five new people, it's not surprising that he feels anxious. Ronan wants to kick himself for not asking earlier if it would be okay.

"Take a seat at my desk and I'll get you a coffee—be nice everyone." Ronan thinks that having his own space and a place to sit might help Dustin relax.

Ronan leads the way to his desk and pulls out the chair for Dustin, very aware that the eyes of his team are on him.

"Once things are settled, maybe you can describe the *Sanguis* demon and its lair. None of us have seen one in person before." Ronan thinks focusing on work, something he knows Dustin is good at, might help distract him from the room full of new people. Ronan squeezes Dustin's arm gently and goes to get him a drink.

It's weird seeing Dustin draw into himself. He's usually so vibrant, so comfortable with himself, but right now he's fidgeting, ill at ease. Ronan keeps an eye on him as he goes to make tea, thinking it'll be more calming than coffee.

"Is he okay?" Alan asks quietly in the kitchen area.

"New people freak him out sometimes," Ronan explains, not wanting to give too much away about Dustin's personal life.

Dustin had been fine interviewing people for the case, but there was usually only one person, and both Dustin and Ronan talking to them or Dustin went off alone, maybe that had made it easier. Ronan doesn't know a lot about anxiety disorders, but the one thing he does know, is that anxiety is different for everyone. Working the case hadn't triggered Dustin, but meeting the team has.

"Can you tell them what it looks like?" Ronan asks, hoping it'll distract Dustin from his nerves.

"Do you have plain paper and a pencil?" Dustin replies.

"Yes, why?" Ronan waves his hand at Lisa who rolls her eyes and gets Dustin the supplies. Well, she did insist on being in charge of stationery. The rest of them never remembered to order anything new, and Rick and Alan tended to pull pranks on each other involving Post-it Notes, wallpapering things like the inside of Alan's car.

"It'd be easier to draw the *Sanguis* demon than try and describe it." Dustin shrugs.

Lisa hands Dustin some paper and pencils and he thanks her.

"You can draw?" Ronan asks.

"I didn't tell you I could draw?" Dustin sets the paper down on the desk and starts drawing.

"No, you didn't." Ronan goes back to making the tea, but he's oddly surprised he hasn't seen Dustin draw.

"Are you good enough that it'll be better than a description?" Alice asks, looking curious.

"I studied art in college; I was okay." Dustin's focused on his drawing.

"I never asked what you did in college." Ronan brings the tea over to Dustin, who thanks him, but keeps most of his attention on his drawing.

"Well, I didn't finish," Dustin says in a flat tone.

Ronan can't really tell how Dustin feels about it. He's not going to ask now. Besides Harry, who Ronan had do the research, none of the rest of the team knows that Dustin had a breakdown in college.

"So while Dustin works on that, have there been any weird sightings anywhere near where the women have gone missing?" Ronan asks.

"Not a lot of credible ones," Lisa sighs.

"Yeah, the usual crazy people seeing aliens with glowing red eyes." Alice snorts.

"Red eyes?" Ronan repeats, nudging Dustin. "That could be the *Sanguis* demon right?" Ronan says, trying to peer at Dustin's drawing, but the way Dustin is sitting he's blocking the paper.

"It has red eyes in its demon form. It looks like a man most of the time I think, or at least some of the time. Long enough to go places unnoticed to take people," Dustin says.

"So we'll double-check the alien sightings." Alice makes a note.

"So you've had a clear vision of this demon?" Alan asks.

"Yeah, Ronan said what I saw matched the stuff you found," Dustin says, still a little quiet, but he seems less tense now that he has the barrier of Ronan standing beside him. Ronan wonders if having one person he considers a friend close by helps Dustin's anxiety.

"That'd be my research, based on what Ronan said you guys found. I'd put money on this being a *Sanguis* demon, even though I've only read about them and have never known anyone who's seen one. They are very rare and very deadly," Harry explains.

"No placing bets on our cases," Ronan orders.

"You're no fun," Harry complains.

"You never win anyway," Rick points out.

"I won once," Harry argues.

"No arguing, children," Alice tuts.

"We don't want to scare off the psychic," Alan adds.

"He survived a week with Ronan, I think he can handle a little bickering, can't you kid?" Lisa grins.

"Yes, I can, but I'm not a kid," Dustin points out.

"He's twenty-one." Ronan had thought that made Dustin young when they first met, but having spent time with him, Ronan has changed his mind. Dustin is wise beyond his years, aged by his life and visions.

"Way to make me feel old," Alice groans.

"Oh honey, women age like wine, we only get finer as we get older." Lisa smiles.

"I'd have to agree." Alan grins, and Ronan knows Alan's taste runs toward older women.

"I'm done," Dustin says shyly, handing over the piece of paper.

Ronan's not sure what he expected, but the drawing is incredible. So detailed, so lifelike, of a man with bat-like features, almost cat-shaped almond eyes. It looks real enough to jump out of the paper.

"This is amazing," Ronan says softly.

"You don't have to say that," Dustin says, hunching into his coat.

"I'm not just saying it. This is an amazing drawing. It could be in a book on demons." Ronan hands the drawing to Alice first.

"This is a scary-looking fucker," Rick says when it reaches him.

"And it matches what the all books say," Harry adds.

"So we're agreed on what is taking these women?" Alan asks.

"It seemed to fit, but I'm sure now, seeing this." Ronan nods.

"And you've seen its lair?" Harry asks

"I think so. I've seen where the women are being kept." Dustin nods.

"About that, you've said they are all in one place right?" Harry says, tapping at his keyboard as he speaks.

"Yes." Dustin looks curious.

"Well, I was thinking. He must be getting them from one state to another. Ronan, you said he had a car with a trunk, but that couldn't move up to eleven women around at one time," Harry says.

"I can't believe I didn't think of that," Ronan groans, feeling guilty because he knows he's been distracted.

"So I was thinking of looking into rentals of large vehicles, trucks and stuff, to see if anyone's been traveling to all the states we have missing women from." Harry grins.

"Great thinking, maybe look into motor homes too. And any abandoned or stolen cars in the cities women went missing, in case it's stealing the cars it uses in the kidnappings," Ronan orders.

"It's quite smart, then?" Rick asks.

"From what I've read, it's as smart as most humans," Lisa answers.

"Smart and strong, with a taste for female blood and spinal fluid." Alan pulls a face like he's grossed out by the demon or rather what it feeds on.

"Why just women?" Alice asks.

"The books speculate it's something to do with hormones. They will kill men, and they will feed off them. But they prefer women,"

Harry explains.

"Sucks to be a girl," Rick says and Lisa throws a ball of paper at him, breaking the wasting paper rule.

"Right, we need to find the lair, that's the most important thing," Ronan says, getting things back to their goal.

"I found something that might help. One book says they like to leave marks. They'll claw the area around the entrance to their lair, so the door to where the women are being kept might have claw marks," Harry says, sounding a little excited about his discovery.

"That's a good lead; look up vandalism reports and animal damage to property, in case people have reported the scratches." Ronan remembers the scratches on the tree he'd seen—lots of those might draw attention.

"We have a lot of work to do. This case should have priority, so if you need anything from any of us…" Alan offers.

"Yeah, my cases can wait," Alice agrees.

"For now we just need to find places the lair could be, then investigate, maybe take Dustin close to see if he picks anything up," Ronan suggests.

"I think this place will have a vibe—that much fear and pain, it has an energy. I should feel the women," Dustin says.

"You can do that? Feel an emotional imprint of a place?" Lisa asks.

"Yes." Dustin nods.

"How powerful are you?" Alan asks.

"I don't know, I've never met another psychic to compare," Dustin says, running a hand through his hair. His hand trembles just a little, giving away, at least to Ronan, the strain that Dustin is feeling being with so many new people.

"But you have pretty strong visions?" Rick sounds curious, but then it's not every day they have a genuine psychic in their office.

"I see things clearly, which I know not all psychics do. Sometimes I just get flashes; sometimes I get the whole story. I'm not sure how it works." Dustin shrugs.

"Let's stop interrogating Dustin and get some research done. I'm going to work from home, so I can take Dustin back. Get in touch if you find any possible sites for the lair and I'll go look," Ronan orders. He doesn't think Dustin would enjoy spending the rest of the day with strangers.

"We'll be in touch soon." Harry nods.

"Hopefully we'll find something before another woman is taken," Alan says as Ronan straightens up.

"Hopefully. Come on, Dustin. We could do with some food and rest. It's been a long week." Ronan says good-bye to his team.

Ronan remembers to mention the kittens to Harry, who says he definitely wants the details. Then he leads the way out, followed quickly by Dustin, who seems relieved to be out of the office.

"Are you okay?" Ronan asks as they get in the car.

"I'm fine," Dustin says.

"Are you sure? You didn't seem too comfortable in there," Ronan says, not starting the car—he wants all his attention on Dustin.

"I... sometimes it's hard for me to be around a lot of people I don't know. I get so nervous and anxious I just want to hide. I'm so worried everyone will think I'm a crazy freak. I don't do well in social situations until I get to know people, and even then I can get tense," Dustin explains.

"I'm sorry. I should have thought about that before taking you to meet the team." Ronan could kick himself.

"It's fine. I liked meeting your friends. It was another insight into a mystery. Did you know you relax the minute you're with them? Your energy changes," Dustin tells him.

"I'm not a mystery. My energy changes? How?" Ronan asks, starting the car.

"You feel the same around them as people seem to feel around family they like. This mix of happy, relaxed, proud. I can't explain it, but they're your family," Dustin says.

"You're right, they are. Most people don't notice that, the way I feel about them. I was thinking of picking up some groceries and cooking at home, nothing fancy, just a break from eating out all week. That okay with you?" Ronan asks.

"You're offering to cook me dinner and you're asking if that's okay? Of course it's okay. I'm happy to help if I can. I'm not a bad cook, but I don't bother much at home," Dustin admits.

"I like cooking, even when it's just for me. But I do cook for the rest of the agency a lot," Ronan says, heading toward the grocery store.

They drive to the store, talking about nothing important, and then head inside to grab some fresh food. It feels strange to be shopping for food with Dustin, oddly domestic for a man he's only known for a week. Ronan can't remember the last time he went to the store with another person.

It isn't long before they're driving back to Ronan's home. Once they are there, they unpack together in the kitchen. Ronan starts cooking. Dustin helps with a lot of the prep, but after a while Ronan gets him to sit down with a drink while he finishes off their dinner. Dustin just keeps him company; it's nice having someone to talk to while he cooks.

Ronan has a question he wants to ask, but he waits until they are both at his kitchen table with spicy chicken and rice, and a glass of white wine each.

"You're really good at art. Have you ever thought about trying to make it a career?" Ronan asks.

"I actually have sold a few paintings and drawings. There are a few galleries that are happy to sell my work when I bring them something. I do it sometimes, when I want to boost my funds or when one of the shelters needs something. I like it better than taking money off my parents," Dustin says honestly.

"Have you thought about art school?" Ronan thinks this might be a sensitive question.

"I've thought about it a dozen times, more. But I always come back to no. I didn't handle college well. School was a lot of pressure; I don't do that well like that. I like the freedom I have now. I set my own timetable. I don't have to live by rigid rules. I don't have to stress about grades and keeping teachers happy. I think I'm better out of school. Is my life perfect? No, but school's not the answer for me," Dustin says very candidly, instead of getting offended that Ronan asked, which was what he'd worried would happen.

"You're amazing at it even without going back to school. Could you do something for me?" Ronan asks.

"Thank you. What do you want me to do?" Dustin asks.

"I'd like a picture for the office, maybe one of the whole team? Could you do that?" Ronan would love a picture off all his friends and him for their workspace.

"I could totally do that for you. I'd like pictures of you all to work from. I can draw you well, but I'd like to have more details for them, even though I'm pretty good at drawing from memory." Dustin smiles.

"I'll pay you, of course," Ronan starts, only to be cut off.

"Don't be stupid. We're friends, right? We do favors for friends; let me do it as a gift. I'll be insulted if you try to pay me," Dustin says.

"But… not to be rude—I've seen your place, where you live. I'd feel bad not paying," Ronan admits.

"Well, let's call it a favor for a favor. You make sure those kittens get homes, maybe even deliver them to their new homes, and I'll do the drawing. You'd really help me out and probably save me money," Dustin reasons.

"Are you sure?" Ronan still feels a little bad. He has a feeling that original art of the quality Dustin produces costs a hell of a lot more than a few tanks of gas to get some kittens to new homes.

"Yes. I choose to not have a lot of money, you know. I could have more. I like a simple life. With my abilities, I could make a lot, but I'd rather help people. I saw what lots of money did to my family, and it didn't make my parents happy. I just… do you get what I'm trying to say? I'd appreciate your help more than your money," Dustin says.

"You don't want to be rich because of the way your family handled money. I get that, but maybe you could let yourself have more. You can still help people from a nice apartment, even if you give away more than you spend on yourself. You should let yourself have nice things." Ronan can easily remember waiting outside Dustin's apartment, with the drug deal going on up the street and the graffiti all around. It hadn't seemed nice, and as an ex-cop it had worried Ronan—it didn't feel safe.

"Maybe. I keep thinking of making changes, but then I get scared that'll fuck everything up. I've managed to get a balance. I'm helping people, and I'm not living my parents' life. That's all that mattered to me for a long time. But maybe I can make some changes without it all going to shit." Dustin bites his lip.

It's clear he's been thinking about this. Ronan hopes he decides he deserves more in life than he lets himself have.

"I don't think you'll ever be like your parents, not from what you've said about them. You could be the richest person in the world and you wouldn't be like them. Dustin, in one day you find out everything supernatural is real and that same day you agree to hunt it to save women you've never met. You're not like them, I know it" Ronan is sure Dustin will never turn into a snooty, uncaring person.

"Thanks. I just… I really don't want to end up like them. I'd like to have kids one day maybe, and I never want to be like my parents. I don't want my kids to hate me," Dustin says.

"You want kids? I don't know about kids. My job's so dangerous, but I do like them. Thanks for letting me be so nosy," Ronan says, finishing off his meal.

"Well, I'm going to be nosy back." Dustin looks like he's a little bit worried.

"Okay, ask, it's only fair." Ronan has no idea what Dustin might ask.

"I saw a collar in my vision when I touched you that first day. A cat's collar. What did that mean? Why was it important enough to stand out?" Dustin asks.

"It belonged to my sister's cat. Mr. Mittens. He pined after she died, wouldn't eat—he died, I kept the collar." Ronan still has that collar in a drawer in his bedroom. He doesn't have many things left of his sister's. His mom had thrown most her things away, redecorated her room, tried to erase her from their lives.

"I'm sorry. I wouldn't have asked if I knew it was connected to your sister. I know it hurts you to talk about her," Dustin apologizes.

"It's okay; I should talk about her more. My mom doesn't talk about Sarah, and I hate her for that. I don't want to be like my mom, pretending that Sarah never existed." Ronan sighs, taking his plate to the sink. He hears Dustin move, and senses him getting close. He turns to take Dustin's plate and wash that as well.

"It's clear you're not trying to forget her—some things are just too painful to talk about. I get that," Dustin says.

"When things are painful for you to talk about, you seem to talk about them anyway," Ronan points out, grabbing their glasses to pour them both more wine. Two glasses each won't get either of them drunk, so they'll be fine to work in the morning.

"I guess I'm a masochist," Dustin jokes, getting his wine from Ronan and taking a seat back at the table.

Ronan sits back down too.

"That's not it, though. Why do you push through the pain?" Ronan asks.

"I learned the hard way that bottling the pain up is no good for you. I pushed down everything that hurt me, locked it inside my head, and it festered; it ended up hurting more," Dustin sighs.

"That makes sense. I... would it be too much of a downer if I told you about my sister? If I tell you how Sarah died?" Ronan can feel a lump in his throat just at the thought of it, but the idea that keeping in the pain could lead to it getting worse makes sense, and Ronan doesn't want that.

Chris knows, and the agency, but no one else living knows what happened. Ronan knows he should talk about it more freely, but he's not sure why he's thinking of telling someone he's known a week. Ronan didn't tell any of his friends that soon. But Dustin is different; there has been an honesty between them from the start.

"You can tell me, but only if you want to," Dustin says, taking a sip of his wine.

"It's not a long story, really. Sarah was ten; she was the most beautiful person, full of light and joy. She was the apple of my dad's eye. I guess we all spoiled her, even Mom. We were all so happy when Sarah was alive, a perfect family." Ronan can hardly keep his eyes on Dustin, but he's determined to get this story out. More people should know about Sarah. She shouldn't be forgotten. She was like an angel long before she was taken from them.

"What happened to her?" Dustin asks, reaching out and taking Ronan's hand, which is clenched into a fist.

He hadn't even noticed, but when Dustin gets him to loosen his fist so they can hold hands, Ronan can tell from the feeling in his joints that he'd been clenching his fist awhile.

"I didn't know what it was until years later, but now I know it was a water spirit. We heard Sarah screaming one day. Me and my dad were in the yard when we heard; we came running inside. Sarah was already in the bath when we got there. It was full even though no one had filled it. Sarah was under the water, in all her clothes." Ronan stops, taking a breath.

"My dad and I tried to pull her out of the bath, but it was holding her down and it was stronger than both of us. It drowned her. It let go once she was dead. It just killed her, for no reason. I... ah... read later that they get energy from killing children." Ronan takes a drink of his wine with his free hand.

"I'm so sorry. Losing her like that must have been awful," Dustin says softly.

"I was right there. I was touching her and there was nothing I could do. I think that's what my dad couldn't take, that we couldn't save her. He tried, but it just dragged him down. He stopped leaving the house—stopped doing anything really—and then he killed himself. They were both gone and Mom might as well have been gone too," Ronan sighs. His throat feels tight and a part of him feels like curling into a ball, or crawling into a bottle. But he's not going to do that. He fought past that when his father had given up, because it's not what Sarah would have wanted.

"Would it be cool if you maybe told me some stories about her? Sarah. But happy stories, from before?" Dustin asks.

"I'd actually like that. I've haven't talked about that stuff in a long time." Ronan hasn't had anyone ask to hear about before Sarah died.

Ronan thinks of his favorite stories from when he and Sarah were growing up and he shares them with Dustin. Ronan talks for a long time, and before he realizes it, it's close to midnight and he can see the tiredness in Dustin's eyes. Ronan says he's going to bed, to encourage Dustin to do the same.

Ronan finds he can't sleep, even though it's quite late. He tries for an hour, but his mind is so full of emotions. It's been a long time since he felt so laid bare, and he just can't work out what it is about Dustin that makes him different. Dustin is damaged, a little strange, kind, and talented. He's different from the other people in Ronan's life.

Ronan gets out of bed and goes for a walk around his house. He wonders if Dustin is awake too. He knows he shouldn't be thinking the thoughts in his head, but he can't seem to help himself, the closer he gets to the room where Dustin is.

He can hear whimpering and clear sounds of distress. He's worried, so he opens the door and rushes into the room. He's not sure what he expected to find, but all he finds is Dustin sleeping. As Ronan watches, he sees Dustin moan unhappily again and start to fight against an invisible enemy.

Ronan remembers Dustin saying he has visions in his sleep sometimes, so Ronan goes over to the bed and shakes Dustin awake. He tells himself he just wants to know what Dustin may have seen, but really he doesn't want to leave Dustin so clearly distressed.

"Dustin, are you okay?" Ronan asks, leaning over Dustin, only to be surprised with a shockingly strong right hook that catches him on the cheek and knocks him back.

"Ow, fuck," Ronan grunts, rubbing his cheek. His usual reaction to being hit would be to hit back and defend himself, but he's knows he's not under attack and that Dustin probably didn't mean it.

"Oh my God, did I just hit you?" Dustin asks, sounding alarmed and turning on the bedside light, which blinds Ronan for a few seconds. When he can see again, Dustin is sitting up in bed, his covers a mess, looking very worried.

"Yes, you did hit me," Ronan complains—his face is throbbing.

"I'm so, so sorry. I will totally understand if you want me to leave your house or if you want to punch me in the face." Dustin looks like a kicked puppy, and it makes Ronan want to do unspeakable things to him, which isn't his usual reaction to that look.

"It's fine. I'm not going to kick you out or hit you. It was an accident, right?" Ronan is pretty sure it was.

"Of course. I'd never hit a friend. I don't ever hit people unless I'm defending myself. I'm not a violent person, I swear," Dustin says in a rush.

"Were you having a vision?" Ronan asks, because if Dustin saw someone being attacked he might wake up feeling the need to defend himself.

"No, just a bad dream. I get them a lot. I think it's because of the visions, though. I see so many awful things, parts of it gets stuck in there," Dustin says. He looks a little pale, and some of his hair is matted down with sweat.

"It was a bad dream, wasn't it? You still look shaken up." Ronan reaches out and runs a hand through Dustin's slightly damp hair. The silky purple strands slide through his fingers.

"You're trying to make me feel better, when I'm the one who hit you. Are you okay?" Dustin reaches out, finding the sore spot on Ronan's cheek.

He winches a little at it being touched—he's sure it's going to bruise.

"It's fine, but you do pack quite the punch for a little guy," Ronan says with a laugh.

"I'm not little, but I'm still sorry I hit you," Dustin says, looking to see what damage he caused.

"I don't know how I'm going to explain the bruise tomorrow if we see the rest of the agency," Ronan comments.

"Don't want them to think a 'little guy' beat you up?" Dustin jokes.

"They'll probably be surprised. I mean, I've trained to fight my whole life. And you don't look like a fighter. We train together as well, and Lisa and Rick are ex-Army. They train really hard. They keep us on our toes," Ronan explains.

"Your whole life?" Dustin asks.

"My dad was ex-Army, remember? He was big into fitness and knowing how to fight if you needed to. He raised me like I was a soldier. Which might be why I'm as straitlaced as you say I am," Ronan says, winching slightly at the pain in his face.

"I hurt you," Dustin says. He looks like he couldn't feel worse about it.

"You didn't mean to, and you said sorry," Ronan says. There is no point in lying and saying it doesn't hurt. He's sure that macho crap would annoy Dustin anyway. It's a fist to the face; of course it hurts.

"Sorry doesn't make it hurt less," Dustin says.

He reaches out again, his fingers just hovering over the sore spot on Ronan's cheek. He guesses it must be red, maybe even already bruising.

"You could kiss it better," Ronan jokes, trying to make Dustin smile.

He hates the sad look on Dustin's face. What he doesn't expect is for Dustin to go to his knees so he can reach, before pressing a tender kiss to Ronan's cheek where it hurts. It's oddly sweet, considering Dustin is the one who punched him, and Ronan is a grown man. No one's kissed his bruises since he was a little boy. He doesn't remember his chest feeling tight when his mom did it.

"Anywhere else hurt?" Dustin asks, with a glint in his blue eyes.

Ronan isn't sure whether he is looking at an angel or the devil himself.

"If I say where I'm tempted to say, I think you'll hit me again." Ronan grins, because in all fairness the ache building in his dick could be considered a kind of pain, so it wouldn't just be a line.

"Don't be a pig. I'm just starting to like you," Dustin says, his eyes drifting to Ronan's mouth.

"Okay, no cheesy come-ons. But hey, only just starting to like me? I thought we were friends," Ronan says, trying to sound offended.

"We are friends, but you were a little straitlaced to start with. I think if I'd hit you the first night we stayed in a motel together, you'd have reacted differently. I don't think you'd have hit me back—you were never an asshole—but before, looking at you was like looking at a closed door. Now you keep opening it a little more, and I like that," Dustin says honestly.

"I wouldn't have hit you back for an accident. But I don't know if I'd have reacted the same. I don't think you'd have kissed it better at the start of the week," Ronan says, trying to resist the urge just to kiss Dustin and pin him to the bed, slide his hands under the cotton T-shirt Dustin is wearing, and see where this attraction he has been feeling could lead.

"At the start of the week I didn't even know you were gay. Besides, I owed you one." Dustin smiles.

"Owed me one?" Ronan asks.

"A kiss," Dustin says, and Ronan is reminded of his slip up in the motel room.

"I shouldn't have—" Ronan starts, only to be cut off by an annoyed Dustin.

"I know, you shouldn't have kissed me, it wasn't professional. Do you live by the rule book?" Dustin huffs.

"I was going to say I shouldn't have stopped," Ronan says softly.

"You mean you regret stopping the kiss when you did?" Dustin looks surprised.

"Yes," Ronan admits. He's been thinking about what could have happened over and over.

"You shouldn't regret it. I think it was the right thing, at the time. We hardly knew each other. Even though it pissed me off in the moment that was mainly sexual frustration talking," Dustin explains.

"I make you sexually frustrated?" Ronan asks, feeling a little bit smug. Dustin is gorgeous, like a supermodel—he could have picked up a man in any state they'd been to, but he hadn't. And he's saying he wants Ronan? It's an ego boost.

It's not like Ronan is ugly or has found it hard to get men into bed, but Dustin is something special. Even with his social anxiety holding him back, he's friendly and outgoing. He's also handsome, talented, and kind. Yes, Dustin definitely wouldn't have trouble finding a man to sleep with if he was looking.

"Don't be dense, of course you do. I mean, the cop type isn't normally my thing, but you're not like other cops I've met—even if you do like your rules. I think if I'd met you when you were a cop I'd still have wanted to jump your bones," Dustin says, with a shy smile.

"That would have been illegal." Ronan realizes he's tried not to think too much about their age gap.

"What would have been?" Dustin asks.

"If we slept together when I was a cop, I'd be in jail. You were sixteen, so maybe you wouldn't have tried to jump my bones." Ronan shakes his head.

"You didn't meet me when I was sixteen." Dustin grins.

"Bit of a wild child?" Ronan asks.

"Kind of. I'd already been arrested a few times. I might have found a cute cop a challenge. I used to like to push people's buttons, especially when I was in trouble. If you'd have arrested me, put me in cuffs? Yeah, I think teenage me would have had a very inappropriate reaction." Dustin smirks.

"You know you're not supposed to enjoy being handcuffed, right?" Ronan is glad he didn't meet Dustin back then—he's certain he wouldn't have been able to handle him. As a detective, and as a young cop, he'd had people make passes at him, mainly to try to get out of trouble. But Dustin—clearly turned on, in handcuffs—may have tested his resolve. He likes to think he would have resisted. Ronan has never slept with someone who was underage, but he thinks, even though he wouldn't break the law, faced with Dustin then he'd have made an ass of himself.

"Tell that to my dick." Dustin grins.

"Please don't talk about your dick when I'm trying to be good,"

Ronan groans.

"Now, where is the fun in that?" Dustin asks.

"You're a hellion. I should have known you'd be trouble when I found you at a crime scene." Ronan can feel his resolve weakening. He's trying to cling to the fact that sleeping with someone you're working with is never a good idea, but it seems his body—well, his dick—isn't too worried about the potential for this to blow up in their faces.

"It's not like I broke in! It was a patch of grass behind a building. Do cops really think some tape is going to keep people out?" Dustin asks. As he speaks, he's still up on his knees facing Ronan. His hand moves forward until he's clutching Ronan's forearm.

Ronan isn't sure if he's steadying himself, wants contact, or both.

"You have a point. But I know for a fact you've been found in places where there was more than tape. Do you pick the locks or bribe people to let you in?" Ronan asks, curiously, very aware of the hand on his arm and how close Dustin's body is to his.

"Kind of neither. I guess you could call it lock picking." Dustin holds up the hand not on Ronan's arm and a paperclip flies off the bedside table and into his hand; it then untwists until it's a straight piece of metal.

"You manipulate the metal in the lock with your mind so it opens? Do you have any more hidden talents I should know about?" Ronan asks, as the paperclip seems to refold itself and float back to the bedside table. Dustin rubs his forehead and Ronan remembers how using his power over metal hurts Dustin.

"Well, I may have a few talents you haven't seen, but I don't know if you want to know about them," Dustin says with a raised eyebrow.

Ronan feels his face flush as he imagines what kinds of talents Dustin may have.

"Never think that I don't want to know. I'm just not sure if it's sensible to obtain that knowledge," Ronan says honestly. It's taking all of his control not to kiss Dustin.

"Why is it so important to be sensible all the time? Wait, don't answer that, I know. It was the way you were raised, Army Dad, then police training, being sensible and following the rules has

134

worked for you. But that doesn't mean you always have to be sensible—let go for once in your life," Dustin urges.

"I don't know if I'm brave enough to go from following every rule to taking what I want. I've known you a week, we're working on a case together," Ronan says.

"Those sound like excuses, not reasons, to me. I don't want to be a pushy asshole, but I want you. I don't care that I just met you or that after this case I might never see you again. There are no certainties in life, so I think people should take what they want while they can. And bullshit to you not being brave enough. You hunt monsters for a living. You're the bravest man I know," Dustin says.

Ronan lets it sink in; Dustin has as excellent point. Anything could happen tomorrow, so why not enjoy tonight while he has it? Something good is within his grasp—even if he loses it later, he should grab hold of it for now. And like Dustin has said, Ronan isn't a coward. If he can face down the dangers of the supernatural world, he can do this.

"Stop overthinking everything," Dustin says.

"Fuck it," Ronan mutters.

Ronan reaches out and places one hand on the back of Dustin's head, the other around his waist. He uses both to pull Dustin to him, so he can place a kiss on Dustin's soft, pink lips.

Dustin kisses back. He grabs hold of Ronan, pulling him close and down onto the bed, which isn't small but really isn't meant for two grown men. Ronan hears it groan under their combined weight.

"Wait!" Ronan says, pulling out of the kiss.

"Damn it, not again!" Dustin complains, clearly thinking that Ronan is calling a stop to things like before in the motel room.

"No, it's not that. I don't want to stop. My bed is bigger, and my bedroom has condoms and lube—I'm assuming you didn't pack those things?" Ronan asks.

"Shit, I didn't even think of that. No, I don't have any stuff. Your room?" Dustin suggests.

"Yeah, I think that sounds like a better idea." Ronan takes Dustin's hand, helps him off the bed, and leads the way to his bedroom.

"Just so you know, I won't be mad at you if you back out. Not gonna lie, I'll be really disappointed, but not mad, and we'll still be friends," Dustin says as they reach Ronan's bedroom door. Which seems like another step in their relationship, like things will be changed between them if they walk into Ronan's room together.

"I feel the same. Any point you want to end things, no hard feelings," Ronan says, pushing open his door, relieved when Dustin follows him into the bedroom.

"I hope there are some hard feelings," Dustin says with a pointed look at Ronan's crotch.

"I can't believe you went there," Ronan groans. He can't remember ever joking with a lover before sex. He likes it.

"I couldn't resist. Now, are we going to talk all night?" Dustin asks.

"You are so mouthy," Ronan says, and it's not a compliant. He's really starting to like it when Dustin gets mouthy.

"Maybe you should shut me up?" Dustin suggests.

Ronan doesn't ask how; he doesn't need to. He crowds into Dustin's space and kisses him again, deeper this time. He wraps his arms around Dustin and pulls him closer, until their bodies are touching all along their fronts. It's a simple kiss, but it feels like fireworks going off. To be close to Dustin, to have Dustin moving against him as they kiss, feels better than Ronan imagined.

Dustin's hands make their way under Ronan's T-shirt, sliding over his skin, gripping at his back, and Ronan breaks the kiss long enough to pull his T-shirt off and over his head, tossing it to the floor.

"Good idea." Dustin grins, stopping Ronan with a hand to the chest when he comes in for another kiss. Once Ronan has backed off slightly, Dustin strips off his own T-shirt. The first thing that Ronan notices is what Dustin said was true—he is all muscle, lean but solid. The second thing he notices is the nipple piercings.

"You have your nipples pierced?" Ronan isn't sure why he's shocked. Dustin has about six pieces of metal in either ear—it's clear he likes piercings.

"Do you like them?" Dustin asks, running his hand over his chest and flicking one of the silver barbells.

"I've never been with a guy with nipple piercings before, but yeah, on you? I like them. You look amazing," Ronan says, a little breathless.

"Thanks. I'm really kind of glad you've kept up the cop-slash-Army workout thing, because your body is..." Dustin trails off, but he reaches out and runs a hand down Ronan's chest, making him shiver.

Without another word, they are kissing again and while they kiss—with the few brain cells Ronan still has working—Ronan backs them up toward his bed, only stopping when they bump into it and fall onto the mattress.

"That was slick." Dustin grins before Ronan kisses him again.

"Well, this may surprise you, but I'm not a virgin. I might be a straitlaced ex-cop, but I know what to do in the bedroom," Ronan teases.

"Prove it," Dustin challenges.

Ronan can't help but smile. He kisses Dustin again, giving everything he's got, as if it were the last kiss he was ever going to have with anybody, and when he lifts up to let Dustin breathe, Dustin looks a little dazed.

"Well, you sure as hell can kiss," Dustin pants.

"I can do more than kiss, but it seems like a good place to start," Ronan says, leaning in to kiss Dustin's neck, trailing a path down to his collarbone, and ending with a nibble, before getting bold and going lower to explore the piercings.

Nipple piercings may be new territory for Ronan, but he's heard stories, seen porn. He thinks the best course of action is just to go with what feels right. He's sure that Dustin would tell him if he didn't like it. So Ronan starts exploring them with his fingers first, feeling the cool metal against Dustin's hot skin. He starts to wonder what Dustin's skin might taste like, how the metal will change it, so he runs his tongue over the barbell, and is pleased when Dustin shudders. It makes him feel powerful.

"So the piercings really do make your nipples more sensitive?" Ronan asks, playing with the cool metal bar with his fingers while he talks.

"Yes," Dustin hisses.

"Cool. Are you pierced anywhere else, other than your ears?" Ronan looks down the length of Dustin's body, to his cotton-covered groin.

"I'm not that brave. I hear it's great once it's healed, but I do not like the idea of a needle near my dick." Dustin shrugs.

"I don't blame you," Ronan says before claiming another kiss.

Ronan feels Dustin's hand run over his stomach, then dip beneath, easily finding his cock. Dustin wraps those long artist's fingers around his girth and strokes gently, teasingly.

"Fuck," Ronan groans. It's been a little while since he felt a hand that wasn't his own on his cock and it feels different, better than when he's touching himself.

"I was hoping," Dustin says cheekily.

"I'm on board. It's been awhile. Is there a polite way to ask which way you like it?" Ronan asks. He's never known how to do that. It's not that he's shy in the bedroom; it just feels awkward.

"Not sure how polite it is, but I know I want to feel this inside of me," Dustin says, jacking Ronan's cock a little more roughly.

"Not like I'm going to say no to that." Ronan grins. He doesn't mind bottoming, but he prefers to top and the idea of fucking Dustin's pert little ass really appeals to Ronan.

"I'm glad we're on the same page. I've been thinking about you fucking me," Dustin admits, as Ronan slips his own hand into Dustin's pajama pants and wraps his hand around Dustin's cock, which is a little thicker than he expected, given how slight Dustin's frame is.

"Yeah? You've been thinking about that?" Ronan finds the idea surprisingly sexy, that Dustin's been thinking about him the way he's been thinking about Dustin.

"I jerked off in your shower thinking about you fucking me," Dustin says, thrusting up into Ronan's hand.

"Shit, I'm never going to be able to use that shower again without getting a hard-on," Ronan groans.

Hungrily, he kisses Dustin again. Ronan wants to be closer to Dustin, needs to feel every part of him.

"I should have just gotten out and come to your room. Hell, I should have jumped you the first night we shared a room, but I thought you might shoot me." Dustin grins, pressing a sucking kiss to Ronan's jawline. He has a feeling that, come tomorrow, he's going to be wearing more marks than the bruise on his face.

"I wouldn't have shot you; I don't wear my gun to bed," Ronan jokes.

"Don't be an asshole. Did you want me, too?" Dustin asks.

"Wasn't sure I liked you, but yeah, I noticed you, wanted you.

Even at the crime scene, I saw that you were beautiful. I didn't let myself think about fucking you until later, but I've thought about it, every night. Having you in the same room drove me crazy," Ronan admits, nipping at Dustin's earlobe, and then sucking a mark behind Dustin's ear, partly because he wants to kiss the sensitive skin and partly because he wants to mark Dustin.

He doesn't want everyone to know whatever happens here tonight, but he wants to be able to look at Dustin tomorrow and see proof of what happened.

"Drove me crazy too. I haven't been this sexually frustrated since I was a teenager. And speaking of that, can we get rid of our pants?" Dustin asks.

"Yes, I want to feel all of you," Ronan says.

Together they help each other get the rest of their clothes off, throwing them to the floor. And then they are both naked, legs tangling together as Dustin arches up for another kiss. Ronan gets lost in the kiss and the feel of Dustin's warm body against his, Dustin's thick cock pushing against his stomach.

They make out and stroke each other's bodies, learning them, finding what parts make the other person shudder or moan. Ronan finds out that Dustin likes the skin of his lower belly stroked; he likes to be touched roughly as well, pinned down and held in place. When Ronan's cock starts to leak, he lifts up off Dustin for a few minutes, finding lube and condoms.

Ronan's going to ask Dustin how he wants to do this, but Dustin answers with his body. Dustin rolls over so he's flat on his stomach with his legs spread. Ronan has to stop for a moment and just stare, because Dustin is a remarkable sight laid out like that. His back is long and pale, slim, tapering at the waist. And his ass— his ass is perfect, the skin pale and unblemished, perfectly shaped.

"What's wrong?" Dustin asks, turning his head to the side, moving a pillow to get comfortable.

"Nothing, it's just that you're incredible. Finding it hard to believe you want to be in bed with me." Ronan doesn't have self-esteem issues. He knows he's good-looking, but he's older than Dustin and so much more reserved.

"Why? You're hot, smart, and brave. Why do you want a screwed-up college dropout? Dustin asks.

"Those things don't matter; I want you." Ronan wants to tell

Dustin he thinks he's perfect, but that feels like too much, too soon. He might be ignoring his rule about sleeping with people he works with, but that doesn't mean he's going to start acting stupid. He doesn't want Dustin to think he's hooked up with an old, clingy fool.

"Exactly, it doesn't matter to me either. Now if we could get back to the touching, I'd really like that." Dustin grins.

Ronan hopes that their differences really don't matter to Dustin, and maybe they don't, because after all Dustin is here with him.

"Can I open you up? Or do you like doing that yourself?" Ronan asks.

"I like being fingered. You have nice hands. I'd like it if you did it, if you want to," Dustin says.

"I'd like that." Ronan opens the lube, and slicks up his fingers.

He strokes his lube-free hand over Dustin's ass cheeks. The skin is smooth and soft, and Ronan kind of wants to bite it, so on a whim he leans in and nips the perfect flesh. Dustin jumps a little, but Ronan hears the way his breath quickens.

"Like that?" Ronan asks, as he trails his fingers between Dustin's ass cheeks, slicks up the crack, and starts to probe Dustin's hole.

"Really, really did. I didn't think biting was my thing, but then no one ever bit my ass before." Dustin sounds a little breathless.

Ronan leans in and gently bites again, at the same time as he presses his lube-slicked finger into Dustin's hole. Dustin makes a happy little noise in the back of his throat. Ronan pushes his finger in deeper and leans in again, but this time he sucks a hickey into the swell of Dustin's ass instead of biting.

"You don't have to go so slow," Dustin tells him.

"I don't want to hurt you." Ronan isn't porn star huge, but he's big enough that he could hurt someone who wasn't prepared. Dustin trusts him with his body and Ronan doesn't want to betray that trust by hurting Dustin.

"You won't. Besides, I like it a little rough," Dustin says quietly.

"How rough?" Ronan asks, as he starts to add a second finger, wiggling them a little to loosen Dustin up.

"Not like BDSM kinky rough. I just like to feel it the next day. Not pain, but a few aches, maybe some bruises. I'm not asking you to hurt me, I don't want that, but you don't need to treat me like glass either," Dustin says. It's clear he knows what he wants and what he likes. Ronan isn't sure he was that confident in the bedroom when he was twenty-one.

"I think I can handle that," Ronan says, pressing a kiss to the bottom of Dustin's spine before thrusting his fingers deeper. He fingers Dustin until he's relaxed little more, then he pulls his fingers out and gets a condom on.

"Come on, I'm ready," Dustin complains.

"Don't rush me," Ronan says, swatting Dustin's ass cheek.

"I'm not; I just really want to feel you," Dustin says, arching his back.

"Okay, okay." Ronan moves closer to Dustin and positions himself. With one hand on Dustin's hips, he uses the other hand to guide the tip of his cock until he's pressing against Dustin's hole, and he starts to push.

Dustin moans, arches his back more, and moves with Ronan. They move together; Dustin presses back as Ronan pushes forward. Ronan can't help the sounds that spill from his lips, broken moans and grunts as he fucks Dustin, and is met on every thrust.

It feels amazing. Dustin is warm and tight around his cock, and in that moment, Ronan doesn't think he has ever felt anything better. After a while, he changes position slightly so that he can get a hand underneath Dustin and start jerking him off, instead of leaving Dustin to rub off against the bedding.

"You feel so good, fuck." Ronan grunts.

He's not going to last long; the pleasure he is feeling is too intense.

"Damn, should have done this the first time you kissed me," Dustin groans.

"You're so tight; you're going to make me come," Ronan pants.

"Do it. I want you to. I want you to come. I want to feel you, see you lose it," Dustin gasps.

Ronan keeps thrusting, trying to keep a rhythm with his hand, but he knows he's a little sloppy, because he's doing what Dustin asked him to; he's losing it. His hips start to move out of time, and he's just thrusting wildly. He feels a little bad that he's going to come first, but when his orgasm hits he can't find it in himself to feel too bad. Pleasure shoots through his body like an incredible electric shock.

He collapses down onto Dustin's back as pleasure hums through his veins, and he presses kisses between Dustin's shoulder blades. Once Ronan has his breath back, he pulls out carefully and rolls Dustin over, pushing his legs farther apart and higher up, and then Ronan leans in to suck the head of Dustin's cock into his mouth, while wrapping his hand around the base and stroking.

"Holy fuck, please never stop doing that," Dustin moans.

Ronan feels a flash of smug pride. This isn't his first blowjob, and he likes to think he's built up a talent over the years, maybe a talent that men Dustin's age might not have. He likes the idea of being better at this than Dustin's previous lovers, a thought he isn't going to explore, not now.

Ronan takes Dustin as deep as he can, dipping down until his lips meet the ring of his fingers, and Dustin's cock bumps the back of his throat. Ronan swallows around it, only almost gagging for a second. Dustin doesn't seem able to keep still, his legs twitching, stomach fluttering, and hips stuttering. Ronan pins Dustin's hips down with his free hand, worried at first he's being too rough, but then he remembers that Dustin said he'd be okay with a few bruises, and he adds a little more strength, holding Dustin in place while he sucks.

"I'm going to come," Dustin warns

Ronan lifts his head; he keeps jerking Dustin off, while claiming his mouth in a kiss.

Dustin doesn't seem to mind his own taste in Ronan's mouth, because he kisses him back deeply, thrusting up into his hand as they kiss. Dustin moans into the kiss when he comes a second later, his hips jerking roughly. Ronan kisses him through it. He slows the kiss down, easing it to a slow, sweet stop as Dustin goes still.

"That was amazing," Dustin says softly, as Ronan pulls away to deal with the condom.

"I can't remember the last time I came that hard," Ronan says, lying down beside Dustin. He's waiting for things to get awkward now that the rush of pleasure is gone, but Dustin just makes room for him, and throws an arm casually over Ronan's waist. His hair is wild, his lips are swollen, he looks disheveled and decedent, and totally beautiful. Ronan is still having a hard time believing that Dustin is in his bed. Dustin is like some rare, exotic creature, something that you don't see every day, unique. Ronan doesn't know what he did to catch the eye of someone so special.

"I know I've been teasing you about being a straitlaced, rule book kind of guy since we met, but you really know how to let loose in the bedroom." Dustin grins.

Dustin's head is next to Ronan's on the pillow, and Ronan can't help leaning in and kissing him, stroking his purple hair off his face.

"Is it still okay to kiss you?" Ronan asks, uncertain. He doesn't know the rules here. They didn't really talk about what was happening here.

Ronan doesn't know if this was a onetime thing or what.

"Of course it's okay to kiss me. You've been inside me, you've sucked my dick—I think we can handle kissing," Dustin teases.

"Sorry, I'm bad at this. I've never slept with someone I worked with or someone who was a friend first. It's always been meet, date, sex. Or sometimes meet, sex, good-bye," Ronan explains.

"I figure we keep it simple for now. We don't want this thing between us to get in the way of the case, right?" Dustin asks.

"Right," Ronan agrees.

"So when we're working on the case we act professional—no kissing, no sex. But when we have downtime, that stuff's allowed. Right now, we are friends who have sex, and work colleagues. If either of those things changes, well, we'll deal with that when it happens," Dustin suggests.

"When did you get so reasonable? When I was your age I'd have freaked out after sleeping with a friend," Ronan admits.

"We're different people. I think you don't normally sleep with friends because that's like breaking a rule. Which is one of the places where we differ. You like following them. I love breaking them." Dustin grins.

"I think it's a really good thing I'm not a cop, or I'd have ended up in some very conflicting situations." Ronan shakes his head.

"We covered how that'd go. You'd arrest me and I'd make a pass at you," Dustin laughs.

"I thought that was just when you were sixteen?" Ronan frowns.

"Nope, if you were a cop now and you arrested me I'd totally make a pass at you. Get you into trouble, convince you to break some rules." Dustin grins.

"I have a feeling you're going to be a bad influence," Ronan groans.

"I'm an awesome influence. I was thinking, it'd be kind of stupid for me to sleep in my own bed. Is that okay with you, if I stay the night?" Dustin asks, sounding nervous as he leans over Ronan to grab a tissue off the bedside table to clean up his stomach.

Ronan takes it from him and cleans his hand.

"I'd like it if you stayed. But I'll be careful if I wake you up. I don't want to get punched again," Ronan says, rubbing his sore cheek.

"I'm so sorry about that," Dustin says, looking mortified.

"I was only teasing—I know it was an accident." Ronan decides to make sure Dustin knows there are no ill feeling by kissing him again.

"Mmm, as much as I like that, we should probably stop before I demand a round two. We need to get some sleep so we can go monster hunting." Dustin sounds content, and he stretches out, arms above his head, toes pointed, looking like a lazy and very satisfied cat.

"Smart and sexy. Okay, bed," Ronan says firmly.

They both get up so they can get under the covers. Ronan realizes he hasn't shared a bed for the night with someone since his last relationship, which was over a year ago. In that time, he's had sex, but he never stayed the night with them or brought them home to his bed. It just doesn't seem strange to invite Dustin into his private space, his home, and his bedroom. Because as different as Dustin is, it doesn't feel like he is out of place.

"When was your last date?" Ronan asks curiously as they both make themselves comfortable, fitting their bodies together.

"I don't really know. I don't get asked on dates a lot." Dustin shrugs.

"I don't believe that. You're gorgeous," Ronan says. He's seen the way women look at Dustin; he's sure men probably react the same.

"I get asked to go to bed with people a lot, but dating, not so much. More when people know more about me. The psychic thing freaks people out. Those who don't believe think I'm nuts or a scam artist, and those who do believe worry that I'll read them all the time," Dustin explains.

"That must be difficult. I guess I was a little worried you'd read me at one point, but I saw quickly that you weren't the type to read a person without their permission. I can't imagine you using your powers against someone you were dating." Ronan is sure of that.

"Thank you. I wouldn't, and it hurts that people don't believe me. I can't help that I have visions, but I don't think it should stop people from trusting me," Dustin sighs.

"I trust you. Now, it's late, we need to sleep. The guys might have a list of places for us to check out tomorrow." Ronan hopes they do.

"And if they don't?" Dustin asks.

"I guess we drive around and hope you pick something up," Ronan suggests. It's not the best option, but it is better than doing nothing.

"Okay, I hope you don't snore," Dustin says, scooting down in the bed a little until he can put his head on Ronan's chest. His fluffy, purple hair tickles Ronan's chest a little, but it's nice, and Ronan wraps a loose arm around Ronan's waist.

"I don't snore," Ronan promises, pressing a quick kiss to the top of Dustin's hair. It smells like vanilla; it must be the shampoo he uses, but Ronan likes it—spicy and sweet, it suits Dustin.

Ronan falls asleep to the scent.

Chapter Eight

One moment everything is peaceful and warm—cozy even—when suddenly there is noise and movement as Ronan starts cursing and grumbling as he jumps out of bed. Dustin just stays where he is, letting Ronan hunt for the missing phone. He stretches, yawning, feeling a few little aches and pains, which make him smile with satisfaction. Half of him can't believe they slept together—the other half is damn glad that they gave into temptation.

Dustin is feeling relaxed, until he senses the mood in the room shift. Ronan's emotions are strong enough that Dustin can pick them up; he's upset and pissed off. Dustin sits up in Ronan's bed and looks at him sitting on the edge of the bed. He can only see Ronan's back, but that is tense.

"All right, we'll be right there," Ronan says, and then he hangs up.

"What happened?" Dustin asks.

"One of the women, Charlotte Carter, they found her body this morning." Ronan sounds pissed off—Dustin doesn't blame him.

"I thought the *Sanguis* demon kept its victims?" Dustin doesn't get it.

"It kills them eventually, uses them up. I said we'd go down to the crime scene. They're not going to move her until we get there," Ronan explains.

"I'll go get dressed," Dustin feels a little shell-shocked. He's not sure why. He's had visions of people dying before; he's helped the police find bodies. It's just that Dustin had really thought they would get all the women back alive—damaged maybe, but alive.

Dustin had felt her, Charlotte, he'd felt her life force, her fear. Knowing that she is dead, it doesn't seem real.

"Try and be quick, they can't hold things forever, and I'd like to see the scene as they found them. You don't have to come if you think seeing the body will bother you," Ronan offers.

"No; I mean, of course I don't want to see her like that. But
I need to; I could see something. I want to try and help," Dustin
says, getting out of bed. He feels like he owes Charlotte this much.
Even if he sees nothing, he'll go.

"All right. Meet me in the car," Ronan suggests.

Dustin grabs his pants and pulls them on, so he's not walking
around naked, and he heads back to the guest room without another
word. Dustin makes sure he takes his meds, and then he quickly
gets dressed.

He's outside by the car in less than half an hour and Ronan's
waiting, looking as neat and well put together as always, apart
from the bruise on his cheek, that is. They get in the car together,
and Ronan must know where he's going, because he takes them
straight to a mall parking lot, about forty minutes from his house,
without a map or satnav.

It's obvious that they're in the right place because of all the cop
cars—the lot is closed off, but when Ronan tells the cop standing
guard who they are, they are waved through. Ronan drives to
where most of the police cars are parked, and parks his own car.

"Ready?" Ronan asks him.

"I think so," Dustin says softly. He can see a crowd of cops,
detectives, higher-ups, medical people, the coroner, all in one
place, and he knows the body must be there.

"If you need to leave, if it gets to be too much, just come back
to the car."

"I'll be fine. I'm not some delicate little flower, and this isn't
my first body," Dustin points out.

"Fine, I'm just being careful," Ronan says, and then he gets out
of the car. He seems a little offended.

Dustin can't worry about that now, though; he has to focus.
They walk toward the crime scene, and a man who must know
Ronan comes over, looking grim.

"Ronan," he says with a nod.

"Chris, this is Dustin McPherson; Dustin, meet Chief
Wilkinson." Ronan makes the introductions and they both nod.

"What happened to your face?" Chris asks Ronan.

"Long story. Can you tell me what you know so far?" Ronan
quickly changes the subject, and Dustin thinks he's a little
embarrassed. He doesn't want to think that Ronan doesn't want to

tell one of his old cop buddies that he got the bruise from a man a lot smaller—and a civilian, without his training—sucker punching him.

"She was found dumped in the trash can down the alleyway beside the store. The medical examiner thinks she died of blood loss sometime in the early hours. She has claw marks and puncture marks. Do you have any idea what did this?" Chris asks.

"Pretty sure," Ronan sighs.

"I don't want to know, do I?" Chris frowns.

"Probably not," Ronan says.

"Right, well, I'll clear a path for you two," Chris says. And then he does just that—people clear out of the way, and Dustin follows Ronan to where Charlotte's body is laid out on the ground on a sheet.

The first thing Dustin notices is how pale she is, probably because she's been drained of her blood. Her blonde hair is a tangled, unwashed mess, her nails are badly broken and dirty, and she has smears of dirt all over.

"I'm going to look at the trash can, see if anything else was left behind. Can I have a copy of the security footage? Send it to Harry?" Ronan says to Chris.

"I'll have it to you by noon. Um, I don't know how this psychic thing works," Chris says, looking at Dustin and he seems skeptical. He's also giving Dustin a once-over. He can't see much with the huge coat Dustin has on, but his boots are showing, and his hair peeks out under his hat. Dustin knows, at this crime scene, he's the one thing that looks out of place.

"Can I have some latex gloves? I'd like to touch the body," Dustin tells Chris.

"I'll be close, holler if you need help," Ronan says, heading toward where the body was dumped.

"Here are some gloves." Chris hands Dustin the gloves.

Dustin pulls off his wool gloves and stuffs them in his pocket; he then puts on the latex gloves.

As he moves forward, he can feel several sets of eyes on him, and he knows that people are wondering why he's here and who he is.

Dustin tunes them out and goes over to Charlotte's body. He kneels down beside her. She doesn't look peaceful, doesn't look the way Dustin was told bodies were supposed to look. It doesn't look like Charlotte died peacefully; it looks like she died in pain, fighting, and terrified.

"I'm sorry we were too late. All I can offer is that we'll get the bad guy, I promise," Dustin says quietly to Charlotte, looking at the cuts and bruises on her body. She's in the sweater and leggings she was wearing when she was taken. But they are dirty and ripped, stained with blood, and God knows what else.

Dustin braces himself, and then he places his latex-covered hand on Charlotte's hand. He doesn't have to work for the vision; hasn't even properly opened himself up for it when the images start rushing in.

The first thing he's aware of is pain, lots of pain, back and neck on fire. It hurts, and she's weak, but she keeps fighting. Dustin sees it, the *Sanguis* demon coming for Charlotte again. It drags her out of the cage by her hair. One minute Dustin feels like he's watching what is happening, the next he feels like it's happening to him. It keeps switching, which is confusing, but all he's sure of is the demon feeding and feeding, until everything goes black. Dustin feels Charlotte's life end, her spark snuffed out at the hands of a demon.

"Dustin, Dustin!"

He can hear a voice calling him, and then a hand on his, pulling it off Charlotte's and breaking the connection.

Dustin blinks—he's kneeling on both knees, and he can feel the sweat cooling on his skin. He blinks to clear his vision and when he looks to the side, he realizes that it was Ronan calling his name. He's no longer at the trash can. He's right by Dustin, with Chris next to him, and some spooked-looking officers behind them.

"What?" Dustin says. He feels a little confused, like his head is still somewhere else. He feels like he's still in that dark basement.

"I've been trying to get you to open your eyes for ten minutes. You went really pale and, I don't know, nothing felt right." Ronan looks shaken.

"You're the real deal, aren't you?" Chris says, looking surprised.

"You thought I wasn't?" Dustin asks, steadying himself before slowly getting up off his knees.

"I wasn't sure. But the way you looked, no one can fake that.

149

And I felt it too, something in the air that went away as soon as you stopped touching the body," Chris says, looking baffled.

"I've had people say they've felt something with a strong vision. Shit," Dustin curses as he feels his nose start bleeding.

"Does anyone have any tissues?" Ronan asks, while Dustin cups his hands to catch the blood, to try and not contaminate the crime scene.

Someone finds tissues and Dustin mops up the blood and pinches his nose to try to stop the bleeding.

"Are you okay?" Ronan asks, and he sounds concerned.

"I'll be okay," Dustin sighs.

"Do your visions damage you?" Chris asks.

"They hurt and cause pressure. But no real damage. When I was younger, doctors thought they'd turn my brain to mush and kill me before I was twenty, but they realized any damage was healing." Dustin shrugs. It had been scary, thinking his visions would kill him, but that's in the past, Dustin has moved on. He no longer panics at every nosebleed.

"Do you want to sit down?" Ronan asks.

"No, I'm okay. I think the bleeding's stopping." Dustin sniffs, dabbing at his nose. For now, he's okay.

"Here, have some water." Chris offers him a fresh bottle and Dustin takes it. He opens it and drinks some of the cool liquid—it wakes him up a little bit, refreshes him, and helps him focus a little more—it clears the fog.

"I don't want to rush you, but I'm guessing you saw something?" Chris asks.

"I saw her last moments. It was like I was with her when she died," Dustin says softly, looking back at Charlotte on the ground. She had been so alive once, so vibrant. She fought even when she was weak from blood loss, hunger, and having her spinal fluid tapped.

"Are you okay?" Ronan asks again.

"Not the first death, remember. I've seen last moments before. I saw some details though. Through Charlotte's eyes," Dustin says, trying to remember every part of his vision.

"What did you see?" Ronan asks.

"Water bottles, he bought a lot of water somewhere, maybe you can find big orders?" Dustin remembers as he looks at the icy bottle in his latex-covered, bloodstained hands.

"I'll get someone on that," Chris says.

"She could hear something; it sounded like she was near a road? A highway, a busy highway." Dustin rubs his forehead, and then curses when he realizes he's getting blood on it.

"Here." Ronan takes a tissue from him, and the bottle of water; he wets the tissue, and then carefully cleans the blood off Dustin's forehead.

"You might want to ditch the gloves," Ronan suggests.

Dustin peels off the gloves, unsure what to do with them, but Chris orders an officer to dispose of them.

"Thank you," Dustin says, putting his warm gloves back on.

"No problem. Did you see or hear anything else?" Chris asks.

"The walls were blue inside, not sure that's helpful. Dark blue. And not something I saw or heard, but I could smell damp, and mold, and the smell of dead mice. I had a mouse die in my apartment once, it smelled like that," Dustin explains.

"We can look for places that have mice infestations near highways, maybe along the 41 or the 180. And places with reported damp problems. Might be worth checking with the health department. The women could be some place they closed down," Ronan suggests.

"Any information you need that Harry can't get, just let me know," Chris offers.

"There's not much Harry can't find, but thanks, I'll keep it in mind if he does get stuck. We'll let you take the body now, but we'll come see you again once the autopsy has been performed, to see if it shows anything we need to know, if there is trace evidence on the body," Ronan says to Chris.

"I might be able to get another vision from Charlotte," Dustin offers.

"You can get more?" Chris asks.

"Maybe, no guarantees. But then, there never are. But I'd like to give it a shot once my head's had a chance to clear and take in all of what I saw." Dustin isn't sure he'll be able to see more, but he wants to. He wants to get to the other women before they are killed; he doesn't want to face another Charlotte.

"Okay. Ronan, look after him and get him something to eat and make sure he's okay. These visions could be key," Chris orders.

"Are you telling me to babysit?" Ronan asks.

"I'm not a child, I don't need a babysitter," Dustin adds. He doesn't need to be babied by the man who had fucked him through the mattress last night.

"I know that. You're both valuable resources. Dustin, we are relying on your visions to help find this thing. And Ronan, it's more than likely you or one of your people will kill whatever this is. I doubt the FBI will catch it, and I have faith in my cops, but they don't know how to hunt the things you do. You're both important. I want you both to take good care of yourselves," Chris says.

"We'll be careful," Ronan promises.

"Really? Looks like you've been getting in trouble," Chris says, looking pointedly at Ronan's bruised cheekbone.

"That was an accident, not a fight." Ronan shrugs.

"Who accidentally hit you?" Chris asks skeptically.

"I did," Dustin admits.

"You hit Ronan?" Chris looks shocked.

"It was an accident." Dustin still feels bad about it. He's not a violent person, even though he's had lessons in several martial arts most of his life. The only reason he had lessons was because his parents thought it was a good pastime for a young man, to keep him out of the house.

"I woke him up from a dream, and he lashed out, half asleep. I would've called you, bitching about him, if we were at each other's throats. We've been getting along fine. It was an accident, but the guy has a good right hook." Ronan smiles as he says it. He looks almost proud.

Dustin wants to snort at Ronan saying they've been getting along fine. He has bruises on his hips in the shape of Ronan's fingertips that suggest they have been getting on better than *fine*.

"Not sure why, I just thought of a psychic as a peaceful hippie But then I read the police report about the marriage protest," Chris says—at the same time, he signals someone and Charlotte's body is covered and a gurney brought over to take her away.

Dustin hopes they take care of her, give her the kindness she didn't have when she passed.

"That guy deserved it. I'm normally a peaceful guy, I swear. He was harassing this young couple; I could feel their despair. I had to do something, so I hit him," Dustin admits.

"Good for you. It's good knowing Ronan has some backup." Chris looks pleased.

"I don't need backup, and his job isn't to fight." Ronan doesn't look at all happy at the suggestion.

Dustin isn't sure why—at first he thinks maybe it's some macho thing, Ronan just not liking the idea of needing another man's help, but then Ronan glances at him, and there is a hint of fear in his eyes.

Like maybe he's afraid of Dustin getting hurt.

"I know his job isn't to fight, Ronan, but it's good to know that he can do it if he needs to. I worry about you, always going off alone to hunt these things, things you don't even like to tell me about." Chris clearly cares about Ronan. He's not just Ronan's ex-boss, using him to clear a case. He acted like they were both just resources, but that's not the case when it comes to Ronan.

"I'll have his back," Dustin says—even though he knows it's not what Ronan wants, it's what he wants. Dustin wants to save these women, and for Ronan to not get killed.

"Come on, you need to rest, especially if you want to try for another vision later. Don't pretend it doesn't take it out of you," Ronan says.

"He's bossy, isn't he?" Dustin says to Chris.

"It's taken you a week to figure that out?" Chris grins.

"I hate you both. Come on, there's a burger place near here." Ronan touches Dustin's arm briefly, before nodding good-bye to Chris and heading for his car.

"Take care of him, and yourself," Chris says, before waving good-bye.

"I will," Dustin promises, following after Ronan.

There are still a lot of cops watching them when Dustin gets into Ronan's car. Dustin isn't sure he'll ever get used to being the freak show.

"You feeling up to lunch? Or should I take you back to my house to rest first?" Ronan asks.

"I guess I should eat before I nap. Will they have the autopsy results today?" Dustin has worked with cops before, but he knows every case is different.

"Probably tomorrow. So you can take it easy. We'll have the

evidence to go over, but that's mainly watching tapes and stuff, nothing difficult," Ronan explains.

"I'm not that delicate. I know it must freak people out a little, the way I go pale, the way my nose bleeds. It looks bad, and it does take a lot out of me. But I'm still not made out of glass. And it'll take more than a few visions to break me," Dustin says, as Ronan drives away from the cops.

"It was kind of scary, seeing you look that way. You've never looked like that before, in the other visions I've seen you have," Ronan points out.

"This one was more intense. Before, I was picking up on old energy, old fear, whatever was left behind. This was new, fresh energy. She hadn't been touched and moved by dozens of people. There was just her imprint and it was strong. Feeling all that I did, all the details, it takes more out of me," Dustin says honestly.

"I get that. It makes sense that you'd get more from a body than a crime scene." Ronan seems to understand.

They drive to a burger place that opens early and park outside, before heading in and grabbing a table. They sit opposite each other and take menus at the same time.

"So you admitted to Chris that you were the one who bruised my cheek," Ronan says after they order.

"Did you not want me to?" Dustin asks. He wonders if Ronan doesn't want Chris knowing he was in Dustin's room or maybe he doesn't want Chris to think he isn't tough, something stupid like that.

"I was worried he'd get pissed at you or think something was up. Chris is protective. I got bruises on a case once, a case I didn't tell him about. I was dating a guy and Chris thought maybe the guy had given me the bruises, it got a little messy. I didn't want Chris thinking you'd meant to hurt me." Ronan shrugs.

"Chris seems like a good guy, more than just an ex-boss." Dustin would be jealous if he thought Chris was gay, but he didn't get that vibe, and Ronan has already said he's happily married with kids.

"I guess he's always been a mentor to me." Ronan nods.

"I never had a mentor. What's it like?" Dustin asks.

"I dunno. I wasn't good at letting him in for a long time. I didn't want a replacement Dad, you know?" Ronan sighs.

Dustin can imagine it'd be hard, having a Dad you loved, and then losing him. But it's good that he found another role model, one who didn't leave him. Dustin isn't judging Ronan's dad for his suicide, because he can't say he wouldn't do the same thing. He's never had a child, so he can't imagine in his wildest dreams what it would be like to see that young child murdered.

"Only guys I had who wanted to be like a 'Father' to me were guys wanting to play 'Daddy' if you know what I mean, and that's never been my thing." Dustin rolls his eyes.

"Really? I never got a lot of that. I guess I went from my dad's Army lifestyle to the police academy. I was not giving off the vibe that welcomes that kind of guy." Ronan snorts.

"And I do? Give off the, 'I need a Daddy' vibe?" Dustin asks with a raised eyebrow.

"No," Ronan says quickly. Probably sensing Dustin's offense.

"Then what did you mean?" Dustin asks.

"Well, you're beautiful now, but you have the 'pretty' thing going on. I can imagine when you were younger. You'd have been young and pretty, cute as hell. That attracts the type who wanted you to play the baby twink," Ronan explains.

"Do you think I'm just some twink who needs taking care of?" Dustin asks.

"Seems to me you take pretty good care of yourself. You have your own place; you work helping people in tons of different ways. I'm not saying I think your life is perfect, but you have it together. You don't need some guy's money or anything else," Ronan says.

"Good. You're right that my life isn't perfect. I want to make changes. I wish I didn't need meds to get through my days. But some macho guy telling me what to do isn't what I need." Dustin doesn't think Ronan wants any guy calling him Daddy. He might be a little bossy, but he doesn't want to rule his partner's life. Dustin is sure of that.

Before they can talk about it more, their food arrives and the subject changes. Dustin knows some people have boyfriends or husbands they call Daddy and it works for them, that Daddies aren't always bad guys, but they just aren't for Dustin, just like sub/Dom relationships work for some people, but they're not Dustin's thing.

Relationships have always been hard for Dustin, and he thinks he should warn Ronan. Because he likes Ronan, a lot. He wants things between them to last longer than a night, but he doesn't know how to ask for that. He can't just say he's fucked up, but he'd like Ronan in his life, because what guy would want that?

They've agreed to keep it professional while working, and to enjoy each other's company in their downtime. Dustin guesses he'll see how that goes.

"Are you okay?" Ronan asks as they eat.

"Yeah, just distracted I guess," Dustin lies. He doesn't want to tell Ronan that he had been thinking about him, and what might happen between them now that they have slept together.

They eat their food, talking about the case, the new things Charlotte had shown them. And then they head back to Ronan's home. When they get there, Ronan suggests they work in the family room so that Dustin can relax on the couch and watch TV. Dustin feels bad about the idea of leaving Ronan to work on his laptop while he does nothing, but he is tired, so he unbuckles and pulls off his boots and sits down, curling his legs under him.

"Here," Ronan says softly, and he unfolds a blanket that had been resting on the back of the couch, and drapes it over Dustin, tucking him in.

"Thank you, but I'm not that tired," Dustin says, even as a yawn betrays him. He's not sure how to feel about Ronan doing things like this. They are kind and tender; he doesn't want to read too much into them, though.

"Stop being so stubborn and have a little catnap. I'll be right here if you need anything," Ronan says, pointing to the spare space on the couch.

"Does being good get me a reward?" Dustin asks, cheekily.

Ronan leans in and kisses him quickly on the lips.

"Think of it this way, it might be better if you had some energy later." Ronan raises an eyebrow suggestively.

"Why not skip the nap and go straight to that?" Dustin smiles.

"Because it would really hurt my ego if you fell asleep in the middle of me fucking you." Ronan grins.

"Like I'd ever do that." Dustin leans up, freeing a hand from the blanket to loop around Ronan's neck, pulling him closer, and stealing a kiss.

Ronan kisses back, moving closer, and Dustin encourages

Ronan to lower his body, until they are both on the couch, separated by the blanket Ronan had put on him. Dustin can still use his hands, and he uses them to pull Ronan closer, to deepen their kisses.

They make out on Ronan's couch until Ronan gets a text and pulls back, breaking the kiss. Dustin wants to complain about being cockblocked by a phone again.

"I have to check that. It could be Chris or Harry with news. And despite your libido being awake, and certain parts of your body, you look half asleep," Ronan says, getting up carefully.

Dustin is tired and the lazy kisses seem to have only relaxed him further. Even though his cock is hard, he's more than ready for a nap. His eyes are only half open.

"Okay, you win. I'll nap," Dustin agrees.

Ronan adjusts the blanket so it's covering Dustin properly again, and then he takes a seat with his phone and laptop on the other end of the couch.

"Is the text anything important?" Dustin asks, moving a pillow to make himself more comfortable. His eyes are heavy and not even the idea of sex is keeping him up, so to speak. He only had a little sleep last night and the vision has taken a lot out of him.

"Just Harry saying he's sent some lists to my e-mail, the stuff we asked for. By the looks of it there are a ton of buildings to narrow down," Ronan sighs.

"If you need help just wake me up," Dustin says, sure his sleepy voice makes him sound less serious.

"I will," Ronan promises.

Dustin curls up comfortably and closes his eyes. He doesn't fall asleep right away. He listens to the faint sound of Ronan typing on his laptop and eventually it lulls him to sleep.

Dustin only sleeps for about an hour, but he feels better for it and joins Ronan in research for the rest of the day. They have dinner together that night, and then when it comes to bedtime things get a little weird, when they had been so comfortable.

They're in the hallway, having left the kitchen, and they could part ways like they had the other night, or they could do things differently.

"Um, you don't have to come to bed with me, if you want to sleep instead," Ronan says hesitantly, his hands coming to rest gently on Dustin's biceps.

"I'm not sleepy." Dustin leans in and kisses the corner of Ronan's mouth teasingly.

"So, my room?" Ronan asks.

"Not yet." Dustin smiles wickedly. And he pulls his arms out of Ronan's grip.

"What are you doing?" Ronan asks. His face changes when he realizes Dustin is going to his knees right there in the hallway.

"Oh." Ronan sounds surprised.

Dustin reaches out once he's on his knees and unzips Ronan's jeans slowly, peeling them down his strong thighs, enough that Dustin can dip his hand into Ronan's underwear and pull his cock out. Ronan's breath comes out heavier and his hands come to rest in Dustin's hair, tangling through the strands, but he doesn't try to pull Dustin forward, he just rests his hands there.

Dustin leans his cheek against Ronan's thigh, breathing in his scent. He nuzzles at Ronan's trimmed pubic hair, building the anticipation. He then uses just a hint of his tongue to run over Ronan's already hardening cock.

"Please," Ronan says. Ronan is a strong man; it feels good to have him saying please so quickly after Dustin goes to his knees. It makes him feel powerful.

He could tease Ronan longer, but Dustin isn't really in a teasing mood. He wraps his hand around the base of Ronan's cock, and then lowers his mouth over the head, sucking as he does. Ronan's head thumps back against the hallway wall and he groans. Dustin would smile if he didn't have his mouth full.

Ronan is pretty well-behaved. His hips move a little, but he doesn't try to fuck Dustin's face, which Dustin only likes to do if he's ready for it, if the guy asks. Ronan just stands there, stroking Dustin's hair and letting him take his time, exploring every inch of Ronan's cock.

It feels good, warm and heavy in his mouth, slightly salty, a hint of something that is purely Ronan. Dustin uses his tongue and lips to tease Ronan's flesh, and he sucks as much of Ronan's length as he can. Dustin has had a fair bit of practice at this sexual activity, and he knows he's good at it, but it is still gratifying to hear Ronan moaning and gasping, swearing under his breath.

Dustin isn't sure how long he stays on his knees, because he feels kind of lost in the activity, but he notices when Ronan's grip in his hair gets tighter, when his curses get louder.

"I'm going to come," Ronan warns.

Dustin has plenty of time to pull off, but he doesn't want to. He wants Ronan's taste to fill his mouth. So he keeps sucking, just drawing back a little so he won't choke when Ronan comes. A few seconds later, Ronan swears loudly and his hips jerk wildly as he comes. Dustin moves with him, drinking in every drop, before moving back to take a deep breath.

Dustin is still catching his breath when Ronan hauls him to his feet, and kisses him roughly, pulling Dustin as close as he can, before letting him go so they can both breathe, roughly.

"You swallowed," is the first thing Ronan says once he is breathing normally again.

"Well, I didn't want to make a mess of your hallway," Dustin lies.

"I could have cleaned it up, you didn't have to," Ronan says, his hands stroking up and down Dustin's back.

"Okay, I wanted to," Dustin admits.

"It felt amazing," Ronan says, and something about his voice makes Dustin think that maybe no one has swallowed when Ronan came before. Dustin feels a little smug being the first, glad that he gave Ronan something he hasn't had before.

"Want me to take care of you?" Ronan asks, running his hand over the front of Dustin's groin, and Dustin shivers at the pressure through his jeans on his hard cock.

"Yeah, but in your bed, if you don't mind?" Dustin's knees are a little sore—he could use a lie down in a comfortable bed.

"Of course I don't mind." Ronan takes Dustin's hand and leads the way to his bedroom.

They help each other out of their clothes, dropping them to the floor once again, and then they fall into bed together, kissing and touching. Dustin quickly decides he wants to get fucked again, so instead of rushing to get off, he fools around with Ronan, working to get the other man hard again.

Ronan fucks him face-to-face, on his back with his legs in the air, and Dustin doesn't come until the sun starts to come up, but it's worth the wait. Dustin feels almost brainless afterward, and he thinks maybe the phrase "having your brains fucked out" is accurate here.

Dustin feels boneless. He lets Ronan clean him up and get him tucked under the covers, and they get comfortable together. Ronan strokes his hair and it's so relaxing. Dustin is already feeling thoroughly fucked—it's not long before Dustin is drifting off to sleep.

Later Ronan wakes him up and suggests they take a shower together. Dustin is more than happy with the idea. They fool around in the shower and end up jerking each other off until they both come, then they finish washing and go to the kitchen for breakfast.

Ronan calls the medical examiner and finds out that Charlotte's body has been autopsied, and they can come for the results and to see the body again.

"Are you ready to do this again?" Ronan asks.

"Yeah. Can't say I'm looking forward to it, but I'm ready." Dustin nods.

"I want to go into the agency today, but you don't have to come if you don't want to," Ronan offers.

"Why wouldn't I want to?" Dustin asks.

"I noticed you didn't really enjoy meeting the team. It's not a problem," Ronan says, washing up his coffee mug.

"You noticed? Did they notice? They probably think I'm an asshole, right? I was just nervous." Dustin hadn't wanted Ronan's friends to think he was an idiot or a fake or some crazy. He wanted to show that he could be useful. And he'd wanted them to like him, because they're clearly all important to Ronan, and he likes Ronan.

"They didn't think you were an asshole, trust me, they just thought you were shy. But I don't want to make you do something that makes you feel uncomfortable," Ronan says. He's a lot more understanding than a lot of people have been about Dustin's anxiety issues.

"I was really nervous, but I have no idea how long this case is going to last. I might need to work with them. I need to get used to them. They seemed like nice people. It'll probably get better the more I'm around them." Dustin doesn't want to have to hide from Ronan's friends, his family.

He knows this thing between himself and Ronan probably can't last very long, but he doesn't want their time to end up being any shorter because he can't get along with the people who matter to Ronan. Dustin doesn't want to think of things coming to an end, though—he finds it makes him feel very low. He's attached to Ronan more than he had thought, or ever expected.

"Okay, but if you need to leave, just tell me and we'll leave," Ronan offers.

"If I made it through high school unmedicated, then I can hang out with five new people now that I'm on meds," Dustin says.

"Ouch, high school must have been hard," Ronan says, turning to face him.

"It was hell. I didn't like talking to people, I had no real friends, and I was a gay freak goth. I told you I wasn't popular. But the point is, I dealt with all those people every day, and I volunteer with people at several shelters without too much trouble. I can do this." Dustin isn't just telling Ronan, he's telling himself. He's dealt with all these other social situations; he can deal with this one.

They finish cleaning up, and then head out for the car and drive to the medical examiner's office. Ronan deals with getting them in. He knows several of the staff members—who seem pleased to see him, and confused by Dustin's presence—but no one asks why he is there.

The medical examiner is an older African-American woman, still good-looking despite her age. She looks very solemn and serious, but then, with her job, Dustin doesn't blame her.

"Hello, detective." She smiles.

"Mary Vines, this is Dustin. Chris said he's told you about him working with me?" Ronan introduces them to each other.

"Yes. I must admit I am a little skeptical; I've never met a psychic before. But then, I've never seen a body like this one," Mary says, not unkindly.

"I can guarantee he's the real deal, but what did you find?" Ronan asks.

"As you told me to suspect, the body was almost completely drained of blood and spinal fluid. The scratches have very little blood in them. I've determined they were made before the blood was drained," Mary says, opening a file.

"Anything else?" Ronan presses, because what Mary has said so far only confirms that it was a *Sanguis* demon that took

Charlotte and the others.

"She was fed—not a lot, but her stomach contents included ham and bread. She was hydrated. I also found some materials under her nails. There was iron and dirt. I've studied them and I've found some components in them similar to dirt found at a crime scene along the 180 highway," Mary explains.

"We suspected that was the right area, thank you." Ronan nods.

"Now, this is going to seem weird, but can I see the body?" Dustin asks.

"Chief Wilkinson warned me you'd need to do that. Some gloves are over there." Mary points. Going to one of the metal doors in the wall, she opens it, and pulls out a tray, revealing a body covered in a white sheet.

Dustin goes to the box of gloves and puts a pair on. He's seen a body after it had been autopsied before, a few times in fact, but it doesn't mean that Dustin is keen to see Charlotte's body again. He feels like he failed her. He had seen her, he had seen her alive— other than the kidnapped women being kept with her, Dustin was the last human to see her alive. He'd wanted to help her, so many people were trying to help her, and they had all failed; he had failed.

"Are you all right?" Ronan asks, and Dustin snaps back into the room.

"Fine. I'm ready." He doesn't want to tell Ronan he feels like a failure.

Dustin walks over to the body and Mary folds back the sheet to show Charlotte's face and shoulders. Dustin can just see the top of where the Y incision was cut and then sewn up.

"Do you need anything? I don't know how this works." Mary looks like she might be open-minded, but he's not sure.

"Nothing. If you could both just stay quiet, though. And if my nose starts bleeding, take my hand off of her," Dustin instructs.

"Try not to get any blood on the body. I'd hate to have to explain how a psychic contaminated the body in court," Mary says, because she still thinks this case will go to court, that there will be a human bad guy, who somehow did this to Charlotte's body.

"He'll be careful," Ronan promises.

Dustin takes another step forward and reaches out. He can still feel energy coming from Charlotte's body before he has even touched her. He can feel the fear coming off her; she'd been terrified when she'd died. Dustin takes a breath and presses his hand to Charlotte's shoulder.

He feels a searing pain in his neck, and when he opens his eyes, he is face-to-face with a demon. Dustin knows he's not really in the room with it, it's not really biting him, but it feels real. He can see its flat nose, its crinkled, bat-like face—he can see its glowing red eyes. His heart starts to race, and his fear mixes with Charlotte's.

Dustin can see the room, the cages, the dirt floor, the stairs leading up to the door. Dustin tries to take in as many details as possible, but he only sees inside. And then, once again, he feels Charlotte die, feels her fear fading along with her life force, and then he's back in his body in the morgue.

"I'll never get used to that," Dustin says softly. He steps back as his nose trickles a tiny bit of blood, and Ronan hands him a wad of tissues. He's really good at looking out for Dustin when he has visions, and after, like yesterday when he'd cleaned the blood off Dustin's forehead. It makes Dustin feel cared for, but he's not sure if he's reading too much into it.

"Used to what?" Mary asks.

"Feeling someone die," Dustin sighs.

"That explains the way you looked. I work with death every day, and you… it looked like you were dead for a second." Mary frowns.

"I told you he was the real deal," Ronan points out.

"I'm starting to believe you," Mary admits.

"Well. Thank you for letting me see Charlotte again," Dustin says, ditching the tissue in a trash can.

"No problem—I hope you find her killer." Mary sounds like she cares. It must be hard to keep caring after seeing so much death.

"Thanks." Dustin nods.

"We'll let you get back to work," Ronan offers. They say goodbye and leave Mary's office, not speaking until they are back in Ronan's car.

"Did you see anything?" Ronan asks when they have buckled up.

"I saw her die again, I saw the room they were kept in, but I didn't see outside the building. There's not a lot inside that really tells you where it could be," Dustin sighs.

"Let's go to the agency and do some research, see if we can narrow it down with all the information we have," Ronan suggests.

"Okay," Dustin agrees.

"You can still wait at my house if you'd like. I wouldn't be upset," Ronan offers.

"Do you not want me to come?" Dustin asks, because this is the second time Ronan has asked this. He's starting to feel like maybe Ronan doesn't want him around.

"Of course not! I want you to come, but I don't want you to feel uncomfortable and tense right after having a vision. I know you're shaken up." Ronan sounds like he means it. So maybe Dustin is just being paranoid.

"I'd like to come. It might not be as bad now that I've met them once. I can never tell for sure what will set off my anxiety, but first meetings are always worse than meeting people again," Dustin says honestly.

They drive to the agency's office, and when they walk in, Dustin can only see three people—Harry tapping away at his computer, which has several more monitors than the others, then Lisa and Rick, both at their own desks.

"Alice and Alan had to go out on a case," Harry explains before anyone asks.

"What case?" Ronan asks.

"Bodies going missing from morgues in Oregon. They're worried it's some kind of voodoo going on," Lisa says without looking up.

"So voodoo is real?" Dustin asks. He's not surprised by anything after his time spent with Ronan.

"I thought you'd have known that," Rick says.

"I was actually a skeptic about most supernatural things. Even though I have visions, I'd never seen anything supernatural until I saw Ann Beth and ended up looking into this case," Dustin explains.

"A skeptic psychic." Rick shakes his head, looking bemused.

"I've seen the demon in my vision. I find myself believing now," Dustin tells him.

"Welcome to our world." Lisa smiles.

"It's a freaky world," Harry adds.

"Well, we're here to get some work done. We're down two hands, so we need to work hard to narrow down where the women are being held. If we don't have anything more specific by tomorrow, I suggest we drive down the 180 and see what Dustin picks up," Ronan says, pushing Dustin toward his desk, and pulling over another chair so they can both work at it.

The five of them all use computers to look into the area they suspect the women are being held. The police and FBI are doing their own investigations, and Ronan gets updates throughout the day from Chris about places they have searched and come up empty.

They get some ideas, but nothing certain before Ronan tells them to give up for the day. Harry suggests they all go out to grab some dinner so they can keep talking about the case. Ronan looks at Dustin like he expects Dustin to say no, but Dustin isn't actually feeling as anxious this time—the work has been distracting him.

So Dustin nods that he's okay to go. He's glad that Ronan cared enough to ask him, instead of making him go to the meal without asking. Lisa and Rick share one car, while Harry jumps in with Dustin and Ronan.

They go to a local restaurant, and all order their food. Lisa orders a bottle of red wine for those who are not going to be driving that night.

Lisa and Rick end up telling him about their time in the Army, and the whole story of how they had come to believe in the supernatural. It's strange, being around a group of people who all believe in the supernatural. Dustin doesn't work with anyone who really knows about his abilities. He keeps them secret in case people think he is crazy.

It's nice, being able just to be himself, to not hide who he is. And he likes these people—they are cool, and they do a great job. They help people who have no one else to help them. Dustin kind of wishes he did more of that. He likes helping people, but in his daily life, he doesn't use his abilities to help people; you don't need visions to re-home a dog.

After dinner, Ronan drives Harry home, and then they go back to Ronan's home. They don't really talk about it this time, but they end up going straight to Ronan's bedroom. Dustin ends up on all fours on Ronan's bed, getting fucked vigorously. His orgasm hits him so hard he's left shaking for long moments after.

They tangle together in the sweaty sheets, and Dustin falls asleep feeling sore and satisfied.

Chapter Nine

"So, I'm like a psychic bloodhound?" Dustin asks from the passenger seat. The high neck of his coat and woolly red scarf hide the hickey Ronan knows he left on Dustin's neck last night. He hadn't meant to. He'd just gotten carried away, and he likes marking Dustin, a fact Ronan isn't going to think about.

"Well, I wouldn't put it like that. I drive us around; you try to get a vision. First we drive the length of the 180. Then we drive around buildings that fit the information we have, like places that have had mice infestations," Ronan says, reasonably.

"It involves us driving around with me hanging out the window? Sounds like you're using me like a bloodhound." Dustin rolls his eyes.

"You don't have to hang out of the window, just, will having it down help? I don't know how easily you can pick up the women's energy." Ronan knows Dustin is powerful, more so than any psychic Ronan has met before, but he doesn't know if driving along the highway will work, if Dustin will be able to read people in the buildings.

"I don't need the window open—glass won't block the energy, just like latex gloves didn't when I was touching Charlotte's body. Skin-to-skin contact can be better, and it's easier to feel things if I'm not wearing wool gloves, but it depends on what I'm trying to feel," Dustin explains.

"Well, let me know if you can feel anything." Ronan starts driving. He doesn't turn the radio on, because he doesn't want to distract Dustin, and he doesn't talk much for the same reason.

Ronan does watch Dustin, though, trying to read his face, but it looks blank. Dustin has accused Ronan of being a closed book, but Ronan thinks that Dustin can be just as bad. They've spent the last three nights in the same bed, but Ronan isn't sure he can read Dustin any better now. He can read his body; he knows what Dustin likes in bed, but that's it.

A part of Ronan is worried, because he thinks he may be developing feelings for Dustin and he has no idea how Dustin feels. Ronan knows the other man is attracted to him, that's become clear to see, but Ronan doesn't know, if it wasn't for the case, if they would spend any time together. Ronan would quite like to see Dustin again after this case ends, but he has a terrible feeling that Dustin will go home and just get back to his life, cutting off all contact.

They drive up and down the highway until it starts to get dark, when Ronan sees a sign on one of the buildings, saying it is condemned, and he decides to pull off the highway, and into the path leading to the old warehouse.

"I can feel something," Dustin says as they get close to the building.

"What can you feel?" Ronan asks.

"Fear, lots and lots of fear," Dustin says softly.

Ronan stops the car, and looks up if this building is one on their list, and it is.

"Let's have a closer look," Ronan suggests.

"Okay," Dustin agrees, but he doesn't look like he is really listening to Ronan.

They get out of the car, and Ronan draws his gun, so he's ready for any surprises. He starts walking the perimeter of the building, with Dustin following behind him. It's clear Dustin can feel something that Ronan cannot see, because the building looks normal enough, old and dirty, all closed up, far from the road.

Ronan isn't sure they have the right place, despite Dustin's reaction, until he comes to a door in the back; around the doorframe are scratch marks, like the book about the *Sanguis* demon said there would be.

"I'm going to call in backup," Ronan says, holstering his gun so he can get his cell phone out and text Chris to bring some of his more believing officers, ones that won't get themselves killed by doing anything stupid.

While Ronan is texting, Dustin goes over to the door, and runs his hands over the grooves in the wood made by the *Sanguis* demon.

"I can feel it," Dustin says.

"The demon, is it here?" Ronan asks.

"I don't know if it's inside, but I know it's been here." Dustin frowns.

Ronan swaps his cell phone for his gun again.

"Did you bring your knives like I told you?" Ronan asks.

"Yes." Dustin nods.

"Have one ready or you're not coming inside," Ronan orders. Even though he's not sure that anything is in this building, let alone anything dangerous, Dustin's visions have never been wrong so far, so Ronan doubts they are wrong now.

Dustin unstraps a knife from his arm and holds it carefully.

Ronan walks ahead of Dustin, testing the door, but it's locked. He doesn't want to kick down the door, in case the *Sanguis* demon is inside—Ronan doesn't want it to know they are coming.

"Dustin, can you open this lock?" Ronan asks.

"I can try." Dustin moves to Ronan's side and puts the hand not holding the knife over the lock.

It's silent for a few moments, and then Ronan hears a click, and sees a small trickle of blood roll from Dustin's nostril. He must not have a tissue, because he just uses the sleeve of his sweater to wipe it away.

Ronan pushes the door open and takes the lead. It's almost pitch-black inside, so he pulls out the small flashlight he carries in his jacket, glad that, unlike Dustin, he hadn't left his coat in the car.

The small amount of light from his flashlight reveals stairs, but doesn't show the rest of the room—Ronan sees a light switch, but doesn't want to risk alerting anything that they are there. Slowly, he starts to make his way down the stairs, Dustin following just a step behind.

Once they are in the room, Ronan lifts his gun in one hand and his flashlight in the other and starts to look around. He hears a noise before he sees anything—weak crying. Ronan follows the sound and the beam of his flashlight finds a cage with a woman in it. She startles at the light shining on her, Ronan hurries over to her. Even though she is dirty and thinner, Ronan recognizes her as Jade Able.

"Jade, I'm a private investigator. The police are on their way. Is the thing that took you in here?" Ronan asks quietly.

"It comes at night," Jade whispers in a weak voice, and Ronan tenses, thinking of the dark sky before he'd entered this windowless room.

He moves his flashlight around, and he can see more cages, more women. He turns to find Dustin, to ask him to start opening the cages and chains with his powers. When Ronan turns to look for him, Dustin is still near the stairs—in the beam of the flashlight, Ronan can see that Dustin is pale and his eyes are unfocused. Ronan realizes this place has triggered a vision.

Ronan takes a step toward Dustin and hears one of the women scream. A second later, he sees movement, and then something is close to Dustin. Ronan fires, but it doesn't stop. Dustin is knocked off his feet by a blur of movement. Ronan sees a manlike figure as his heart races and he fires at it again.

Glowing red eyes land on him and Ronan fires again. He hears a shrill noise, and then the figure is retreating, rushing up the stairs at an inhuman speed, and out into the darkness. Keeping his guard up, Ronan rushes over to Dustin. He can smell the tang of copper in the air, and knows Dustin is bleeding even before he reaches him.

Ronan drops down beside Dustin, who is clutching his stomach, and Ronan can see blood seeping through his fingers.

"Let me look," Ronan says, forcing himself to sound calm, when really he is panicking.

Dustin lifts a shaky hand, and there is a slash in his sweater, and two deep gashes in his stomach where he has clearly been clawed by the *Sanguis* demon. The slashes are bad, but not dangerously deep, by the looks of them. They'll need stitches, but they won't be fatal.

"You'll be okay." Ronan doesn't get why it attacked Dustin first. Ronan had a gun, he was near the women, and Dustin had just been standing there, in a trance, not a danger to the demon. And then Ronan remembers the blood on Dustin's sleeve from his small nosebleed. Everything he read said blood was the most important thing to a *Sanguis* demon—maybe it had smelled the blood.

"Did you hit it?" Dustin asks.

"I'm not sure, it was fast," Ronan admits.

"Ronan?" A voice calls out, and it sounds like Chris.

"Down here—the women are here, and Dustin is hurt. You're going to need a bunch of ambulances, and be careful. I don't know if it's still here, I didn't get it," Ronan warns. He hasn't found blood or a body.

Lights go on, officers come streaming in, and the room goes from nearly silent to full of noise—the officers and the kidnapped women. Soon there are sirens filling the air as ambulances arrive. Someone gets a bolt cutter to free the women, and another officer gives Ronan a blanket to wad up and press against Dustin's bleeding stomach.

"You did a good job," Chris tells him.

"I didn't get it," Ronan sighs.

"There are ten women alive down here, Ronan. They need a doctor, a good meal, and probably a ton of therapy, but they are alive. You two found them alive," Chris points out.

He's right. They have a victory here, ten women still living, but Ronan still feels like he has failed, because the *Sanguis* demon is still out there.

Ronan helps Dustin get up the stairs to be seen by a paramedic, who insists on taking Dustin to the hospital along with the women. The women are half starved, missing pints of blood and most of their spinal fluid. Ronan goes to the hospital with Dustin, who's given a bed, lots of medication, and stitches.

"How are you feeling?" Ronan asks, still worried even though he knows that Dustin is okay.

"Weird," Dustin says, sounding half awake.

"That would be the painkillers," Ronan explains.

"No, I can feel something." Dustin frowns, touching his stomach lightly.

"What?" Ronan asks.

"I think I can feel the *Sanguis* demon—I can feel its energy," Dustin says.

"Is it close?" Ronan asks, hand on his gun, worried for Dustin, the women, and the staff in the hospital if the *Sanguis* demon has tracked them here.

"I think it's in the basement of the hospital. I can see sheets, laundry, I can smell chemicals, and I can hear tumble driers. I can feel it, Ronan. It's like I'm inside of it. I think I can feel its energy because it cut me," Dustin says in a rush.

"Stay here," Ronan orders.

He doesn't wait for Dustin to answer. He heads out of the room, asks a nurse the way to the basement, and heads in that direction.

Ronan finds the right stairs and heads down. He isn't sure he's in the right place until he hears those industrial tumble driers that Dustin had talked about.

Ronan raises his gun and walks toward the noise. As he moves forward, he notices something on the floor—blood. Ronan kneels down to check if it's still wet, still warm. Which it is—it's more blood than the *Sanguis* demon cries, so Ronan thinks he must have hit the demon with one of his shots back in the warehouse.

Ronan is just straightening up again when something solid barrels into him, knocking him off his feet. Ronan holds onto his gun, not wanting to drop it, and quickly scrambles to his feet, only to come face-to-face with glowing red eyes. Dustin was right—the *Sanguis* demon had followed them, followed its victims here.

The *Sanguis* demon hisses at him and charges, and its razor-sharp claws shred right through Ronan's jacket sleeve and into his arm, which makes him drop the gun.

"Damn it," Ronan curses. He goes to grab the gun, but the *Sanguis* demon blocks him. It bares its teeth and launches at Ronan.

They both end up on the floor, wrestling, Ronan trying to keep the creature's teeth away from his throat, but his arm and shoulder take hits, getting bitten, and his chest is getting clawed as he tries to get free, tries to get his gun. Ronan punches the demon as hard as he can in its jaw, which gets its mouth away from him for a second. Ronan tries to roll away, toward his fallen gun.

The *Sanguis* demon grabs his leg, claws biting in deeply as it tugs on Ronan. He yelps in pain. He snags the gun with his fingertips, pulling it closer, yelling out in pain as he gets hit with claws over and over. He can smell his own blood in the air.

Ronan twists his body, gun up, so he can fire toward the *Sanguis* demon. He nails it in the shoulder, blood spurts out, and the demon lets out a horrible scream. It gives Ronan enough time to find his feet, but when he does, he finds he can hardly put his right leg down. The leg of his pants is shredded and stained with blood, a lot of blood. His left arm is equally useless. But he's right-handed and that's what matters. Ronan holds the gun steady to fire, and shoots, hitting the *Sanguis* in the chest.

But it doesn't stop the *Sanguis* demon. It just gives an enraged shriek and charges toward him and slams him hard into the wall.

Ronan only just keeps a hold of his gun, for all the good it's doing. Ronan had thought shooting the demon would incapacitate it. Instead, the angry creature slams Ronan into the wall so hard he hears a rib crack a second before the blinding pain registers, blooming in his chest.

Ronan kicks out at the demon with his good leg, and then knees it in the groin, and it seems the books were right about the *Sanguis* demon having humanlike genitalia, because it hisses and stumbles back.

Hoping that quantity of shots over quality might be the way to go, as soon as the *Sanguis* demon has taken a step back, Ronan starts firing, emptying his clip into the demon, blood and bullet casings going everywhere, and the demon roaring like nothing Ronan has ever heard before.

It seems to slow the demon down, but it hasn't stopped it—and it sure as hell has pissed it off. The ugly, twisted face is fixed in a snarl, showing off its wolf-like teeth. They are both covered in blood, and Ronan can see the *Sanguis* demon breathing in the air and the scent of blood, and its eyes glow brighter.

"Here." Dustin's voice comes from behind him and before Ronan can question it, a knife is being pressed into his hand.

Ronan doesn't look back at Dustin, he just summons all of his strength and limps toward the demon as fast as he can, and the demon closes the gap by prowling toward him. Ronan's a good fighter, this isn't the first time he's had a knife in his hand, but it's the first time he was aiming for just a creature's heart.

"Stay back, Dustin," Ronan orders, already horrified that Dustin is down here with the demon again.

Once he's warned Dustin away, Ronan launches himself at the demon, punching with his injured, weaker arm, and slashing with the knife. The *Sanguis* demon grabs him, claws puncturing more holes in his flesh. Ronan uses the pain, lets it turn to anger—when the *Sanguis* demon slams him into a wall again, Ronan lets himself be thrown. He keeps the knife hidden behind him, and lets the demon come close, using himself as bait.

The *Sanguis* demon leans in, fangs exposed, ready to sink into Ronan's neck, but Ronan strikes quickly, thrusting the knife in his hand up into the demon's chest—it roars, jerking back, but Ronan follows it, keeping the knife buried to the hilt. The *Sanguis* demon hits the floor, mouth still fixed in a snarl, and its eyes wide open, and, as Ronan watches, the bright red lights in its eyes fade.

"You're hurt," Dustin says, coming forward, holding his own bandage-covered stomach.

"Stay back, I want to make sure it's dead," Ronan orders. He moves close and pulls the hunting knife out of the *Sanguis* demon's chest. The demon doesn't even twitch, but Ronan stabs in again, just to be sure.

"It's dead. Can I help you now?" Dustin asks.

"I won't be able to walk back up those stairs, but you could hurt your stomach helping me. Go get Chris and the other officers. They can deal with the demon's body, get it to the right people, and help me," Ronan says, leaning against a wall. He's aware that he's hurt pretty badly—bite marks, claw marks, heavy bleeding, and broken bones. He needs help, but he hates asking for it, and no way is he risking hurting Dustin more. He has risked Dustin enough today taking him to the warehouse, and then Dustin had known he wasn't carrying a knife, because he'd left his jacket with every weapon other than his gun at Dustin's bedside. He'd been so distracted by Dustin getting hurt that he had screwed up, and risked getting him killed.

"Okay." Dustin seems hesitant to leave, but he does, heading down the hallway and away from Ronan. Once Dustin is out of sight, Ronan allows himself to slide to the floor, his leg not wanting to hold him anymore—the pain is intense.

Ronan isn't sure how long it is before officers appear, and Chris is at his side, helping him to his feet and out of the hospital basement. As soon as Ronan is back in the brightly lit hallways of the hospital, the staff descends on him. Chris outright lies to them, saying that it was an animal attack outside the hospital, but then they can't exactly tell the truth.

"You could have been killed," Chris hisses as Ronan is poked and prodded, examined on a gurney.

"We need to take your detective into surgery. There is damage to an artery in his leg, as well as the muscle—he needs emergency repairs." The doctor aims his statement at Chris, not Ronan, and Ronan is about to complain, but then he goes from woozy to very sleepy, and then nothingness pulls him down.

Ronan wakes up in a bed in a small ward. There are two other beds along the same wall as his, his being in the middle, and three exactly opposite. There is an officer on guard at the door, and in a chair beside Ronan's bed is Dustin. Someone must have gotten him new clothes, because he's wearing a pale-blue T-shirt that isn't at all his usual style, and loose, green jogging pants that look too long for him.

Dustin looks like he's in a world of his own, but then, before Ronan can speak, Dustin turns to face him, like he had known Ronan had woken up.

"Why are we under guard?" Ronan asks.

"Hello to you too." Dustin sounds a little annoyed.

But Ronan has a feeling it's going to get worse, because there is something he has to do here. Maybe Dustin won't even care.

"Is the *Sanguis* demon still alive?" Ronan presses.

"No, Chris made sure, he got someone to get a bigger knife and they cut its head off. Then the FBI took it for study, but I'm not supposed to know that. If asked, the FBI have made it clear they won't be admitting to dissecting a demon," Dustin explains.

"How are the women doing?" Ronan asks.

"Better than you'd think. The demon kept them quite healthy. I think they'll all be having trouble sleeping for a while. I gave the women from Oregon the names of some good psychiatrists," Dustin says with a slight smile.

"The case is over, then," Ronan says. He's not going to ask Dustin about how his surgery went; he'll ask a doctor. He doesn't want things to get more personal here. Ronan could have gotten Dustin killed twice today. He's very aware of that. It makes him feel sick and helpless, and he doesn't like feeling that one bit.

"Yeah, apart from Charlotte, we got them all back alive, so pretty good job." Dustin looks worried.

"Well, I'm not going to be driving for a while with my leg, but I'm sure Chris can arrange an officer to take you to pick up your stuff and then back to Oregon." Ronan does his best to sound like he doesn't care that Dustin will be leaving now and going home. He thinks he does a good job of keeping emotion out of his voice.

"Rushing me out the door so quickly?" Dustin asks softly.

"Your life is in Oregon, mine is in California, a quick fling isn't going to change that," Ronan says simply, even though it doesn't feel simple at all.

He wants to ask Dustin to stay, but he doesn't want to face rejection, and he also doesn't want Dustin in his world—it's too dangerous. He wants Dustin to go back to his safe life, helping abuse victims and animals.

"'Quick fling?'" Dustin repeats, looking at Ronan with a hard-to-read face.

Ronan just nods, because that was what it was. He might want it to be more, but it was like a one-night stand that got extended really, and Ronan would be a fool to read more into it.

"Funny, I thought I'd made a friend. And I thought you'd changed. You haven't changed." Dustin shakes his head.

"Don't act like this is something it's not. We both got what we wanted at the time. And now it's over," Ronan says, harshly; he feels like an asshole.

He does care about Dustin, more than he would care about someone he was just sleeping with, but that's why it's best to send Dustin away, before either of them get hurt again physically or emotionally, because Ronan has a feeling that, along with his other powers, Dustin has the power to break his heart.

"I should have seen this coming, and not because I'm psychic. But because of who you are. I should have known you'd never want more than a few orgasms before you went back to your straitlaced, rule-abiding world," Dustin says, standing up carefully. It's clear by the way he's moving that his stomach is bothering him.

Ronan wants to ask Dustin if he's okay, how his injuries are, but that would only confuse things. It's better if Dustin thinks he doesn't care, instead of realizing Ronan cares far too much, considering how long they've known each other.

"Don't act like you were looking for more than sex," Ronan says sourly as Dustin starts to walk away. He knows Dustin liked him as a friend, was attracted to him too, but that doesn't add up to a relationship. It's friends with benefits at best, and Ronan isn't that kind of guy. Not long term.

"I guess we'll never know," Dustin says softly, and he walks away without looking back.

Ronan tries to shake off the feeling in his chest and the pit of his stomach. He tells himself it's the drugs, but it feels an awful lot like regret.

***

They keep Ronan in the hospital for over a week—finally the day arrives where Chris comes to take him home.

"Thank you for doing this," Ronan says as Chris takes Ronan's bag and puts it his trunk.

"No problem. You okay to get in with your leg?" Chris asks.

"I should be fine." Ronan has seen a physical therapist about his leg. The guy had shown him how to move it carefully, without damaging it and putting too much strain on the healing muscle.

They both get in the car and Chris starts driving.

"I've had something I've been wanting to say, but I wanted to wait until you got out of the hospital. It didn't seem right to pile more crap on you while you were only starting to heal." Chris sounds very serious.

"What is it—is everything okay? Your family?" Ronan asks. He's seen everyone in the agency in the past week, a bunch of cops, Chris, but not Chris' wife or kids.

"No, it's fine, everything is fine. The kids just went to visit their aunt. This is about you," Chris explains.

"Am I not getting paid for the case?" Ronan has had to fight for his payment before, but he got the women back—even if the police don't have proof that the case is solved, it is solved.

"Nothing like that." Chris waves his hand.

"Then what?" Ronan pushes. He doesn't have the energy for guessing games; he's still healing. This case had landed him more stitches than he's had ever had before, between the slashes from claws and the bite marks from those teeth, he's going to have some impressive scars.

"You're an idiot, that's what," Chris says.

"Because I went into the basement without backup? I do that all the time, you know it's part of my job," Ronan points out.

"As stupid as I think you going in without help is, it's not why I think you're an idiot this time." Chris shakes his head.

"Why am I an idiot, then?" Ronan asks, baffled.

"You're an idiot for not asking that boy to stay," Chris says, cutting to the chase.

Ronan instantly knows the boy Chris means. He means Dustin,

who Ronan hasn't seen or heard from since he sent him away. Which is good, it's what he wanted, but somehow every time he thinks of Dustin or somebody mentions him, Ronan feels like he has a lead weight in his chest.

"I don't know what you mean," Ronan lies, because Chris wasn't supposed to know about Dustin. Ronan hadn't said anything about him to Chris.

"Don't try that with me, Ronan. I know you better than that. Which is why I knew, the minute I saw you two together, that something was going on. Am I wrong?" Chris asks.

"We slept together; it was nothing," Ronan says, looking out of the car window to avoid eye contact.

"Don't tell me it was nothing. I saw the way you looked at him, like he was something special. You were captivated," Chris insists.

"It was just a fling that I shouldn't have had while I was working," Ronan says just as firmly.

"If it was just a fling, why have you been so miserable since Dustin left?" Chris asks.

"I've been in pain; I've been healing. I haven't been miserable," Ronan lies again.

"Bullshit. You cared about Dustin when he was here and you care about him now that he's gone. Why's it so hard for you to admit that?" Chris asks.

"I got him hurt, Chris! He was clawed up because I wasn't watching him closely enough, and then he shows up in the hospital basement, hurt, because I forgot a knife and he knew I needed it. I could have got him killed," Ronan says in a rush.

"I might call him a boy, but he's an adult, and in charge of his own safety. You're not responsible for him, or what happened to him. Yes, he got hurt, but everyone on your team apart from Harry has been hurt at least as badly," Chris points out.

"Dustin isn't a part of my team. He's not a monster hunter. He's a psychic consultant. He's never supposed to get near the danger, and I took him right into it," Ronan groans.

"He took himself into the danger. And from what I've read, this isn't the first time. He's been to crime scenes before, searched buildings for the bad guys. The only difference is your bad guy had claws and teeth instead of a gun. So you sent him away in some stupid attempt to protect him?" Chris asks.

"Maybe." Ronan wouldn't even admit that much to most people, but Chris isn't most people to him.

"So for the first time in years you actually like someone, and you've pushed him away?" Chris looks at him like he's the biggest idiot in the universe.

"It's safer," Ronan argues.

"For who, him or you? Because I think you are just protecting yourself from rejection if you'd asked him to stay and he'd said no," Chris accuses.

"I..." Ronan doesn't know what to say to that, because it's true. He was afraid, if he asked Dustin to stay longer, he'd say no, say that Ronan was crazy. By being the one to push Dustin away first, he had thought it wouldn't hurt, but he's been left with this ache anyway.

"You could call him?" Chris suggests.

"Never got his number and I was kind of an asshole to him. He won't want to hear from me," Ronan sighs.

"You're a private detective, you could find out a phone number," Chris says, pulling up outside of Ronan's house.

"Just leave it, Chris, I don't need you to meddle in my life like this." Ronan gets out of the car.

Chris follows him and gets Ronan's bag for him.

"I don't mean to meddle, but I'd like to see you happy," Chris says, handing the bag over to Ronan.

"I am happy. I have friends and a great job. I don't need more." Maybe Ronan would like more, doesn't mean he needs it. His life was fine before he met Dustin.

"Just think about it, Ronan," Chris suggests.

"I will." Ronan isn't lying. He's sure he's going to be thinking about Dustin a lot. He had all week in the hospital, but even when he pictures things being different, he just can't picture things working.

Chapter Ten

"Are you ready to go to your new home today?" Dustin asks a fuzzy orange kitten by the name of Mr. Paws, named for his unusually large paws.

The kitten meows at him and struggles. It clearly doesn't like being put in the box with his brother, another tomcat named Wiggles. Dustin gets them both in the cat carrier, and picks up the other box that has the two girl kittens in it.

Dustin walks out into the main reception room with the kittens, and Chris is waiting. Dustin had been surprised when Chris had gotten in touch about the kittens. He'd offered to come get the ones for his kids and Harry. Dustin wasn't going to pass up good homes for his kittens, so he'd agreed, despite his stupid, achy heart.

It's been three weeks since he saw Chris at the hospital, and unsurprisingly, Chris hasn't changed.

"Hello, Chris. You just have to sign a form over here," Dustin says, putting the kittens down so he can get the form for Chris.

"You're as bad as him. Aren't you going to ask me how he is?" Chris asks, taking the form.

Dustin isn't petty enough to pretend he doesn't know who Chris means.

"How is Ronan? Is he healing well?" Dustin asks.

"His leg has been healing slower than he'd like. But he's hardly limping now. He'll be fine. But he's been like a wounded bear, in a terrible mood," Chris sighs.

"Doesn't deal well with being injured?" Dustin asks.

"He's been injured before, it's not that. He's hurt. I'm kind of hoping you're not as stubborn as he is," Chris says, finishing signing the form.

"What do you mean?" Dustin is confused.

"Ronan misses you. I'm hoping you'll be willing to get in touch." Chris looks hopeful.

"So what if he misses getting laid?" Dustin rolls his eyes. It's clear Ronan must have said something to his ex-boss, because Chris had come here knowing Ronan and Dustin had done more than work together.

"Um, I'm sure he misses that. But I don't think that is the real issue. Ronan really took to you; I could see that. When you were hurt in the warehouse, I saw his face. I've never seen him look like that. Sometimes people just click—I don't think you should dismiss it just because it didn't last long," Chris argues.

"So, what? I go to California to a guy who called what we had a fling? I risk getting humiliated? Hurt? All because you think he feels more for me than he said?" Dustin asks in disbelief.

"I know Ronan better than most people; I know you mean something to him. And maybe you don't have to go there. I could give you his number, you could call him?" Chris suggests.

"Okay, give me his number, I want to call him now," Dustin says, pulling out his cell phone—Chris has made him curious. Dustin hadn't thought things were over between him and Ronan until Ronan had suddenly ended them. He needs to know if what Chris is saying is true—does Ronan really care about him?

"Here." Chris shows him the number, and Dustin dials it, almost holding his breath waiting for an answer.

"Hello, who is this?" Ronan's voice comes on the line, and several memories flood back—being in the car with Ronan, being in his bed. It wasn't even a full two weeks, but it feels like a lifetime passed between them.

"Hi Ronan, it's Dustin." Dustin hopes that Ronan doesn't just hang up.

"Dustin, oh, hey… I ah… I've been meaning to call," Ronan says in a rush.

"Really?" Dustin doesn't want to get his hopes up. He's been trying to forget about Ronan longer than he knew him, but he hasn't had any luck. Mainly because most of him doesn't want to forget about Ronan—Ronan has gotten under his skin, in his head.

"Yeah. I kind of hate how I left things. I was a dick to you, and a coward," Ronan says, surprising Dustin.

"What do you mean?" Dustin asks.

"You have every right to shoot me down. But when you were here, I was developing feelings for you, even though it hadn't been long. I'm not confessing my undying love to you, but it's going to bother me if I don't man up enough to say I do care deeply for you, as well as being wildly attracted to you," Ronan tells him, and all Dustin can do is clutch the phone for a few moments.

"Dustin?" Ronan says softly.

"I guess I half expected you to say to leave you alone, that it was just sex. It wasn't just sex to me, either," Dustin admits, taking a few steps away from Chris, blushing.

"I feel something for you, something strong. I'd like to see where it goes. I know you can't drive, and we live a ways apart, but I can come see you any time you want, okay?" Ronan offers.

"Okay," Dustin says, feeling hopeful.

They talk for a few more moments before Ronan has to go. Dustin puts away his phone, smiling, and goes back over to Chris, who's looking pleased.

"Boy decided to stop being stubborn and stupid?" Chris asks.

"I guess so. I think we're going to try something. Would it be crazy to come with you now? Come see him?" Dustin asks.

"No, I think he'd like that," Chris grins.

"And you wouldn't mind?" Dustin wants to be sure he isn't pushing himself on Chris.

"Of course not. It'll be worth driving you there and back just to see a smile on his face for once," Chris says happily.

"You don't have to bring me back, I can make my way," Dustin offers.

"If Ronan doesn't drive you back, I will, and that's final," Chris says.

"Thank you, you're really good to Ronan." Dustin smiles.

"I care about him like one of my own," Chris admits.

"He needs that; he needs people who care," Dustin knows neither he nor Ronan had good family lives, but their lives were very different. Dustin's parents are still alive, happy to pay him any amount he wants, as long as he doesn't show up and ruin their perfect social life.

"He does—maybe you can be one of the people looking out for him," Chris suggests.

"Maybe." Dustin would like to be in Ronan's life, but life doesn't always work out the way he wants it to. He knows that, but he's still hopeful.

"Are you ready to go?" Chris asks.

"Yeah, let's go." Dustin nods. They take the kittens and head to California.

They stop at Harry's place first to drop off his kittens, because they've been in the car a long time. Then, Chris drops off Dustin outside Ronan's place, saying he'll be back when he's needed, taking his own kittens to go meet their new family.

Dustin builds up his courage and goes to Ronan's door and rings the bell. It's a few moments before the door opens, and then there is a very surprised-looking Ronan.

"Dustin?" Ronan sounds shocked.

"Chris gave me a ride," Dustin explains.

He's prepared for things to get awkward, for Ronan actually not to be pleased to see him, but then Ronan grabs him and pulls him into a hug.

Dustin looks up to meet Ronan's eyes, and finds himself being drawn into a kiss, right there on Ronan's front porch. Dustin doesn't object—if Ronan doesn't care what his neighbors think, then Dustin certainly doesn't. But as things start to heat up quickly, Dustin thinks they'll soon be putting on enough of a show to be arrested.

"We should take this inside," Dustin suggests.

"Yeah, good idea." Ronan doesn't let go of Dustin. He just pulls him inside and shuts the door behind them, and then they go straight to Ronan's bedroom.

Almost an hour later, Dustin finds himself, exhausted, in Ronan's bed, the sheet covering his waist, and Ronan running his fingers over the scars on Dustin's stomach—two diagonal, raised lines, still healing, still pink. Dustin can already tell that they won't fade and will be with him for life. But he's not the only one left with scars from the *Sanguis* demon—Dustin had seen and felt them several places on Ronan's naked body.

"I'm sorry," Ronan says softly.

"What for?" Dustin asks.

"Getting you hurt," Ronan says, placing his hand flat on Dustin's stomach over the scars. He'd been lucky—he could have been gutted, but the demon had had just caught him.

"You didn't hurt me, a monster did. A monster I chose to go after. I would have searched for it if I wasn't with you. I would've searched for it alone, and maybe got hurt worse. You need to get over this," Dustin says.

"It's hard to see someone you care about going headfirst into dangerous situations," Ronan sighs.

"You care about your team like family, and they're often in danger. I know you want to protect everyone, but you can't; you're not Superman. You won't always be there to save the day for the people who matter to you, but I know you'll always be there to pick up the pieces after, for the team and… maybe me? If you want to be there for me?" Dustin asks.

"I do; I want you in my life. But I'm not sure if I could live with seeing you get hurt," Ronan says.

"You already saw me get hurt and you lived through it, we both did. We're okay. We can both help people, it's what we do. We can still do it and be together," Dustin says hopefully.

"I want to try." Ronan leans in and presses a kiss to Dustin's naked shoulder.

Dustin is kind of terrified, more afraid now than he had been in the warehouse with the *Sanguis* demon. He knows he wants to be with Ronan, to have him in his life, but he doesn't know if it'll work. They both have their issues, and over time it might fall apart, but Dustin wants to try, so he cuddles into Ronan's side, hoping, and making the most of whatever time they have.

Epilogue

Four months later

"That way, no, left, my left!" Harry yells.

Ronan twists the desk he is carrying, following Harry's instructions, and finally he and Alan get the new desk through the door.

"Just a little farther, boys," Lisa says.

Alice dives out of the way as they stagger in, and then finally the desk is in place.

"My back," Alan complains.

"Don't be a wuss," Ronan says.

"Yes, boss," Alan groans.

"He's coming," Harry calls.

They all stand together, blocking the desk from view, and Dustin walks in.

"What's going on?" Dustin asks right away.

"Ta-da," Alice says as they part to reveal the desk.

"You got me a desk?" Dustin asks, coming over, and Ronan loops an arm around his waist. They have a "no PDA in the office" rule, but they get away with a small level of affection.

"Well, you've been working with us for a month, seemed like time you have a desk." Ronan smiles—he sometimes can't believe the leap Dustin had taken for him.

After two months of dating long-distance, Dustin had decided to move out of Oregon, to California. There had been a full-time position at an animal rescue center locally, and Dustin had gotten the job easily. So now he's working on re-homing animals and investigating cases of animal abuse.

But he also works at the agency. If he gets a vision, they investigate it with him, whether it is supernatural or not, and he helps them on more difficult cases to get leads. He works with Ronan the most, but he's helped out the others too. It's clear he's part of the team.

Ronan knows he's lucky, though, to have met a man who was willing to uproot his life, change his job, get a new apartment, to try and make what they have work, and it does feel like it's working. Ronan had thought about spending more time in Oregon, had offered to, but his job kept him with the team, even though he travels for his cases. Moving would have been harder for him, but just because it would be easier for Dustin, Ronan had never expected it.

They don't live together yet. Dustin got an apartment close to Ronan's house. It's nicer than his place in Oregon, and Ronan likes that Dustin is allowing himself to have money, without thinking it'll make him like his parents. He's been selling paintings and sketches locally and online.

"I love the desk." Dustin grins, leaning into Ronan's side.

"We'll get you anything else you need, it looks a bit bare," Alan comments.

"You should have a photo of you and Ronan," Alice teases.

The team has taken to Dustin. Ronan had a meeting with them before he asked Dustin to join the team, and they had all been more than okay with it. Harry epically seems to like Dustin, but then, they are closest in age, and they both do the least fieldwork.

"Thank you all." Dustin goes and takes a seat at his desk, grinning.

Ronan likes to see him happy, to know he's a part of that happiness. He thanks Chris often for talking him out of pushing Dustin away and for going to see Dustin. He'd been trying to protect his own heart as well as Dustin's safety, but now they are here, together. Dustin is safe and Ronan's heart is feeling fuller every day.

Ronan watches as Dustin positions his laptop on the desk, and Lisa and Alice give him things like notepads and Post-it Notes. Both women spoil him rotten. They say he needs it because he's the youngest, but Ronan suspects they just find Dustin charming, like most people do.

Ronan is talking with Alan and Rick when Harry calls his name.

"What?" Ronan calls back without looking around to see Harry.

"I think Dustin is having a vision," Harry says.

Ronan turns quickly—Dustin is sitting there silently, face blank, eyes wide. Ronan walks over to him and waits for Dustin to snap out of it.

"Dustin?" Ronan says quietly after a few moments—everyone is waiting, watching.

"Vision," Dustin says.

"What did you see?" Ronan asks.

"I'm not sure, but something's coming." Dustin sounds troubled by his vision.

"It'll be okay," Ronan says confidently, looking at his team.

"What makes you so sure?" Dustin asks.

"Because there is nothing bad enough that we can't face it." Ronan hopes his optimism isn't foolish, but he believes it. He believes they can fight any evil.

Dustin turns to face him, and, ignoring the "no PDA in the office" rule, kisses Ronan full-on the mouth to the grumbling protest of their friends.

"What was that for?" Ronan asks.

"For being you." Dustin smiles, and Ronan chooses to ignore whoever makes the vomiting noise.

He just puts an arm around Dustin and starts talking through what he had seen in his vision, because if there is something coming, they'll be prepared for it and together they will fight it. Ronan knows he has the best supernatural detective agency around and the best boyfriend a man could ask for.

The wall he had built around his heart is still there, but now it has a door, and Dustin holds the key.

ABOUT L.J. HAMLIN

L.J. Hamlin is a twenty-something (getting older every day) author, who has been writing all her life, mainly in notebooks no one else ever saw. Then she discovered M/M groups online and was encouraged by friends to share her stories. After a while (and with a lot of pushing) she grew brave enough to attempt getting published. Now she shares her stories with others and hopes never to stop. L.J. loves cats and pretty much all animals, is a collector of many things, often weird, but most of all books.

Find L.J. online:
Blog: https://www.blogger.com/profile/02717576317697299159
Facebook: https://www.facebook.com/L.j.hamlin91
Pinterest: https://uk.pinterest.com/lizibabes
Twitter: https://twitter.com/LjHamlin

Also Available from L.J. Hamlin and Torquere Press:

ANTHOLOGIES
Dawg Days / Haunted Hotties Volume I / Men in Uniform / Mythologically Torqued Volume One / Santa's Little Kinksters / Snowed In M/M

SHORT STORIES
Adventures of a Yeti Hunter / In Love With Zeus' Son / Nurse Levi / Paw Prints on My Skin / Spirit Wolf / The Christmas Office Party

NOVELS
Blood Visions / Pale Light / The Dusty Hat Bar

SERIES
Lace Series
Black Lace

If you enjoyed L.J. Hamlin's *Blood Visions*, please consider telling others and writing a review.